This book is to be returned on
the last date stamped be

The Brighton Belle
and other stories

The Brighton Belle and other stories

Francis King

Longmans

LONGMANS, GREEN AND CO LTD
48 Grosvenor Street, London W1
Associated companies, branches and representatives
throughout the world

This edition first published 1968

393443

*Printed in Great Britain by
Clarke, Doble & Brendon Ltd
Cattedown, Plymouth*

404250-6

To

Olivia Manning

NOTE

Some of these stories have already appeared in print: THE BRIGHTON BELLE in *Nova*; I LIVED FOR YOU in *The London Magazine* and *Harper's Bazaar*; THEIR NIGHT in *Harper's Bazaar* and *The Weekend Telegraph*; and THE CONTAINERS in *The London Magazine*

Contents

The Brighton Belle

She was the daughter of an earl, she had been rich, she had been beautiful. I think that it was I who first gave her the nickname 'The Brighton Belle'.

She reminded me of one of the old first-class Pullman coaches, once elegant but now dilapidated and ramshackle, that make up that train: its opulent upholstery beginning to sag and to exude a smell of spilled food and drink; its tarnished brass and cracked mirrors boldly stating the meretriciousness at which they had only hinted in their glory; its passage seismic with sudden jolts and tremors.

She lived a few doors up from me, and before we had met at a party, I had often seen her making her unsteady way down the hill, thrusting before her a shopping basket on wheels and stopping from time to time to peer over a fence or hedge into a front window. I used to wonder who she was; and even then, in spite of the soiled and shabby clothes, the large hats with the abundant fruit or feathers on them, and the ankle-strap tart's shoes below the bulging legs, I was certain that she must be someone of distinction. She had a habit of talking and of grimacing to herself as she moved along. Her face was a curious mauve shade, with deep-set eyes around which the mascara was heavily smeared, a small retroussé nose and a pointed chin above a wobbling subsidence of fat. Her hair was fuzzy, an improbable shade of orange, brushed forward over her cheeks to conceal (so our mutual friend Robin Charles, the antique dealer, maintained) the scars of a face-lift performed, as he put it, 'in the dark ages'.

'I only live on the ground floor now. I find it difficult to manage all the stairs. So I let off some rooms—not for the money, of course, but because I like to have young people around me and it gives me an interest in life.' Her cat, a huge neutered Russian Blue, jumped into her lap, which was already streaked with its hairs. She looked around her, kneading its head: 'Yes, I'm afraid that this room is really overcrowded. But I don't like to leave my really valuable bits and pieces in my lodgers' rooms. They don't appreciate them in the first place, and they damage them in the second. . . . Is this tea all right for you?'

'Oh, yes, thank you.'

The tea was so bitter and black that I suspected that she had merely poured more hot water into the pot she had prepared for her breakfast.

'It's a special blend which Jacksons used to make up for my father and for his father before him. It's difficult to get them to do it for me now—they say it's too much trouble. But I drink nothing else.' She sipped and sipped again, drawing the tea between her lips with a curious suck and click. 'A biscuit?' She held out the plate. 'That's a pretty design, isn't it? Chinese. You'll recognise it of course. I had a set of twelve given to me by General Doi when I was in Japan just before the war. You know who I mean by General Doi—the Chief of Japanese Intelligence? This is the only plate that survives.' She examined it from all angles; then she said firmly, as though to defy any secret doubts I might have about its beauty, its date or its provenance, 'It's very valuable.'

After she had poured me out a second cup of the tea, ignoring my insincere plea that I never drank more than one, she continued to talk of her travels in the East. 'Yes, those were the days! When I think how I and my second husband—he was a painter, you know—squandered our money! I remember that in Pekin these Chinese friends of ours, such delightful people,

2

related in some way to Sun Yat-sen, lent us their mansion and we gave a party for more than five hundred guests. We all wore Chinese costume and I had this oh, so lovely embroidered robe-thing of the ninth century, a fabulous shade of peacock blue, and these rubies the size of . . .' After China, it was Japan. 'The Japan we knew disappeared with the war. *Your* Japan must be entirely different. The Emperor, as you probably know, had and still has this interest in marine biology, and my husband, who was Russian, White Russian, had a marvellous idea of ordering for him from Canada or Iceland or somewhere this very, very rare species of crab—two of them to be precise, male and female. And when we were received by the Emperor, I presented the crabs to him. Oh, we had a good laugh about that later.' At that she proceeded to have a good laugh again, throwing back her head so that the sagging chins were drawn taut and closing her eyes, as though to squeeze out of them the tears which eventually began to trickle down her cheeks, tinged with mascara. 'You see . . .' she plucked a handkerchief, far from clean, from the recesses of her bodice—'you see, the English language press, the *Tokyo Times* or whatever it was called, had this priceless headline with a photograph of little me and his Imperial Highness: "Earl's daughter exchanges crabs with Emperor." '

Could the source of the 'good laugh' be what I suspected it to be? Only later was I to be certain that it was.

'I see that you are admiring my darling table.' In fact, I had been eyeing, not the table, but the mildewed banana skin which I could glimpse beneath the papers littering its top. How long had it been there? How long would it stay? 'Yes, it's a lovely little piece—a real gem.' The 'gem' was made of boarding-house bamboo, with dragons clumsily lacquered on to every available plane. 'It came from the Pavilion originally, you know. And that chair too—the one with all those clothes on it. Of course they've been in my family for years and years—

3

since long before I was born. But I've made arrangements in my will that eventually they are to go back. . . .' She broke off, at a knock at the door. 'Poop! . . . Yes? Who is it?' A plump, brown face appeared. 'No, I'm sorry Mr Barzengi, I'm busy at this precise moment.' She enunciated with extreme care, giving an equal value to each syllable. 'I'm busy. Later, please.'

'But, madam, my electric light. . . . It is impossible for me. I am now waiting three days and I cannot continue with my preparation and my teacher . . .'

'Later, my dear. Let us talk of it later. I've called the electrician, I really can't do more. Now can I? Later, later.' She got to her swollen feet, waddled across the room, and gently closed the door on him. 'Oh, these people! It's just not worth one's while to have them. I do it because all my life I've been interested in international understanding. There was a time, you know, when I took a leading part in the World Government Movement. But I feel that to provide a decent home for half a dozen foreign students is really of far more value than any amount of sitting on committees. Don't you agree?'

She had gone to the huge break-front wardrobe in one corner of the room and had begun to tweak out of its drawers one crumpled piece of clothing after another, dropping each on to the floor. 'There's something here that I know will interest you. A bowl, a Sung bowl. It was also a present. From the Governor General of Kyoto. We travelled there, you know, in the Imperial Train. The Emperor put it at our disposal. I shall never forget it! There was this little tea-house actually on the train— can you imagine?—and a lovely young girl, a real geisha, passed the time for us by initiating us into the tea-ceremony. Oh, they don't do things like that now! I bet that you never enjoyed the tea-ceremony on a train. Now did you? . . . Ah, there we are!'

She began to unwind a tightly wrapped bundle, which slowly revealed itself to be a nightdress, grey with grime. 'There now!'

She dropped the nightdress and held the bowl out to the light. 'Now isn't that just the most exquisite thing you've ever seen?'

'Yes, it's rather nice,' I said, compromising between good manners and truthfulness.

'I am right in thinking that you collect Oriental art? That's what Robin told me.'

'I don't really know much about it,' I deprecated.

'Robin tells me that you have a quite marvellous collection.' Robin so rarely praises any objects other than those he himself has for sale that I was sure that he had never said anything of the kind. 'Sung,' she said, turning the bowl round and round before my eyes. 'Exquisite. But what use is it to me? I have nowhere to display it. As you see, I've already got far too many objects. So it lies in this drawer. If you're interested,' her manner at once became both wheedling and anxious, 'if you've really fallen in love with it, then perhaps. . . . I'd like it to go to someone who would appreciate it, really appreciate it, and know its true worth.'

Later I was to become inured to the Brighton Belle's attempts either to sell me objects which both of us knew to be of no value, or to borrow off me money which both of us knew would never be repaid. But on this occasion I was acutely embarrassed. Stammering that of course it was a most remarkable piece, and that it was kind of her to think of me, I concluded that its purchase would, I was afraid, be far beyond my means.

But 'Name a price,' she pursued relentlessly. 'There's no harm in naming a price. As I told you before, what I'm chiefly interested in is finding the right kind of home for it.'

I was glad that at that moment the bell rang and went on ringing until again making that curious exclamation 'Poop!' she had to go out to answer it.

'Lady Dorothy Pawson?' I heard a girl's voice drawl.

'Yes.'

'Oh, Lady Dorothy,' the voice rushed on, 'you won't know

5

who I am. But a friend of mine, Sonia Smith-Borrows, was lodging here with you last year. Remember? Well, she told me about lodging here, and so I wrote you a letter last week asking if you . . .'

'A letter? What letter? Don't know what you mean.'

'Perhaps you never got it. Anyway, Lady Dorothy, I'd so much like to lodge with you. And now that I'm in the Old Fashioned Music Hall on the pier, I'd be awfully grateful. . . .'

'The Old Fashioned *what*? The house is quite full.'

'Oh, I don't mind where I sleep—just anywhere, any odd corner. And I love housework, there's nothing I enjoy more than pottering around the house. So I'd willingly help you. Can't you really find room for me? Please!'

'Well . . .' There was a long silence. Then: 'Well, come in and we'll talk about it.'

Of all the Brighton Belle's friends it was therefore I who first met Cynthia.

Cynthia was no longer young, but she had all the optimism with which the young console themselves for the lack of talent or success. None of us ever learned her age: but references to being in the chorus of this revue with Hermione Gingold or of that pantomime with Nellie Wallace suggested that she was well into her thirties. Her hair, which had a metallic reddish glint in its brown, was loosely waved and usually worn over a ribbon which she tied in a girlish bow in front. She had a wide mouth, which tended to remain half open to reveal teeth with a gap in their middle, a small, beaked nose and eyes set close together under finely pencilled eyebrows. There were times, usually in conversation with male strangers, when she affected a lisp.

'She's a monster,' Robin pronounced. 'What can the poor Brighton Belle see in her? It's a mystery, an absolute mystery.'

Robin's wife, Helga, stopped polishing a table. 'There's no

mystery about it. Cynthia believes every word that Dorothy tells her. And none of Dorothy's other friends can do that.'

'She pretends to believe.'

'Well, if she pretends, then she pretends better than we can —any of us. And that's what Dorothy wants. If the Brighton Belle says that a table has come from the Pavilion, then as far as Cynthia is concerned, that's where it came from. If the Brighton Belle says that an Imari bowl is Sung, then for Cynthia Sung it is. It's as simple as that.'

Things always were simple to Helga's German mind.

'But what does Cynthia get out of the relationship?' I asked.

'She's a little snub.' To Helga the words 'snob' and 'snub' have always been interchangeable. 'And to be on terms of friendship with the daughter of an earl. . . . Besides, she probably has her eye on a legacy.'

'What has poor Dorothy got to leave except her debts?'

'As far as Cynthia is concerned she has a lot to leave—a Sung bowl, a Chinese Chippendale table and countless other treasures.'

'She's a monster,' Robin repeated. 'And we have to accompany the Brighton Belle to Eastbourne tomorrow to see the monster perform in what the Argus calls "a happy family seaside show." Oh God!'

I did not, at that time, know Dorothy (or Dotty, as her oldest friends from the pre-war days would call her) well enough for her to attempt to bully and wheedle me into joining that particular party. But in the months ahead I was often to be her victim on similar excursions. With the same persistence with which she pursued anyone who seemed likely either to buy one of her 'heirlooms' or to lend her money, she would telephone or call at my house repeatedly to force me to accompany her.

'. . . Cynthia has a part in "Ladies in Retirement" at Westcliff-on-Sea,' she would announce. 'It's a semi-professional production. Not quite what one would wish for her, but I tell her that this is the beginning for her in the legitimate theatre.' She giggled. 'Why do they call it the "legitimate" theatre? Those two recent plays by Osborne and Pinter to which you took me might really be called "illegitimate. . . ."' Now I know that you are fearfully busy, my dear, but would you escort me? I hate the idea of going to a benighted place like that all on my own. And the poor child does so value your support and criticism. She calls you "the sea-green incorruptible," you know. "When Francis says that a thing is good or bad, one always knows he means what he says," she remarked only yesterday. Yes, do come with me! I count on you! Please! I really couldn't face that awful journey on my own. And after the show we can have dinner at a marvellous little restaurant run by a charming Spanish couple—a discovery of Cynthia's. You'd never imagine that a place like that could exist at Westcliff-on-Sea. Just the three of us together.'

She knew my interest in food and shamelessly she was now prepared to play on it. But I doubted if the restaurant existed at all; and if it did, I should certainly be left with the bill.

'I'm so busy,' I protested feebly. 'I really can't. . . .' But I knew even then that I should have to give in.

Half an hour later Robin was on the telephone.

'Westcliff-on-Sea?'

'You too?'

'Yes. And Ruby Lamont and Irvine and Delia Morrow and the Quinceys and, well, all the crowd.'

'Dinner at a marvellous little restaurant?'

'Just the three of us together—yes, that's right. Cynthia insists I see her performance. She values my criticism so much.'

'Does she call you "the sea-green incorruptible"?'

'Yes. How clever of you to know that!'

*

8

In the course of the next year the Brighton Belle persuaded us to visit most of the seaside resorts of southern England. We saw Cynthia smiling fixedly at us from the front row of the chorus on this pier and at that Hippodrome; we were present at her first 'starring' performance in a village hall on the Downs; we clapped, when there was no one else to clap, as she pranced forward, simpering, to take a curtsy after rendering 'Somewhere over the Rainbow' in *Aladdin* in East Croydon. Each performance served only to harden us in our conviction that she had no talent at all; but at each performance the Belle herself was enraptured.

'If a Victorian sofa can become a Louis Quinze settee, then why shouldn't poor little Cynthia become a Mrs Siddons?' Robin asked bitterly when we were returning, tired and depressed, from a performance of *The Circle* in Bognor.

The Brighton Belle's final aim was to achieve a West End debut for her protégée, and since one of Robin's most extravagant customers was Sir Charles Otley, the famous actor, she now began to scheme for this eminent if disagreeable man and 'the little girl'—as she had recently begun to refer to Cynthia —to be brought together.

'He would be far more interested in a little boy,' Robin commented when approached. But being basically good-natured (in spite of his venomous tongue) and having a genuine affection for the Belle, he eventually arranged a meeting in his house.

Dorothy, on that occasion, both flattered Sir Charles and astounded the rest of us by managing to remember a host of roles played by the last of the great actor-managers in the 'thirties and even 'twenties. '. . . Oh, I shall never forget that marvellous Joseph Surface in the Komisarjevsky production. It was definitive—that's the only word for it—definitive. And of course it was the same year that you did the second of your Romeos, wasn't it? What an *annus mirabilis*!'

The rouged and raddled old queen told Robin afterwards that he had found Dorothy 'delightful, quite delightful—a *grande dame* of the old school'; but when Robin inquired 'And what did you think of her protégée?' he said 'Who?' and then added 'Oh, you mean that writer fellow who sat glum and said nothing.'

Cynthia, who had also sat glum and said nothing, he had obviously not noticed at all.

But that first failure did not deter the Brighton Belle; nothing, where Cynthia's career was concerned, could ever deter her. She invited Sir Charles to 'an intimate supper' at which I was also present; she went round to his dressing-room at the Haymarket Theatre, pushing Cynthia into it before her but leaving me to wait for them outside (as I much preferred to do in any case); repeatedly telephoned to him and sent him messages by Robin and wrote him letters in a scrawl of green ink.

By this time Cynthia had taken to calling Dorothy 'Auntie', and was playing the part of devoted niece to the old woman far more convincingly that any part she had ever assumed on the stage. She seemed to take a rare pleasure in saying the words 'Lady Dorothy', savouring them as a ham actor might savour 'To be or not to be' or 'Tomorrow and tomorrow'. 'I'm ringing up for Lady Dorothy—Lady Dorothy Pawson. Lady Dorothy's sherry has not arrived yet and her guests are already here.' The 'guests' were merely myself and my dog. 'Lady Dorothy would like the sherry at once—as soon as you can make it. . . . Thank you. Yes, I'll tell Lady Dorothy.' Often what she had to tell Lady Dorothy was that no South African sherry could be delivered until a bill had been paid.

It was no longer possible ever to see Dorothy without 'the little girl' unless it was on a night of a performance; and even then it might well be that Dorothy had decided to go for yet another time to see *Ladies in Retirement* or *Dear Octopus* or *The Corn is Green*. No longer did Dorothy stay on and on when one had invited her to a drink before Sunday lunch, so that the joint began to shrivel and flake away and one grew groggy with hunger and too much alcohol. Cynthia saw to that, and one was grateful to her for doing so. But nor did the Brighton Belle now have the opportunity to regale one with those libellously indiscreet accounts of her earlier life or of the lives of our Brighton friends. Cynthia, who was a prude, also saw to that : with a shocked 'Oh, really, Auntie, no! No, don't listen to her! Isn't she awful?' Once, in an aside to me, after she had stopped Dorothy from telling some particularly scurrilous and risqué story, Cynthia whispered : 'You'd never think from some of the things she says that she came of such an aristocratic family, would you?' Evidently Cynthia did not know that an eighteenth-century squarson ancestor of the Belle had been one of the most outspoken and scandalous of English diarists.

Helga and Robin, whom I invariably consulted when anything baffled me in Brighton, explained Dorothy's theatrical ambitions for Cynthia as a compensation for her own frustrated ones in the distant 'twenties. Dorothy had, after all, been one of Mr Cochran's Young Ladies for a few months, before she had married the first of her three husbands; and years later her friendship with Ivor Novello had brought her a walking-on part in one of his musicals. Probably she had had no more talent then than poor Cynthia now; but at least on the evidence of the fashionable photographs, taken through draped fishing-nets, ropes of paper wistaria or yards of fine gauze, she had been exceptionally beautiful.

Through ceaseless badgering and coaxing, through the half-hearted intervention of Sir Charles and through the last-minute illness of another actress, Cynthia at last got her chance in the West End. The play was a comedy thriller in which a once famous star of the wartime screen had for some time been touring the provinces. From the way in which Dorothy and even

11

Cynthia spoke of the part, I assumed that it was almost as important as that of the former film star. 'In terms of actual lines it's not of course the leading role—Madam has seen to that!' the Brighton Belle announced. 'But in terms of dramatic effectiveness—well, you'll see for yourself.' But before the opportunity came to see for myself, I had to hear for myself too. Dorothy insisted that I should 'run through' the role with Cynthia.

It was useless to say that this was a task for which I was wholly unqualified. 'No, my dear,' Dorothy brushed aside all my objections. 'As a writer, you have this marvellous feeling for words. What you can teach her will be invaluable.'

For the words of the play, unfortunately, I had no feeling at all. They were totally undistinguished.

Cynthia's reading of them on the other hand, did have a bizarre distinction, as she mouthed, grimaced, threw her arms about and showered both the script and myself with spittle. The part was a minuscule one—she appeared briefly as a secretary, taking dictation from the hero in the first act and answering the telephone in the third. But it was apparent that both she and Dorothy regarded this peripheral character as having the same kind of artistic significance as the Gravedigger in *Hamlet* or the Porter in *Macbeth*.

'Isn't she splendid?' Dorothy exclaimed, as I polished the moisture off my glasses. 'I feel that this will be her breakthrough. Madam's going to regret that she ever allowed her in the show.'

This I could well believe.

For days before the first night Dorothy was busy rallying her friends and the friends of her friends. A couple whom she had met for a moment in my house—they were going out as she was coming in—were astonished to receive first a leaflet about the play with a green ink scrawl across it 'Do come! We're counting on You!' and then a whole succession of telephone calls, each more insistent than the last. A schoolmaster and his wife, whose lives were devoted to the cultivation of orchids, they seldom went to the theatre more than once each year. To many of us she sent out letters couched in terms so ambiguous that those who did not know her well (by now I was not one of them) assumed that they were being invited to attend the first night as her guests. When, having accepted, they received a notification from the threatre than an early remittance would oblige, they made far from obliging comments.

I felt myself to be to blame, at least in part, for the accident. If I had not been so eager to escape Dorothy, it might never have happened. She knew that the drama critic for one of the weekly reviews was an acquaintance of mine and, since he lived not far from Brighton, she had been telephoning me almost daily to ask if I had done anything about bringing him and 'the little girl' together. I had made vague promises, but these were not enough for Dorothy, who, as always, insisted on action.

Helga and I had just emerged from the butcher's, when Helga clutched my arm: 'Oh, my lord! There's the Brighton Belle—with Cynthia.'

'And there, thank God, is my bus!'

'And mine,' said Helga, who in fact lived in the opposite direction.

'Can't stop, Dorothy dear. Must catch this bus,' I shouted at her, as she waved from half-way across the road, the traffic swerving and braking around her. 'I'll call you.'

Her swollen legs wide apart and a pink silk umbrella raised in one hand, she shouted: 'Wait! Take the next one! Wait! Important!'

I pretended not to hear, as Helga and I scampered for the bus.

When I swung myself on after Helga, I realised that the Belle was hobbling behind us, still shouting my name, while

Cynthia, lurching under two heavy shopping baskets, brought up the rear.

Approaching from the back of the bus, where neither the driver nor the conductor could see her, Dorothy raised a foot on the platform and gripped at the rail. But simultaneously the bus jerked off. 'Oh, poop! The fool! The bloody fool!' Dorothy bellowed. Frantically I rang the bell, while Helga screamed 'Let go, let go!' But with astonishing persistence, Dorothy continued to cling on, as she was dragged, one leg on the platform and one on the ground, forwards by the bus. I tried to catch hold of her and pull her aboard; and simultaneously Cynthia raced up from behind and began to push.

It was all so quick—a matter of seconds. The bus began to halt, passengers jumped to their feet; the Brighton Belle's grip weakened on the rail, I made repeated efforts to cling on to her and drag her aboard the platform, as though she were a stranded dolphin, while she herself kept gasping: 'Bloody fool, bloody fool!'—her huge floral hat askew and one shoe now off the foot which was being dragged along the road.

Then she was away from the platform altogether, her knees bumping horribly along the road and her hands going down with a slap, slap, one after the other.

When we hauled her to her feet, she seemed dazed, but otherwise all right apart from some superficial cuts and bruises.

'You shouldn't have started, you bloody fool!' she panted at the conductor, as a crowd collected around her on the pavement. 'You might have killed me.'

'And you shouldn't have got on to a moving bus from behind the platform.'

'I did nothing of the kind! The bus hadn't started. Had it?'

She turned to me for the confirmation which I could not in good conscience give her; but a red-faced woman in the crowd took up: 'That's right. The bus hadn't started. Criminal! You might have killed her, the poor old lady.'

'Well, take my number then. Take my number.' The young conductor histrionically pulled forward the lapel of his jacket. 'Take it, if you want to. Go on.'

'How can she take your number, the state she's in?' the red-faced woman demanded, squaring her shoulders. 'Write it down for her.'

Eventually we got Dorothy home in a taxi. Cynthia bathed the grazes on her knees, elbows and palms, Helga made a cup of the 'special' tea (which appeared to come in bags), and I kept urging the Belle to allow me to call a doctor.

'No, no. . . . Not necessary, not necessary at all. Helga sweet, do put the teeniest, weeniest dash of rum in this tea. That's all I need. In the Regency chiffonier over there. That's an angel! No, just a little bit more than that. I want to be able to taste it, after all.'

Eventually she had recovered enough to return to the subject of the critic.

'Wouldn't you like to call him now—from here? Why not?'

'Oh, he never gets home until the evening.'

'Well, call him in London—at his office.'

'He doesn't have an office.'

'Well, call him where he is.'

I gave a sigh and called him. Fortunately no one answered.

Perhaps the accident really had nothing to do with the stroke; perhaps it would have happened anyway.

I had just gone to bed, shortly after one o'clock, when I was brought to the door in my dressing-gown by a repeated ringing of the bell. Cynthia was there in pyjamas and a raincoat, her face shiny and creased and her eyes bleared with sleep. 'It's Auntie,' she moaned. 'She's had a queer turn. I'm awfully worried about her. She doesn't seem able to talk at all—I can't get anything out of her. Oh, do come quickly.'

So for the second time that day, I had to attempt to heave up Dorothy, whom I found propped against her bed, her puffy, blue-veined legs outstretched before her, with the skirt of her nightdress rucked above the knees, her chin on her raddled chest, and her mouth horribly twisted. But this time Cynthia and the frightened Mr Barzengi, wearing a checked cap and with a blanket draped about him, were there to help me. Even so the weight was formidable.

The Brighton Belle kept trying to say something; but each time all that emerged was a kind of hiccoughing gasp.

Then suddenly, my ear to her mouth, I realised what she was croaking: the name of the critic to whom I was to introduce 'the little girl'.

The next day Dorothy was able to enunciate an occasional word with the greatest of difficulty. 'Theatre . . . rehearsal . . . rehearsal. . . .'

'Yes, what about your rehearsals, Cynthia? I can stay with Dorothy—I can bring my work over here—if you have a rehearsal in London.'

'Oh, I've withdrawn from the play,' Cynthia replied in a rush of embarrassment. 'I've already told them. I rang up this morning.'

'Withdrawn!'

'It won't be all that inconvenient—it's such a small part, they were probably quite relieved. I wasn't much good in it.'

Dorothy's eyes, the skin around them streaked with mascara as though with coal-dust, all at once became frantic in the terrifyingly immobile face. She made a sound as of retching and repeated it three times before she got out 'Go. Must go. Rehearsal. Go.'

'Now, shush, Auntie, shush!' Cynthia got to her feet. 'I'm going downstairs to get you some supper, while Francis sits with you. All right?'

Dorothy scrabbled at my hand and then gripped it tighter and tighter. 'Make—her. . . . Must—make—her. . . .'

But from then on no one could make 'the little girl' leave the Brighton Belle for more than a few minutes on end.

Robin, always cynical in his ascription of motives, said that it was obvious—of course 'the little girl' was determined to get all Auntie's money. 'She daren't let her out of her sight for a moment. Even when that cousin called to see her, did you notice how Cynthia watched her like a lynx? And Helga—who after all has known the Brighton Belle longer than any of us—says that she and Dorothy are never left alone together for even a moment. . . . Well, that poor creature is going to get a nasty shock when she realises that Auntie's heirlooms are, in fact, quite valueless.'

'You talk as if Dorothy were going to die.'

'Well, isn't she?' Robin retorted brutally.

Robin was, of course, right—he usually is; Dorothy died after a second stroke, some four months later, having spent the last three weeks of her life in a coma during which Cynthia, with the assistance of the district nurse, attended to all her needs. Many of her friends joined the doctor in urging that the Belle should be placed in a hospital; but Cynthia would have none of that. 'No, she hated hospitals,' she would say. 'She hated illness. I'm certain that she would like to stay here.'

'But Cynthia, she's taking nothing in—nothing in at all,' I argued. 'It doesn't matter to her whether she's . . .'

'I think that she'd rather be here.'

Cynthia raised a cigarette to her mouth with a hand that trembled slightly and puffed at it, exhaling the smoke as soon as she had drawn it in. She had asked me for the cigarette; she never smoked as a rule. 'Filthy habit,' she used to say, as she swept up the ash scattered by the Belle over the lacquer dragons on the table reputedly from the Pavilion. 'Why do you have to do it?'

'It's the only pleasure left to me,' the Brighton Belle would answer.

Cynthia choked and began to cough, banging with her knuckles on her bony chest, until tears came to eyes, already red-rimmed with the ones she had shed that morning. 'Poop!' she spluttered. 'Poop!' I had never heard her use that expletive before.

She was wearing trousers and a dark blue polo-neck sweater, and her hair, no longer flashing those curiously metallic glints of red, hung straight in a bob, its brown streaked with grey. 'I like a womanly woman,' Dorothy used to say, glancing at her. But poor Cynthia was no longer that. The months of constant attendance on her dying friend had both aged 'the little girl' and given to her a masculine toughness and hardness.

'So that's it, Francis,' she said. 'That's it.'

Quite what was what, I was not clear.

'Now you must start your career again,' I said encouragingly, if fatuously.

'My what? Are you off your nut?' She puffed again, two or three times in rapid succession, at the shrivelled end of her cigarette and then stared down at its tip. 'I have no "career" and you know that.' She seemed to enjoy my embarrassment. 'So Auntie wanted to believe that I had. Well, why not? But I was never good enough for anything but the chorus—and the back row at that. Right?' She gave a hoarse laugh. 'Oh, I could see what all of you thought of my dramatic ambitions —or, rather, the poor old dear's ambitions for me. Of course I could see! Well, you were right. Just as you were right about all that furniture, which anyone in their right senses could tell had come from a junk-shop. But if she wanted to believe . . . Well, she had to have something. There was so little left for her. Three marriages and all of them unhappy—no children—

18

precious little money. Nothing really but that handle to her name. And what good was that? It didn't even get her any more credit.' She stubbed out the cigarette. 'I shall be sick if I go on with that. . . . No, not even a single bottle of South African sherry.'

'Then what are you going to do?'

Cynthia slumped yet lower in the chair and covered her eyes with a hand on which the veins stood out. 'Do, oh, God knows! I don't want to *do* anything any more.' She shook herself, straightened in the chair and, with an effort, smiled at me. 'All I want to do is sleep, and sleep, and sleep. . . . But I miss the old girl, you know. There was something—she had something. . . . You could tell at once. See her, staggering down the street, half-drunk, and you could tell at once. She was a lady, a real lady. I suppose that's what got me.' She put a little finger to the corner of an eye, to wipe away the tear that had formed there : the lady-like gesture of someone who would never be a lady.

'I'll go on running the lodging-house,' she said. 'Because that's what it was—a lodging-house. If she could make a little money out of it, then I can do much better. That's what I'll do. We'll continue to be neighbours. That'll be fun won't it? But— oh dear . . .' again the little finger brushed the eyelashes, 'it won't be the same without the Brighton Belle. It won't be the same for any of us.'

It was the first time that I had heard her use the nickname; she was to call Dorothy nothing else from then on.

19

I Lived for You

'*I* don't mind at all,' Mrs Parrish said. 'But it's just the sort of thing that would upset poor Gerald. We have to think of Gerald.'

Her granddaughter, Caroline, saw no reason why they should think of the coloured servant at all; but it was better not to exasperate the old woman, to whom exasperation came more and more easily with the passing of the years. She therefore went out into the garden at the rear of the house and shooed her two young children, both of whom were entirely naked, back through the open french windows into their bedroom. 'You must never, *never*, do that again,' she said in a loud, cross voice. Then she added more quietly, so that Mrs Parrish should not hear : 'At least not in this house.' At home, the children, who were two and four, were used to running about without any clothes.

There were many things that they and their mother were not allowed to do in the Brighton house because of Gerald. There were many things that Mrs Parrish did not allow herself to do because of him. She no longer swore, as in the presence of her former housekeeper, Miss Carfrae, now dead; she no longer slopped around the house in her dressing-gown until lunch-time and even later; and her bouts of drinking had become increasingly furtive and guilty.

Gerald, her relatives all told each other, had done the old woman a world of good; he had given her a new lease of life; they could not imagine how she had ever managed without him. But neither these considerations nor the abstracted saintliness of his manner could make them like him. He was, each of them was convinced—though they never mentioned this to each other—after Mrs Parrish's money; and since they were after it themselves, an unacknowledged rivalry was bound to exist.

Gerald came from the West Indies and, when asked his age, used to answer with his benignly remote smile, 'Now you'd better ask my mother that, hadn't you?' As said by him, the reply could not be taken as an impertinence; but it secretly annoyed those who had put the far more impertinent question. His hair was a wiry black streaked with grey, and he brushed it straight back from his bulging, unlined forehead, over his ears, to make a bush at the back of his head. Perhaps it was this bush of hair, always slightly redolent of macassar oil, which made his neck seem so fragile and long. His liquid eyes were beautiful—everyone agreed on that—and so were his hands. One of the grandsons claimed, on the flimsiest of evidence, that Gerald used the hands to massage Mrs Parrish when she had her bouts of fibrositis; but this seemed unlikely. Gerald was always so fastidious, he always shrank from any contact with others, perching himself on the edge of the back seat of the car so that no part of his person or even his clothes would have to touch either of the two children when Caroline and her husband gave him a lift to the market. Waiting at table, he wore gloves.

'I can't see the point of the gloves,' one of Mrs Parrish's sons remarked. 'In Florence my Bruno puts on gloves, and that's just as well, because he has such awful hands and the nails are never clean. But Gerald's hands are marvellous.'

'Perhaps it's because they are so marvellous, that he wants to protect them,' his mother replied.

Gerald had now been with her for almost a decade.

After the death of Miss Carfrae there had been a bad period of almost a year. Mrs Parrish had first employed a former

21

buyer from a London store, whose hair was dyed an improbable shade of orange and who never stopped talking, either to Mrs Parrish or to herself; then a succession of sluttish daily women, who left her either because she found them dishonest and dirty or because they found less exacting and better paid work in the hotels; and finally a Scots couple who each night banged around in the basement set aside for them and each morning emerged from it bleary and indiscriminately scarred and bruised.

The couple left after a scene, in which they had discovered to their amazement that 'the old girl's' language was a match for their own; and Caroline had then come down for a week 'to help out'. But she found Mrs Parrish, as she wrote to her husband, 'Impossible, quite impossible', and not even the thought of the legacy which would, they hoped, eventually pay for them to send their elder child to Eton, could persuade her to stay. So she put an advertisement for her grandmother in the *Brighton Argus*, explained that she really must leave because she didn't like to entrust the children to Nanny for too long, and returned to London, vindictively glad that the old woman would now have to cope for herself.

A number of applicants for the job appeared; but either Mrs Parrish told them point-blank that she considered them unsuitable or her tone, hectoring and peevish, made them decide that they themselves would be better suited elsewhere. The house grew dustier and untidier; an indefinable smell, both musty and sour, began to envelop it; the milkman was annoyed to find a greenish sediment in the bottles left out for him and the dustmen were surprised to find that often no dust-bins were put out for them for several weeks on end. From time to time Caroline or one of the other relatives would come down for what they called a 'blitz'. All of them were secretly convinced that, like the beautiful old Regency house, the once beautiful old woman was entering on her final dissolution. She was drinking heavily and blatantly, with no attempt, however perfunctory, at concealment; she was eating hardly at all.

Then Gerald appeared, in answer not to the advertisement in the *Argus* but to one, put up many weeks before, on a newsagent's board and now grown faint and streaky from the rain which had seeped into it.

'It's no use your applying,' the old woman panted crossly, as she swayed before him on the doorstep, one ringed hand raised—–there was some ink on the bony wrist and the nails were far from clean—preparatory to slamming the door shut. 'I said quite distinctly—I mean, I wrote, my granddaughter wrote, quite distinctly—"Housekeeper".'

'I wish to be housekeeper,' Gerald said. 'That is my wish.'

It was then that he gave that benignly remote smile of his, the full lips slowly parting to reveal first the teeth, white against purple, and then the pink gums above them, while the black eyes grew oddly unfocused as though at the advent of some deep-seated pain, not for himself nor even for his interlocutor, but for the whole of the suffering and striving world at large.

Mrs Parrish hesitated; then she said 'Well, come in for a moment. Though it's really no use. I had a woman in mind.'

'I can do anything that a woman can do, madam,' he replied in his deep, sing-song voice, pressing against the door to click it shut, since she had failed to close it properly.

He mounted the stairs behind her to the first-floor sitting-room; then rushed ahead of her on the landing to pull open the door.

She was disconcerted by the way in which, as she interrogated him, he automatically began to tidy the coffee table before his chair : tipping the contents of all the ashtrays together into the largest of them; folding up the papers; and then placing the magazines one on top of the other, with a rapid glance at the date to make sure that he had them in the right order.

Yes, he could cook; at present he could prepare only simple

dishes but he was willing to learn. No, he had never done work of this kind before, but he was sure that he could do it to madam's satisfaction. A reference? He frowned at the pile of magazines, biting on his lower lip. Well, of course, there was the chief nurse at the hospital.

'The hospital?' Mrs Parrish took up, alarmed. She was convinced now that he was a madman, either escaped or discharged prematurely from a lunatic asylum.

Yes, he explained gently, he had been working at a hospital; he lived in the male nurses' hostel. 'But I do not care to be with those people. Such a life does not suit me—such a life in the hostel. And I have been unlucky in my lodgings—when I have lived in lodgings.'

As he continued talking, Mrs Parrish inspected him surreptitiously; the frayed but neat blue pin-stripe suit, its trousers sharply creased but a little too short for him so that even when he stood up his socks remained visible; the black tie and the shirt with the old-fashioned detachable collar, cream against the white; the belt with the silver snake clasp. But even then she had the uncomfortable feeling that it was not she who sat in judgment on him, but he on her. Her hair, she realized, was a mess; and glancing at her reflection in the lid of a silver cigarette-box at her elbow she saw to her horror that the lipstick was smeared at one corner of her mouth.

'My only desire is to serve. Please allow me to do so.'

To her own amazement, but not to his, she acceded to a request which, she was soon to learn, was totally sincere.

To serve did, indeed, seem to be his sole desire. She would go down to the kitchen at 11 o'clock at night and find him on his hands and knees, scrubbing the floor. On his days off he would often tell her that he had decided to remain at home in order to prepare some dish for a dinner party on the following evening. He had asked her to buy him a number of cookery books—the only extravagance to which he subjected her—and from these, not from any instruction she or Caroline or any other of the children or grandchildren had been able to give him, he had learned to become a superb cook. Mrs Parrish offered to get him in a woman for the rough, but he invariably replied that he preferred to have the house to himself.

Mrs Parish and her family were all curious about Gerald; but they discovered little. He spoke of a brother in the vaguest of terms—he had some unspecified business in Barbados and every six months or so a flimsy letter would arrive for him, so thin that, as she fingered it, Mrs Parrish used to wonder if the envelope contained anything at all. Gerald apparently had no friends, though he would chat with assistants who served him at the shops. His room—both Mrs Parrish and her family would peep into it from time to time when he was out—contained nothing personal : no photographs, no ornaments except those that Mrs Parrish put there, nothing except a calendar, the date neatly torn off each day, an inkwell and a dipper pen, a canvas garden chair which he had bought for himself, evidently preferring it to the armchair provided by Mrs Parrish and, most important of all, his religious books.

What was his religion? They never discovered. He had second-hand volumes on Zen Buddhism and Theosophy and Gurdjieff and Subhud; he had tracts, also usually second-hand, containing instruction in the Roman Catholic faith; he had ancient parish magazines and copies, often with their covers missing, of *The Divine Word* and *Spiritual Healing* and *Psychic News*. Mrs Parrish would turn over the new acquisitions, shaking her head in wonder; her children and grandchildren would giggle over them and tell each other that Gerald was 'really quite dotty'. He never went to church, as far as any of them knew.

Mrs Parrish had never, until then, been a tidy woman. With the prodigality of those who have had money all their lives without ever being obliged either to earn it or safeguard it,

a

she allowed food to rot in the larder until it had to be thrown away; newspapers and magazines to accumulate unread on occasional tables, chairs and even the carpet; clothes to grow musty in soiled, jumbled heaps in cupboards or the corner of drawers for lack of a single button or because of a seam that needed stitching. To all that, Gerald put an end.

He seemed to enjoy nothing more than to wash, iron and repair her clothes; so that garments, the existence of which she had wholly forgotten, would suddenly appear, as though new, on hangers or neatly folded. He also spent patient hours on bringing order to the chaos of her dressing-table, her bed-side table and the two desks, one in her bedroom and the other in her sitting-room, into the drawers of which she had the habit of stuffing any papers too complicated or too tedious for her to deal with. She became furtively ashamed of the squalor and untidiness which she created, to be removed each day by this gentle, perpetually smiling servant; and the very fact that he never complained or showed the slightest exasperation or disgust seemed not to alleviate her shame, as one might suppose, but merely to intensify it.

'Caroline, dear,' she would say, 'do take care where that cigarette ash is falling. It makes so much more work for poor Gerald.' Or: 'Children—you'd better ask poor Gerald for a dustpan and brush and do something about that mud you've brought in.' Or, to the eldest of her sons, a brigadier in his fifties: 'Can't you clear up some of the mess in your room? I hate to have Gerald see it like that.'

There were, however, curious periods—so widely spaced apart that each of them came to Mrs Parrish with the shock of a disagreeable novelty—when the smooth precision of this process of tending both to the house and its octogenarian mistress would suddenly suffer unaccountable checks and hesitations. Gerald would become absentminded, forgetting Mrs Parrish's bedtime glass of milk with a dash of brandy in it, or omitting to lock and bolt the front door last thing at night, or leaving a shopping-bag on the counter of a shop; his hand would tremble as he stooped over her with a dish of potatoes and he would give a series of peculiarly extended sighs while he moved about his cleaning; his clothes would look dishevelled and even dirty, he would stammer and swallow as he talked to her, and in his eyes, usually so placid in their indiscriminate benignity, would lurk an expression of anxiety and even panic.

Such occurrences, of which there were one or two each year, always reminded Mrs Parrish of the occasional breakdowns of her dishwasher. This was an expensive machine, the best on the market, and day after day it carried out its tasks without any trouble. But then, suddenly and inexplicably, its quiet murmur would become a sequence of strident moans and grunts; it would shake as though in rage or terror; and the dishes which were taken from it emerged covered in bits of macerated food, detergent and grease. A mechanic would come round and at once the machine would resume the ordered tenor of its existence, its brief aberration forgotten. But there was no mechanic for whom to send to deal with Gerald.

'Do you think he drinks secretly?' Caroline's husband asked, when a visit to Mrs Parrish had coincided with one of Gerald's 'turns' (as Mrs Parrish called them).

'Nonsense! Gerald never touches a drop.'

'Perhaps he gets homesick from time to time?' Caroline suggested.

'This is his only home. He has told me that more than once.'

The smell of burning potatoes crept up the stairs. Normally Gerald never burnt anything in the kitchen.

Mrs Parrish had been to London to the christening of one of her grandchildren. Gerald had, as usual, driven her to the station in her old but capacious and comfortable Armstrong

Siddeley and had settled her in the first-class Pullman carriage with a pile of magazines, most of which she would leave unread on the table when she reached Victoria. One of her sons was to meet her.

'Don't forget that the carpenter is coming in to mend that window frame.'

Gerald said that he would not forget; and Mrs Parrish herself knew that it was unnecessary to remind him.

'Well, then, have a good rest for the three days,' she dismissed him. But she also knew that, whether she was present or absent, Gerald would never rest.

Gerald met her again at the station, and as he dropped her hatbox while taking it from the carriage—gaily it rolled on and on ahead of them, with Gerald making no attempt to retrieve it—Mrs Parrish realized, with the mixture of shock and unease she always experienced on these occasions, that this was the beginning of another of his 'turns'.

In the car she questioned him about the weather in Brighton, but his answers were almost inarticulate. Turning round to stammer an answer to another of her questions—this time about the window frame—he all but drove into the back of a van in front of them. Mrs Parrish decided that it would be better to be silent.

It was then that she noticed his neck. It was a cold afternoon—the month was March and an icy wind was blowing off the sea—but in spite of that the brown skin under that outthrust bush of hair was glistening with sweat. She watched fascinated and yet obscurely horrified, as a trickle ran down the line of his jaw and then fell, with a plop, on to his collar, which—she also now noticed—was far from clean.

They drew up at the house in Brunswick Square—although there was plenty of room, it was some time before Gerald succeeded in getting the car alongside the kerb, between a lorry and a motor-bicycle—and Mrs Parrish then waited for him to open the door for her, as he usually did, and to help her down. But he was carrying out the luggage.

'Gerald!' she summoned him sharply; until at last, with dragging footsteps, he came to her. His face at the window, as he stooped to open the door, shocked her both with its expression of despair and with its greyish pallor. He supported her to the top of the steps, unlocked the door, pushed it open, mumbled something and then ran back to the car. Mrs Parrish went in, first pulling the pins out of her hat and then removing it from her head, which had unaccountably started to throb. She put her hat down and knew even then that something was amiss, though she failed to realise that it was the carriage-clock which had disappeared from its place on top of the hall table where the hat now rested. Fearfully she went into her bedroom, on the ground-floor, switching on the light although it was far from dark, as though in an effort to dispel a premonition.

The photograph, the photograph of her long-dead husband in its silver frame! The ivory and gold brushes! The little Fabergé box in which she kept pins! She put her hands to her lips to stop their idiot trembling and, aghast, gazed around her, her fur first twitching on her shoulders as she swung hither and thither, and then writhing to the floor.

'Gerald!' she called weakly. Then she screamed 'Gerald! Gerald! *Gerald!*' on a note of shriller and shriller panic.

But Gerald did not come.

She tottered out into the hall and saw the two suitcases and the hat-box standing in one corner. The front door swung open on a gust of icy wind. She went to it, picking her way over the parquet as though it were treacherous ice, and peered out. The car was still outside; there were some children playing beyond it on the lawns; an old man limped by with a mongrel dog on a length of rope. But she could not see Gerald.

She shut the door and called again.

Breathlessly she began to mount the stairs to the upstairs

room, his name now becoming a kind of plaintive mewing as she continued to repeat it. 'Oh—oh—oh!' Again, in the sitting room, she pressed her hands to her lips. All at once she had experienced a terrible lurching sickness in her stomach and her throat. The cigarette case—the cigarette case which Auntie Janet had given them! The three miniatures to the left of the fireplace! The . . . The . . .

At last she reached Gerald's room, at the top of the house. She pressed a hand to her side and then, with the same hand, knocked on the door. Her rings rattled and scraped on the wood. But no answer came. She fumbled for the door handle, turned it and peered in.

Gerald sat on a straight-backed chair, one hand on either knee and his eyes fixed on the empty grate. Mrs Parrish had never seen the room in such disorder : bedclothes lay on the floor, one of the two curtain-rods hung down from a corner of the window, with the curtain trailing on to the floor, its velvet thick with dust and plaster; the bedside lamp lay in fragments, its shade crushed to a plate-like oval.

'What *is* all this? What on earth has happened? Gerald, tell me! Speak to me!'

Gerald said nothing and Mrs Parrish began to whimper anew : 'Oh, Gerald, what is it? How did it happen? Tell me, Gerald!' while her eyes picked out one fresh horror after another.

Suddenly Gerald slipped off the chair, gliding down on to the curtain at his feet as limply as a doll. Mrs Parrish thought that he had fainted; but he begun to writhe on the floor, burying his face in the folds of the curtain and sobbing incoherently 'I can't. . . . I can't. . . .' while Mrs Parrish looked down at him in amazement and horror.

The police eventually arrived, summoned not by Gerald but by Mrs Parrish. It was also Mrs Parrish who opened the door to them. The bell rang three times, while she waited for Gerald to answer; then she made her way slowly down the stairs herself and let them in.

The senior of the two detectives had a chilly, even contemptuous manner and he made no attempt to restrain his irritation when Mrs Parrish gave way to tears. He surveyed the places from which this or that knick-knack had been looted with the detachment of a dentist examining the gaps in a row of teeth.

Finally he asked to see Gerald, having already enquired what staff Mrs Parrish employed.

Mrs Parrish called 'Gerald, Gerald!' forlornly up the stairs, after she had repeatedly rung the sitting-room bell without receiving an answer. Gerald did not come.

'Perhaps he's gone out?'

Mrs Parrish shook her head.

Again there was no answer when Mrs Parrish knocked on the door. Gerald was standing by the window, and when they went into the room, he did not turn round.

'Gerald, here are the police. They want to ask you one or two questions.'

Gerald leant further out of the window, as though he were about to retch into the street below. He was standing on the end of the curtain, with his arms crossed over his stomach and his shoulders hunched.

The detectives spoke in turn to him, but he would not answer them any more than he would answer Mrs Parrish. At last, still speaking calmly to him though plainly exasperated, they asked him to go with them to the police-station. Mutely he followed them down the stairs, his arms still crossed over his stomach and on his face a look of dazed terror.

Mrs Parrish went downstairs with them, let them out and then descended to the basement to make herself a cup of tea. She sipped at it; then she poured in first one finger and then

31

a second of brandy. She began to cough and as she did so, she suffered an attack of giddiness, so that only by clutching at the side of the kitchen table was she able to prevent herself from falling down.

It had long since grown dark when the bell rang again. Mrs Parrish was by then seated hunched, still in her coat, before the empty grate in the drawing-room, the curtains undrawn and only a single lamp burning on the table beside her.

It was the senior of the two detectives. She wished that it had been the other one, who was younger and plainer and obviously more stupid. The detective said that they had questioned Gerald carefully and that they thought they had got to the bottom of the business. At first he had been unco-operative but, well, at last he had given them the answers to their questions.

'But surely you can't think that he would ever have—'

No, it was not precisely *that* that they thought.

He leant forward in his chair, fussing at the same time with the bowl of the pipe he had asked her if he might smoke :

'Did you realize that your servant was a homosexual ? . . . Excuse me putting it so bluntly.'

The idea had never occurred to Mrs Parrish. But with marvellous dignity she straightened herself in her chair, fixed her clear blue eyes on his face and answered : 'Well, of course, I guessed that he must be. Would any other sort of man become a woman's servant ?'

The detective gave a small smirk; it was a smirk of embarrassment, tinged with disappointment.

He went on to explain how the theft had taken place, and now the chilliness of his demeanour began to thaw out, he gave off a kind of wintry sparkle.

Gerald had 'picked up' (that was the phrase the detective eventually selected after some deliberation) an Irish labourer from a building site in Western Road and had brought him back to the house to spend the night. The labourer had gone berserk, had attacked Gerald—oh, yes, he was quite extensively bruised—and had then looted the house before he had got away.

'Of course, the poor wretch was terrified of calling us in. But I don't know how he expected to hide the thefts from you.'

'I wonder why he didn't tell me at once, instead of allowing me to find out for myself,' Mrs Parrish said quietly.

'It wouldn't be an easy thing to tell.'

'Not all that difficult.' She gave herself a small shake, drawing her pointed chin down on to her breast and then breaking into a sigh.

She barely heard what the detective said after that. '. . . Not to worry. . . . Now we have our lead. . . . Dare say we'll get our man. . . . Not to worry. . . . All come out in the wash. . . . Get our man. . . .' Nor did she see him out.

More than an hour later, as she still sat hunched, shivering and hungry, before the empty grate, she heard Gerald come in. But by the time she had tottered out on the landing, he was already racing up the stairs. She called his name; at the sound, his face, distorted and streaked with sweat or tears, was briefly turned towards her as he hissed : 'Please! Don't talk to me! Don't!'

She deliberated; then she climbed yet again up to his room. But though she knocked on the door repeatedly, cajoled, and rattled the handle, he would neither let her in nor speak to her.

Wearily, she went downstairs, and without eating, got into her nightdress and slipped between the icy sheets. 'My hot-water bottle,' she thought. She gave a little moan. 'My milk.' She buried her face in the pillow. 'The curtains.' At that time these three trivial omissions seemed to be far worse betrayals than anything of which the detective had told her.

Many hours later, half awake and half asleep, her whole

33

body shivering in spite of the central heating and the blankets piled on top of her, she heard a faint creak and then another on the stairs outside her room. 'Gerald!' she called. For a moment she imagined in panic that the Irish labourer had returned. She swung her legs out of the bed and scrabbled with an arm in the sleeve of her dressing-gown as she tottered to her feet.

At the same moment that she opened the door of her bedroom, the front door clicked shut.

She hurried over to the front door; an icy wind whipped at her as she managed to pull it open. Trees plunged like gigantic stallions, their hooves battering the night to whirling sparks, and under them, cringing as he ran, was Gerald, a suitcase in either hand and his raincoat billowing out behind him. She shouted his name; she even ventured out into the road, clasping the folds of the dressing-gown over her shrunken breasts and feeling the hardness and coldness of the pavement beneath her naked feet. But the drumming hooves had beaten him into the darkness of which, without her guessing it, he had always been a part.

Then, passing the hall table (the sobs rising in her throat like terrible effortful hiccoughs) she all at once saw the note lying where the carriage clock had stood for three generations, and would now stand no longer. The paper, blue and lined, seemed to be heavy with the ink in which it was saturated. He had used large, capital letters, which had bitten deep.

Mrs Parrish read, sitting on the edge of her bed with her bare, blue-veined feet crossed one over the other and her whole body shivering:

SORRY. I LIVED FOR YOU BELIEVE THAT.
BUT I CAN'T GO ON. SO ALL THE BEST. FORGIVE.
SORRY.
    GERALD.

She went to the uncurtained window, an old woman in an old, empty house (now at last she saw herself as that, with an access of self-pity) and looked out through the uncurtained window at the thrashing trees, at the empty lawns and at the black sky above them. 'I LIVED FOR YOU BELIEVE THAT.'

But now she knew, after so many years, that it was she who had lived for him.

Mess

Myra, in the overlarge quilted dressing-gown that had belonged to a dead aunt, put her head round the door of the attic room.

'Aren't you coming down, dear?'

'I've already been down,' her fifteen-year-old son answered, without looking up from the work-bench across which he was sprawled.

'Been down! Then you've had your brekkers!'

The boy shook his head, still not looking up as his mother now shuffled into the room, rubbing at her eyes with one hand while the other held the dressing-gown together over her shallow breasts.

'Aren't you hungry?'

'I'll wait until lunch. Whenever that will be,' he added on a note of quiet fury.

'But, darling, we always have brekkers late on a Sunday. You know that. You can't expect us to get up at eight-thirty after a party. And such a party!' The hand that had been rubbing her eyes now went to her temples.

'Yes, I heard it,' he said, pouring a dark brown liquid carefully from one test-tube to another.

'Surely you can get your own breakfast once in a while!'
Myra's voice was now no less accusatory than her son's. The boy went on pouring. 'Roger! Surely!'

'I took one look at all that mess and decided I couldn't face it.'

'What mess?'

'All that mess in the kitchen. And elsewhere. Everywhere. Except in here.'

'Well, *of course* there's a mess after a party. You expect a mess after a party. Everyone has a mess on their hands after a party. . . . What are you smiling at?'

For the first time the boy raised his head, overlarge for his skinny body; his spectacles glinted at her as they caught the sunlight through the window. 'There's always a mess in the kitchen—party or no party. You know that, Mummy.'

'Is it my fault that Patty decided to take off like that without a day of notice? Or that that wreched *au pair* woman decided to be so unhelpful?' She waited for an answer. 'Is it?' The boy shrugged. 'These days people have no sense of responsibility. Think of all we did for Patty. It makes me sick.' She put a hand on her son's shoulder, leaning more and more heavily on him while he scowled down at the test-tube. Then she put a cheek against his, so that he could smell the sour alcohol on her breath. 'Don't be cross, darling,' she coaxed. 'What's been the matter with you these hols? You're no longer the sweet-natured boy you used to be.'

'You've been drinking,' he said.

'Drinking?' She straightened, squinting angrily down at the test-tube in his hand. 'Of course I drank last night. Everyone drinks at a party.'

'I mean drinking now. This morning.'

'Roger, I *haven't*! How dare you say such a thing!'

'I can smell it.'

She made heavily towards the door. 'Well, if you want any breakfast you'd better come down.'

'There's no bread.'

'How do you know?'

'I looked.'

'Bloody hell!' She hesitated; then she said in a coaxingly artificial voice: 'In that case, darling, couldn't you be an angel

37

and jump on your bicycle and go down to the delicatessen and—'

'No,' he interrupted her. 'I'm busy. Can't you see I'm busy? Why can't Daddy go? He could go in the car!'

His mother no longer drove, after an accident when, drunk, she had all but killed an old woman.

'Daddy's not feeling well. He's still in bed.'

'What's the matter with him?'

'He's not feeling well.'

'Then Marje.'

'She and the American seem already to have left the house.'

Myra seldom referred to her daughter's boy-friend in his absence except as the 'American'.

'Perhaps they never came home.'

Myra had already guessed that they had never come home; but she now preferred to ignore this supposition. Twisting the handle of the door she coaxed again: *'Please,* darling. Just for once be helpful. You don't expect *me* to get on your bicycle and go instead? Do you?'

Roger began to snort with unexpected laughter at the idea.

Enraged, his mother stared at him; then all at once she put the fingers of both hands to her lips, letting the dressing-gown fall open on her black lace nightgown, wrinkled up her face and let out one gulping sob after another.

'Mummy! *Please!*'

It was the one thing he could not stand; to see her cry filled him with pity, embarrassment, hatred and shame all at once.

'Mummy!'

She had put her forehead to the door; her whole body was shaking.

'Oh Mummy!' He jumped up, ran to her and put an arm round her wildly jerking shoulders.

'What's come over you?' she got out between sobs. 'I don't understand. I just don't understand.'

38

'All right,' he said. 'I'll go. All right.' First he was consolatory; then in a sudden rage he shouted 'All right! I've said I'll go! All right!'

She clutched at him still; even her tears, smearing his cheeks as well as her own, seemed to smell of whisky.

'You're really a very sweet boy,' she said. 'And we've all been such pals. I don't know what I'd do without you. Such pals.'

Gently but remorselessly he freed himself from her grasp and made for the stairs.

'Oh, darling,' she called after him. 'One other thing. Daddy's *News of the World*. You won't forget Daddy's *News of the World*? They seem to have forgotten to bring the papers this morning.'

'Perhaps they'd bring them if you remembered to pay the bill,' he shouted back over his shoulder. Then he added, pausing on the landing: 'Daddy can jolly well get his own *News of the World*.' As he continued down the stairs, he muttered, now to himself, 'I'll be damned if I'll get it for him.'

When Roger entered the delicatessen, he at once saw that Dick Harrap was standing at the counter. A young, fair-haired man with muscular shoulders and acne on the back of his neck, Harrap was wearing a blue pin-stripe suit shiny at the seat and elbows. In one hand he was carrying what looked like a prayer-book.

'Yes,' he was saying, in a vaguely distracted voice, 'Yes. What else? What else do I need? Oh, some pork luncheon meat —a tin of pork luncheon meat.'

The Jewish owner of the delicatessen scratched at the thick black hair on one of his bare arms, said, 'No pork luncheon meat,' in a good-natured voice, and then added: 'I've got some nice tinned beef, if that's any use to you.'

'Oh, yes, yes. Sorry. Yes.' The acne-covered neck went scarlet. 'That'll be fine.' His purchases completed, Harrap almost bumped into Roger as he left the counter, calculating the change in a sweaty palm. 'Oops! Sorry!' Then he saw who it was and greeted him: 'Hello, Roger! Long time, no see.'

'I was at the baths on Tuesday. I was there all afternoon. You never came.'

'Oh, gosh! Yes. I had to put in some extra work—one of the other blokes ill.' He frowned in an effort at recollection. 'But I told your mother I couldn't make it. I met her coming out of the Druid's Head and I asked her to give you a message.'

'Mummy never gives a message.'

'On principle, you mean?'

Roger, who suspected that his mother had no principles, shook his head. 'She forgets.'

'Anyway, I'll be seeing you this afternoon, won't I?'

'Will you?'

'Of course I will.' By now they were standing beside Harrap's motor-bicycle, Roger resting a hand on its worn seat. 'Your mother asked me to pop in for a cuppa.'

'Oh, good,' Roger said without enthusiasm. He always preferred to see Harrap away from home.

Harrap straddled the machine and kicked its engine into loud, throbbing life. His cheeks and lips trembled at the vibration, his large hands gripped the handlebars. 'Expected to see you at church,' he shouted above the din.

Roger did not confess that he had been to the Roman Catholic Church up the road, but instead merely shrugged his shoulders and pulled a little face.

'Bad boy!' A black-gloved hand waved. 'See you!'

'Don't come too early. We won't have finished lunch,' Roger shouted in warning. But the motor-bicycle had already screeched giddily round a corner.

Marje lay out in a deckchair in the garden, picking tar off her brown suede boots with a twig. The prematurely middle-aged American, whom everyone called Mac, was asleep on the grass beside her, a thread of silvery saliva glinting in the sunlight as it stretched from his openly snoring mouth to his ear. 'That beach,' she said. 'It's a disgrace.'

'Oh, darling, I do wish that you'd cleaned those boots of yours a little earlier. Now we'll have tar all over the carpets yet again.'

'Eucalyptus oil. It only needs some eucalyptus oil. That always does the trick.'

'Fine,' her mother agreed, sucking deeply on the cigarette she held between thumb and forefinger. 'But who's going to go on hands and knees to deal with it? You really are a rather thoughtless girl.'

'Oh, *please*, Mummy! Must you always nag? You *know* that I'm not feeling awfully well.'

'I wish I knew what was the matter with you.'

'Oh, it's just the usual.'

'You really ought to have that little op.'

'Do shut up! When I decide to have the operation, I'll have it. Now let's drop the subject.'

'What operation?' Roger looked up to ask from the flower-bed he was weeding.

'None of your business.'

Perhaps she had to have an abortion, Roger thought with swift distaste. Serve her right! He would always remember coming on the two of them in the dining-room, the curtains undrawn and that heaving and grunting, as though of some dying animal, from the shadows of one corner. 'Beat it!' Mac had said hoarsely and Roger had beaten it, taking the stairs in twos and threes. He had thought that when Mummy and Daddy came home, he ought to tell them; but in the event they were in the middle of one of their rows and he preferred to sit, shivering with anger and disgust, before his test-tubes

D

and retorts, their hysterically acrimonious voices reverberating up the stairwell, rather than go down.

Jack now came limping across the lawn, a silk scarf at his throat and his neatly crimped blond hair appearing as no more than an extension of the lined forehead below it. He was nine years younger than his wife and it was on her money that they lived.

'Where's my *News of the World*?' he demanded, in that parody of a military voice that Roger's schoolmates had been quick to take off.

'Roger forgot to buy it,' Myra said. 'You can have Mac's *Observer*.'

'Christ no! No thanks!'

'How's the head?'

'Hellish.'

'What about a little drinkie before lunch?'

'Well that might help, I suppose. What's yours?'

'Some of that supermarket gin.' Myra raised her glass.

'Gut-rot,' he said. He stooped and pinched Marje's leg. 'How's our Marje?' he asked.

Marje scowled at him. 'Our Marje is not feeling well,' she retorted.

'Too many psychedelic experiences?'

'Oh, pack it in!'

'Anyway that pallor suits you. Yes, it suits you. Doesn't it, Mac?'

Mac had already opened one eye; now he opened the other, frowning up as he brushed away the thread of saliva on the back of a bony hand. 'Christ, I had such a dream!' he exclaimed. 'Wow!'

Roger straightened himself by the flower-bed and began to wander over.

'A nice dream?' Myra asked, lighting one cigarette from another and then tossing the used one over her shoulder.

'Nice? *Horrible*! I dreamed about that witch-wife of mine. And the two brats. Dreamed I was going on a long, long journey with them and they were always getting lost or wanting something. Horrible, just horrible.'

'Poor darling,' Marje said, stooping to run her finger through his thinning red hair.

'What about lunch?' Roger asked.

His mother looked up at him, hugging her trousered legs. He hated to see her in trousers; once she had even worn them when visiting him at school—the other boys had been merciless about the size of her bum. 'What about what, darling?' she asked.

'Lunch,' he almost shouted. 'I'm famished.'

'Poor dear. Yes, I must do something about it.' She got to her feet, still clutching her glass of gin.

'It's gone three. If you put the joint in now, it'll *never* be ready.'

'Oh, let's forget the joint,' she said. 'We can have it for supper. Or tomorrow. I'll make an omelette Arnold Bennett—how about that? There's the haddock from yesterday.'

'From the day before yesterday,' Roger amended.

'I think your mother is fabulous,' Mac said, settling himself once again on the grass. As he said it, with a small sideways smile, it did not sound like a compliment.

'Do you want me to help you?' Roger asked. A moment before he had been thinking 'Slut, slut, slut'; but now as she waddled off across the lawn, with her blouse hanging loose around the trousers that constricted her thighs and buttocks, there was something so forlorn about her that he felt a sudden stab of pity. She was not a bad sort; not really. If Daddy had not had to leave Malaya, if she had not got that sugar-thing that made her have to inject herself, if she would only stop drinking. . . . He knew all the things she ought to do—leave Daddy for a start; and if only she would do them, then of course she could be happy. But she never would. Never.

'Well, that's sweet of you, darling.' She put an arm round his shoulder, splashing gin over his shirt-front without being aware of it, as she propelled him towards the house.

In the kitchen, with its piles of unwashed plates, its garbage bin that had overflowed on to the floor, and the two cats that set up an accusatory miaouing as soon as they entered, Roger asked : 'Hadn't we better clear up first?'

'Oh, *no*, darling. I couldn't bear it.'

'But it's so difficult. . . .'

'We'll do it all after lunch. Everyone will lend a hand. You'll see.'

She had said exactly the same thing the day before and no one had lent a hand and nothing had been done.

'The cats want some food.'

'Yes, I know, the poor sweeties! I meant to ask you to get them some tins when you went to the delicatessen. Never mind —we'll give them some of the haddock.' She took the fish out of the refrigerator, unwrapped it and held it to her nose. Then she extended it for him to smell. 'Do you think that fish is off? It shouldn't be, should it? I mean, salt fish doesn't go off, does it? Smell, darling.'

'I don't want to smell.'

'Oh, come on!'

He sniffed; there was a faint whiff of ammonia. 'Well, it *does* have rather a nasty pong.'

'I expect it'll be all right.'

'We don't all want to be poisoned, Mummy.'

For some reason that he could not explain and that caused him a strange unease, he found himself blushing as he said this.

'Poor Daddy feels queasy enough as it is!' she agreed. But she nonetheless began to prepare the haddock. 'He's rather hurt about your attitude to him,' she said.

'Hurt, Mummy?'

'You used to be such good friends.'

They had never been good friends; Roger had always hated his father and now he had also come to despise him. But he let that go, since he knew that it was important to his mother that the family should seem united.

'We still are,' he mumbled.

'Try to talk to him a little. He feels that you ignore him.'

'It's just—just that I have so much else to think about.'

'You and your stinks! Yes, darling, I know. But Daddy *can* be fearfully interesting. Honestly he can.'

Roger, who had heard his father tell over and over again the same dreary stories about his adventures as a policeman in Malaya, secretly doubted that. But he merely nodded now as he began to collect the knives and forks to put on the table.

'He's not an intellectual. I know that. But you could learn a lot from him. You give the impression of—well—looking down on him.'

'Oh, I don't do that,' he lied quickly. 'But we have so little in common.'

'Things have not been easy for him,' she said, as though in extenuation of his shortcomings. 'Having to leave Malaya like that really wrecked his life.'

'Even if that's true, that gives him no right to wreck yours,' he wanted to answer. But he restrained himself. 'What *are* his interests?' he asked instead. 'I've never really known.'

'What do you mean?' Myra was almost angry. Put point-blank like that it was a question difficult to answer. She could hardly say, 'Sex and drink.' 'Well, there's his golf, dear,' she said at last. 'And he's very interested in politics. And horses. And the countryside. And—and his photography. Oh, you know all this!'

'He never uses the dark-room. It was just a waste of money. I could have had it for a lab.'

'Well, if you're nice to him,' she coaxed, 'then he might give it up to you.'

At that moment the door-bell rang.

'We'd better not answer!'

Roger, who knew that it must be Harrap, was ashamed that his friend should find both his father and his mother tipsy and the lunch still uneaten at nearly four o'clock.

'Of course we must answer it.' Myra could never bear not to pick up the telephone as soon as it rang, not to open every letter as soon as it reached her, not to attend every function to which they were invited. She seemed to live in perpetual expectancy of some surprise that would at a stroke change all their lives.

Mac had loped to the front-door. They heard him say, 'Hi!' and then Harrap's 'Good afternoon,' followed by some nervous clearing of the throat. Mac appeared :

'It's that school-teacher pal of Roger's,' he announced in a voice obviously audible to Harrap, who could be seen through the two intervening doorways, a hand tugging at his collar as though it were too tight.

'Oh, Mr Harrap! Lovely to see you!' Myra hurried through the dining-room, her glass again in one hand. She waved it in the air and more of the gin splashed out. 'We're fearfully late —we're just about to have our *lunch*. Do forgive us. Isn't it awful?'

'Would you like me to come back later?'

'Heavens no. You can share our omelette Arnold Bennett. Or I can make you a cup of tea. Whichever you prefer.'

'Well, I think I'd really rather have a cup of tea. If that's no trouble.'

'Of course you would! Roger—be an angel and put on the kettle.'

'Do let me help,' Harrap volunteered. 'Living alone, I'm really very domesticated.'

46

'One day you must show us your flat.'

' "Flat" is far too grand a word for it. It's only a furnished room. . . . How are things, Roger?' But Roger sensed an absence of warmth in the routine question, as always when Harrap spoke to him in the house. Outside it was different; then the schoolmaster's voice took on a lingering, almost caressive quality and he had the habit of staring at the boy with his pale blue eyes for seconds on end.

Harrap now joined Roger in laying the table; but to the boy's shame there were not enough knives and forks until Myra ran some of the dirty ones under the tap and then wiped them off on a cloth that was used indiscriminately to dry both the crockery and cutlery.

'You must think us a real slum family,' Myra remarked as she handed him the still greasy silver.

'Not at all,' Harrap assured her; but he had been shocked to discover that people whom he had always regarded as rich should live in far worse squalor than his own family in Doncaster, his landlady, or himself.

When at last they had all sat down at the table, Marje raised a forkful of the omelette Arnold Bennett and then put it down again. 'This is off,' she said decisively.

'Oh darling, is it?' Myra wailed.

'Of course it is.'

Mac lifted his whole plate and sniffed at it. 'It smells *very* odd.'

'What do you think, Dick?' It was the first time that Roger had ever heard his mother call Harrap by his Christian name and it gave him a jar. She held out her plate.

Harrap sniffed in turn; then he said with nervous diffidence : 'Smells all right to me.'

Myra jumped to her feet. 'Bloody hell!' She began to gather up the plates, crushing the servings of omelette as she placed them one on top of the other. 'Well, well, we'll just have to make do with bread and cheese and fruit. At least this wine is good. . . . Roger, *do* give me a hand.'

In the kitchen Roger said to her, 'Oh, I'm sick of it!'

'Sick of what?'

'All this—this *mess*!'

'What mess?'

'Never mind.' He was on the verge of tears. Angrily he swallowed and swallowed yet again, his throat aching and his eyelids feeling as though grit were lodged beneath them.

'He's nice,' Myra said, as she unwrapped some cheese.

'Who's nice?'

'Dick.' Roger could see that she was now really drunk. 'I once knew a limerick about someone called Dick. How did it go?' Balancing the cheese-board on the uplifted palm of one hand, like a waiter with a tray, she waddled back into the dining-room, tripped and sent gruyere, Camembert and cheddar tumbling across the carpet. 'Thanks, Dick. Thanks,' she said, as he stooped to help her retrieve the fragments. 'Thanks a million.' Still kneeling, she dusted a piece of cheddar on her blouse. 'I was trying to remember a limerick I used to know. About a young man called Dick. Do you know it?'

Dick shook his head.

'How did it go?' She thought, the hand clutching the piece of cheddar raised to her cheek. ' "There once was a fellow called Dick, Who was known for the size of his prick. . . ." '

"Mummy!"

"What's the matter, darling? You know far worse words than that, I'll bet. . . . Roger! *Roger*!'

But the boy had fled into the garden.

'Now where's he gone to?' Myra asked, lumbering to her feet.

'Leave him,' Marje said. 'Don't worry.'

'What's the matter with the child?' Myra demanded, at last putting the cheese on to the board. 'Did I say something so bad?' she asked Harrap; but, flushed, he did not reply.

'He's a silly little prig,' Jack remarked, pouring some wine into his glass. 'I don't know what they've done to him at that expensive school of his. He usedn't to be like that.'

'We-ell, I can understand it,' Mac drawled.

'Can you?' Myra heaved a sigh. 'I wish I could.'

'Sure I can.' The American cracked the joints of his bony fingers one by one as he began his exposition. 'Reaction. That's what it is. We all—all of us here—reacted against the oppression—and—er—*sup*pression of our family backgrounds. Right? That's what makes us tick. Right? We believe in individualism and a healthy contempt for authority and the need to call a spade a spade—or a prick a prick.' Harrap's flush darkened even further, but the rest of them laughed. 'But Roger here— as I see it—is reacting against our permissiveness. He craves authority. Discipline. Order and conformity and convention and all the rest of the crap we flung out of the window.'

Myra was staring at him in admiration, her pudgy chin cradled in a far from clean palm. 'Oh, Mac, you put these things so clearly. In perspective. Doesn't he, Marje?'

'Well, he ought to,' Marje said acidly. 'After all, he *majored* in psychiatry.' It was obvious from her tone that they were soon due for another of the spells of bickering that afflicted them like a recurrent hysteria.

'Doesn't he put it well, Dick? Don't you think?'

Harrap nodded unhappily. Then summoning courage, he cleared his throat and said, 'I've always regarded myself as a rather conformist person too.' He swallowed. 'Actually.'

'But you're not conformist! Not in the way poor Roger is!' Myra shrilled out. Suddenly on a drunken impulse she put a hand over his. 'Is that tea very horrid?'

It was. But he shook his head, staring fascinatedly into her blotchy but far from uncomely face.

*

Roger sat on a bench and gazed morosely now at the dull grey waves and now at the passers-by. His stomach rumbled with hunger but he had run out of the house without taking any money with him and so could not buy a hot-dog from the stall behind him. At first the smell of vinegar and burning fat had sharpened his appetite; but now it had become so nauseating that he kept telling himself that he would have to move on.

Oh, the mess of it, the *mess*! It hadn't always been like that: not when Daddy had been on his own out in Malaya because Mummy had only just started her sugar-thing and no one really knew what was wrong with her and they had that little furnished house at Bexhill with the sitting-room that had hardly any room in it for the whale-like sofa and two armchairs, all covered in the same curious, shiny grey material. Meals were on time then and the kitchen was clean and for a whole year they had had the same daily woman, that one with the cleft palate and the dyed orange hair, instead of a whole succession of Austrian couples and *au pairs* and chars who flounced out of the house saying that they had just about had enough. What had gone wrong? What had happened? Daddy had tried a number of jobs and, failing at them, had then put Mummy's money into a number of businesses at which he had also failed. Mummy had started to drink more and more and to care less and less what people might think of her. Using all those dirty words she had never used before. Chain-smoking. Not bothering to change the sheets or to wash his shirts for him or to buy anything *proper* to eat. No puddings, unless they were those awful stodgy pies that came in packets. Tins. Sausages. Frozen vegetables when everyone knew that they had far fewer vitamins than fresh ones.

If only she would listen to him he could put it all right. First, of course—pay off Daddy. What did they call it—alimony? That was usually paid by the husband to the wife but there was probably no reason why it shouldn't be the other way round. Sell the house—it was all very well to say that one couldn't live in anything but a Regency house, but who wanted damp in the basement and cockroaches and mice in the kitchen and all those stairs going up and up and up? What they should have was one of those modern flats along the sea-front. Mummy would have to lay off the drink. And inject herself regularly. Marje would have to be told to behave herself. Or else. It was a waste of time for someone like her to go to the university, where all she did was to fool around. A secretarial course. Or she could train to work in a hospital. Discipline was what she needed.

Clutching his stomach, he swayed back and forth in mingled misery and hunger. What was the use? Mummy would never listen to him. He had tried to tell her something of what he felt often enough in the past and she would hug him and say, 'Poor little darling,' or 'You mustn't be so censorious,' or 'Darling you're so young—you must try to understand what it means to be grown up.' If being grown up meant never paying bills or keeping appointments or looking after things, then he preferred to stay as he was.

He jumped to his feet and began to wander aimlessly along the front. His head was throbbing now and, although he could no longer smell the hot-dog stand, he still felt vaguely sick.

Eventually he found himself trailing up the road of squalid rooming-houses and boarding-houses in which Harrap lived. He had not been conscious of making in that direction until all at once there he was, outside the narrow Victorian house with the extraordinary multi-coloured art-nouveau glass porch and the rust-coloured paint that was flaking off like scalded skin. 'Petrada.' He had thought that such an odd name until Harrap had explained to him that the landlady's dead husband had been Peter and she herself was Ada.

Peering into the shed, constructed of tarred clapboard and rusty corrugated iron, that nudged the red-brick side of the narrow, mean-looking house, he was surprised to see Harrap's motor-bicycle gleaming from the shadows. No doubt shocked and disgusted by what he had found at Lewes Crescent he had beat a retreat as soon as he could.

Roger wandered round the side of the house and on an impulse tapped on Harrap's ground-floor window. Then regretting that he had done so, he began to hurry off.

'Hey! Roger! What are you doing here?'

'Oh, you *are* in!' he said feebly, turning. 'I didn't know. I knocked on the off-chance but you didn't seem to hear me the first time.'

'Come in. The front-door's open.'

'But aren't I disturbing you? I'm sure you've lots to do.'

'I have. Thirty-three compositions to correct. But never mind. I can take ten minutes off.'

As Roger opened the front door, the landlady appeared from her sitting-room, gave him a stern, appraising glance and then said, '*Good* afternoon.'

'I—I came to see Mr Harrap.'

'That's all right, Mrs Mills. Thank you very much.' Harrap's voice had the same artificially jolly tone that it assumed when talking to Myra or Marje. 'This way, Roger.'

Since Roger had visited Harrap's room a number of times, he wondered why the older man should think it necessary to tell him the way.

Mrs Mills leant her sixteen stone against the front-door. 'You haven't closed the door properly.'

'Oh, haven't I? Sorry.' The boy turned, flustered.

'All right, I've done it.'

When Harrap had shut his own door, he smiled at Roger and said, 'She's always in a disagreeable mood on Sundays. Don't ask me why.' He picked a box of chocolate peppermint creams out of a confusion of exercise-books and papers and held it out.

'Thanks.' Roger munched. 'That's the first thing I've had to eat today.'

'What?'

'None of the others has any breakfast on Sunday. And I—I couldn't be bothered to get my own. And then—as you know —I rushed away like that before I'd had my lunch.'

'You'd better have a biscuit.' Harrap fumbled in a cupboard stuffed with clothes, most of them soiled, and eventually extricated a tin from under a rugger vest. It had a powder-blue poodle on its lid. 'They're a bit soggy,' he said.

He was right; but Roger did not mind the sogginess, so hungry was he feeling.

'Sit,' Harrap said, lowering himself on to the unmade bed.

Roger sat, not on the bed as Harrap seemed to indicate but on an upright chair, over which a tweed jacket was draped.

'I'm sorry this room is such a slum. I never seem to have a moment.'

'It's nothing compared to our house. That really *is* a slum.'

Harrap gave the boy that long, meditative stare of his, his pale blue eyes seeming to focus not on the eyes opposite to them but on a point somewhere between them and the mouth. 'Poor Roger,' he said at last.

Roger squirmed on the chair, at once touched and yet obscurely put to shame by the other's pitying tone.

'I shouldn't have run off like that,' he said.

'No, you shouldn't,' Harrap agreed.

'It's just that—that . . .' He was at a loss for words, as one of his hands fiddled with a button-hole of the jacket against which he was leaning. All that—that *mess*,' he got out at last, with an involuntary grimace.

Harrap laughed. 'What about the mess in here?' he asked.

'Oh, that's different,' Roger said.

Again Harrap laughed. 'How different?'

Roger did not know; but different it certainly was. He shook his head, drawing his brows together so that his steel-rimmed spectacles edged further down his nose.

'You must be more tolerant,' Harrap said.

'That's what my mother tells me. I try to be tolerant.'

'But you don't really succeed. Is that it?'

Roger jumped off the chair and went to the window. The concrete-paved yard contained nothing but three dust-bins and, in one corner, a number of flowerpots, most of them lying on their sides, out of which vegetation trailed yellow and limp. 'I wish I could get away.'

'Where to?'

'Anywhere.' He turned: 'You know, I must be the only boy at school who prefers school to the holidays.'

'But that's awful, Roger.' Again the pale blue eyes fixed themselves on the boy's face with a curiously withdrawn, yet melting gaze. 'I'd no idea you were *that* unhappy.'

'I wouldn't care if the whole lot of them—' He broke off. He had been going to say, 'If the whole lot of them were dead,' but he now amended this to 'If—if I were never to see any of them again.'

Something in the suppressed passion of the boy's declaration excited the schoolmaster. He got up. 'What a funny boy you are!'

'Am I?'

'Yes. You look so cool—and—intellectual—and in control of things. . . . And yet—really—behind that scholarly exterior . . .' He stood close to Roger now, his large hands deep in the pockets of his creased grey flannel trousers and the weight of his whole body falling entirely on one out-thrust foot, as though in preparation for a spring. 'You say that now —about not caring if you never saw your family again—but what would you do if suddenly you were all alone?'

'I'd manage,' the boy mumbled almost sulkily.

'Would you? How?'

The boy shrugged. 'Oh, I'd manage. I'm not a baby.'

'You could make your home with me. I—I could adopt you.' Harrap's tone was bantering; but his lower lip trembled oddly until he bit on it. 'Yes,' he said, 'I could adopt you. Would you like that?'

Roger did not answer. He had picked up one of the exercise books and was turning the pages over.

'Would you? No great enthusiasm, I see!'

'I ought to go. Perhaps my mother is worrying.'

'You could telephone.'

'No, I'd better go, I think. Thank you.'

In a vaguely cross voice, Harrap said, 'Well, come again. Any time. Whenever suits you.'

He opened the door.

Roger caught his hand. 'Thanks,' he said 'Thanks a lot.'

Then he was gone, hurrying past Mrs Mills's door, which creaked open as he passed it.

As he strode back along the front, his eyes blinking against the wind that whirled dust and scraps of paper in spirals at every corner, Roger felt at once excited and disappointed. Of course it had been only a joke, that suggestion of adoption. But he had been a real idiot, failing to respond. The truth was that Harrap made him feel unaccountably shy; and when he was shy he knew that he sounded cross and—and censorious. Censorious. It was the word that Daddy now used about him often. 'Oh, don't be so bloody censorious,' he would shout. Or, 'You and those censorious airs of yours!'

Just before he reached Lewes Crescent he stopped and looked down from the Drive, first on the crowds on the promenade below, then to the beach, from which the last bathers were preparing to retreat, and finally out to sea. The dying sun had streaked the farthest crimped waves with an orange that faded at the edges of the horizon to yellow; and against this orange the silhouette of a ship slowly moved, its masts jabbing the sky like upended toothpicks. A woman's voice from the promenade was calling shrilly, 'Chang! Come here; come here this instant!' and as he listened to it he suddenly experienced a terrible thirst to be out there on that ship, moving off northwards into the silence and gathering darkness. He forgot that he hated the sea, that he could not swim and that the slightest swell invariably made him sea-sick; nor did he realise that the ship in question was, in fact, a dredger. He imagined himself lying out on a deck-chair, oblivious of the cold, and watching the waves roll away from either side of the stern, their tops glittering in the last light of the sun. A gong would sound out for dinner, all the other passengers would have already gone below; but he would be entirely content where he was. On and on moved the ship; and now, still on the deck-chair, he felt the shadow of the fiord they were entering falling coldly, thrillingly across his body and his eyes went up and up to scale the towering and wrinkled blue-grey rock that hemmed them in, on either side. 'Rock of ages cleft for me. . . .' The words came into his mind; and simultaneously, still lying out on the deck-chair, he felt a hand on his shoulder : 'All right?' It was Harrap's voice; and turning his head, he found him there behind him, his hand on the back of the chair, in a pair of white cotton shorts and gym shoes and a white cotton vest, at the neck of which the blond hair sprouted. (That was how he had first met him, at the public tennis-courts in St. Ann's Well Gardens.)

. . . Roger shook himself. Again that voice, near now, shrilled out : 'Chang! *Will* you come here!' Then, puffing and with one ringed hand pressed to her side, an elderly woman emerged up the steps that led from the promenade to the Drive, her blue-veined legs bare and her arms covered in goose-pimples, with a Pekinese dog panting up behind her. 'The little monkey,' she said, either to herself or to Roger. She stooped with difficulty and attached a lead, while the dog gazed at her with huge eyes that smouldered like topazes in the slanting rays of the sun. She touched her purple hair, cut short in a fringe across her forehead, glanced at the boy and then waddled off with the waddling dog, admonishing him, 'Now walk! Just walk! Don't pull!'

When Roger looked again for his ship, it had miraculously vanished; and a moment later the orange swathe through which it had moved had darkened to mauve.

Myra was washing up alone. Apart from her, the house was deserted.

'Can I help you, Mummy?'

'Oh, there you are! No, I don't want any help. No thank you.'

She spoke in a cold, hurt voice, not looking up from the glass she was turning round and round as she polished it on a grubbily grey towel.

Silently Roger hunted for a clean cloth in the drawer of the dresser and then, having found one that was not actually clean but less dirty than the others, he no less silently set to work. Side by side they stood, Myra breathing heavily as though over some exacting physical task. Suddenly she burst out:

'What's the matter with you? For God's sake, what's the matter with you?'

He did not answer, fishing some knives out of the tepid, greasy water in which they had been lying.

'What poor Dick Harrap thought I really do not know. When there are guests in the house you really might make an effort—'

'Well, what do you think he thought, coming in and finding us like that?' He spoke with the cold fury which, he now knew, always terrified her; and the fact that it terrified her filled him with an exultant sense of power, if also with shame.

'Like what?'

'Not having had lunch at nearly four o'clock. The kitchen full of filth. And that awful meal.'

'Really! How dare you say that! Everyone agrees that I'm a jolly good cook.'

'When you can be bothered. Anyway that fish was bad.'

'Was that my fault? If that bloody fishmonger gives me a piece of expensive finnan haddock which is no longer fresh—'

'He wasn't to know that you'd forget to put it into the refrigerator. And keep it for days on end.'

Myra put down the glass she had been ineptly polishing and put a hand to her forehead. 'Oh stop it, stop it! *Please*! Why can't you be a little more understanding?'

Stubbornly he made no response to this plea, though part of him ached to do so.

'Don't you realise—I'm *ill*!'

'Oh, I know that, Mummy—we all know that. But if you'd remember to inject yourself—'

'How would you like to have to inject yourself—day after day after day?'

'I wouldn't *like* to do it. But if I *had* to do it—'

'Oh, you're so marvellous, so bloody marvellous!'

'I wish you wouldn't swear like that.'

'I'll damn well do what I like.'

He knew that he only had to put a little more pressure on her to reduce her to tears and the prospect of those tears at once excited him and filled him with dread.

'As you wish,' he said.

'You don't know how much I have to worry me.' Her voice broke on the word 'worry'. 'You just don't know.'

'Well, tell me.'

'You're still just a child. You've no idea what I have to go through. Oh, you're so hard. And so—self-satisfied.'

When she spoke of what she had to go through, he knew that she meant his father; but in that case, why not leave him?

'You could make a new start,' he ventured, at last, without looking up at her.

'What new start? What are you talking about?' With sudden violence she turned on him, her face, already glistening with sweat, darkening and growing oddly congested.

'You've got yourself into this rut,' he said with a new gentleness. 'If you could only get yourself out of it. Begin again. It wouldn't be difficult.' He swallowed. 'I'd help you.'

She stared down into the greasy washing-up water; then she jerked out the plug and continued to watch the water as it eddied away. 'There are no new starts,' she said, still staring down. 'That's where you show how young you are. New starts don't happen. They just don't happen.'

Mac and Marje had one of their recurrent quarrels and Marje took an overdose of the sleeping-pills prescribed for Myra. Mac wept by Marje's bedside—passing in the corridor, Roger stopped and with tingling scalp and rising gorge, listened to his abrupt, hiccoughing sobs—and two nights later they borrowed some money, never to be repaid, off Myra and went to Amsterdam with a group of friends from the university.

The next week it was Myra who fell into a coma because she had failed to inject herself.

'But why, Mummy, why?' Roger asked her, when he had summoned the doctor—no one else was in the house—and she had at last been brought round.

Wearily she replied, 'Because I had so much else on my mind.'

'But did you *want* to die?' he demanded, kneeling by her bedside and clutching at a corner of the eiderdown as though he were about to jerk it off her.

Tears trickled from under her eyelids and coursed slowly down her cheeks. She was wearing the black net nightdress and he noticed the curious crease, like a red scar, that ran from between her breasts almost to her left shoulder-blade.

'Did you? Mummy, did you?'

Still she did not answer, only turning herself over and away from him with a deep sigh and then drawing the bedclothes up to her chin.

Three days later it was Jack who was in trouble.

Roger returned home from a visit with Harrap to the King Alfred Baths and, as he slipped into the hall, hoping that no one would hear him so that he would be able to get on with some work in his room in peace, he was assailed by the voices of his mother and father from the kitchen. It was always a source of astonishment to him that they should spend so much time in that room and yet perform so few of the usual kitchen tasks. Hugging the damp roll of his towel and bathing-slip, he leant against the front-door and listened.

'But how could you? How *could* you?' his mother was demanding, as Roger had so often heard her demand in the past; and as in the past his father seemed incapable of explaining. 'You said the last time,' she went on. 'You promised. Have you no control of yourself?'

His father mumbled something too low for him to catch.

'It'll be in all the papers,' Myra went on.

'Don't be a bloody fool! Who's interested in reading that kind of thing in the papers? Happens every day. I'm not that famous.'

'It'll be in the *Argus*.'

'To hell with the *Argus*!' Jack was slowly working himself in to a self-indignant rage, as so often when she caught him out. 'I don't care a damn.'

'*You* don't care! Of course you don't. But what about us? I suppose that you don't care a damn about us either. I just can't understand how you could *stoop* to anything so—so squalid and—sordid—and, oh, puerile.'

'Now that's an end of it!'

'What do you mean—an end of it? It's only the beginning. You might go to gaol. Of course you might! Don't grin at me in that idiotic way. Of course you might! They're not likely to take such a lenient view now that it's the second time.'

'Well, at least in gaol I'd get a bit of peace.'

'Oh, I don't know, I just don't know.' Myra had begun to moan, almost inaudibly from the hall. Then suddenly she was shouting hysterically: 'Oh, don't just stand there! Can't you ever be of any use? If you'd *do* something, you'd have less time to get yourself into trouble. For God's sake do something! Stoke the boiler—or—or lay the table for supper—or peel these bloody potatoes for me.'

Roger stiffened suddenly as he heard the unmistakable sound of a slap, though at first he did not know who had slapped whom. Then he heard his father say: 'Steady, old girl! Steady!' in the threateningly craven voice of a man who feels obliged to challenge an opponent and yet has no intention of fighting. 'Steady on!'

'Let me go! You're hurting my wrist! *Will* you let me go!'

At that point Roger appeared in the door and Jack hurriedly releasing Myra, began to rub one cheek. 'Your mother slapped me,' he said.

Roger looked from one of them to other. 'What's it all about?'

His mother had turned to the cupboard she was tidying. 'Nothing,' she said. 'Nothing to do with you.'

'I heard you shouting at each other.'

'All right. We were shouting at each other. That's something married couples do—shout at each other. All right.'

Jack began to wander unhappily towards the door. 'Your

mother's temper gets worse and worse,' he said. 'She ought to watch it.'

'If anyone ought to watch it, it's you,' Myra turned to scream at him.

Jack bolted.

'What *is* all this, Mother?'

'Nothing. I've told you, nothing.'

'When I came in you were saying something about—gaol.'

Myra, now kneeling by the cupboard as she savagely pulled out jars and tins and then thrust them back again, did not answer.

'You were, weren't you?'

'You'd no business to be listening to our conversation. It was private. Something between the two of us.'

'I could hardly *help* hearing. You were shouting so loudly.'

'Oh, for God's sake let me get on with this job in peace.'

Roger stared down at her; he had never noticed before that she had a small bald patch, the size of a sixpence, at the crown of her head. One of her shoulder-straps had slipped.

Hitching at it with one hand, she held up a jar with another.

'You're always so snooty about the *mess* in the kitchen, but what about this? What's this doing here?'

'It's my killing-bottle.'

'Your *what*?'

He would like to have added, 'Yes, I'd like to put the lot of you in it.' But he merely repeated, 'My killing-bottle. For killing my specimens—my butterflies.'

Myra pulled a face and put the bottle down among the others that contained coagulated grains of demerara sugar, sago, tea to which age had given the colour and consistency of chopped straw, prunes and haricot beans.

Roger was often to wonder later why he had not taken up the jar and carried it to his room.

'Oh, do go away!' Myra ordered irritably. 'Either lend me

a hand or go away! I hate being watched.' Again she hitched at the shoulder-strap.

'Tell me what's the matter,' he pursued.

'Nothing's the matter!' she turned to shout at him, her rage against Jack transferred, as often in the past, to the tall, trembling boy.

'But I heard—' he persisted.

'Well, you'd no business to hear. Now—go away! Go—a—way!' Each isolated syllable was like a blow at the pit of his stomach.

Slowly he went.

Harrap was on his way to the laundromat on foot when Roger passed him on his bicycle. The schoolmaster was carrying a huge polythene bag stuffed with dirty clothes. The brakes of the ancient bicycle—Roger had repeatedly asked, in vain, that Jack should buy him a new one—squealed agonisingly as he came to a halt, one foot kicking at the edge of the pavement.

'Where are you off to?'

Harrap was wearing khaki shorts, smeared with grease, and a pair of sandals that flopped as he walked. Grease was also on one cheekbone, on his hands and on a knee.

Roger had in fact been to Mass but he did not tell Harrap that. 'Oh, just taking a ride,' he mumbled.

'The motor-bike has packed it in again. I've been struggling with it for the last hour and a half.'

'Would you like me to look at it for you?' Once before Roger had been able to mend the motor-bicycle when Harrap had been incapable of doing so. But the older man had seemed almost to resent the assistance then, as he seemed almost to resent its offer now.

'Oh, I'll let the garage have a look at it,' he said. 'I think that one sometimes does more harm than good by trying to put these things right oneself.'

'Anyway let me take that bag for you.'

'It's only around the corner.'

'Never mind. I'll take it.'

Roger dismounted and placed the polythene bag across the handlebars of the bicycle, which he then began to push. The bag had the same animal odour that came from Harrap's body after they had played tennis together or had gone for a long walk; the same odour that clung to his room, even when he was out of it. Through the polythene he could see the soiled socks and the tennis-vest and the grubby pyjamas and pants, and the sight of them all there, pressed against each other, filled him, not with distaste, but with a curious exaltation.

'It's hotting up,' Harrap said.

Roger swallowed and nodded his head.

'We might go for a swim today,' Harrap went on. 'Except that that wind has brought in a lot more tar. I'm going to teach you to do the crawl if it's the last thing I do. You can't go on doing that lady-like breast-stroke.'

Roger blushed.

As they sat waiting in front of the washing-machine, Harrap asked : 'How are things at home ?'

Roger shook his head; he did not want either to think or to talk about them.

'Funny your father doing a thing like that. He doesn't seem the type. . . . Oh, well,' he went on charitably, 'I suppose that at a certain age any of us might make that kind of slip-up. That's why the magistrate asked for that medical report.'

Roger listened in mounting panic. Since he had overheard that conversation between his mother and father in the kitchen he had known that something was seriously amiss; but neither of them had said anything to him and, in spite of their anxious comings and goings, the visit of Mr Bird, their solicitor, and a number of other visits from men he had never seen before, he had, all unconsciously, made no further attempt to discover what was happening. Day after day he would sit up in his room working at what his mother called his 'stinks'; and at meal-times he would merely allow himself to become another particle in the web of boring, viscous silence in which his parents were entrapped. He noticed how his mother seemed to be making up her face with even greater boldness and how —a sure sign that she was deeply unhappy—she would eat more than he and his father ate between them; he also noticed the curious twitch down one side of his father's face, causing him to screw up his mouth as though at some sudden, brief stab of pain.

'Do you prefer not to talk about it?' Harrap asked, leaning forward in his chair, grease-stained hands clasped, and looking into the flushed but expressionless face of the boy.

Still Roger did not answer.

'There's nothing to worry about,' Harrap went on. 'As I said, any man of that age might do the same thing. *I* might at fifty. *You* might,' he added with a laugh.

'Daddy's only forty-one.'

'Really? He looks much older. Doesn't he? Then your mother—'

'She's older than he.'

'Oh, I know it's difficult to imagine how anyone could do a thing like that. You probably think that it's—rather sordid. But honestly it's happening all the time. You mustn't take too serious a view of it.' The boy's curious withdrawn apathy had begun to worry him.

'I think your things are ready,' Roger said quietly.

Harrap leapt to his feet, relieved at the distraction. 'Oh, good show! So they are!'

'Yes, it was in the papers,' Myra said. 'In the *Argus*.' The trowel in her hand tossed up not merely some weeds but also a clump of pansies, which she at once tried to push back into the soil. 'I wasn't going to point it out to you. The less you knew about it the better.'

'Will he go to prison?'

'No. I don't think so.' She frowned, shook herself and then snapped: 'Of course he won't! Don't be idiotic!'

'He might.'

'They'll say he must have medical treatment. That young man at the Brighton General—that psychiatrist—he seems awfully nice. He'll fix it.'

'But what did he *do*?' Roger was standing over his mother as she knelt beside the flower-bed, her knees on a cushion which Jack had long ago ruined by being sick on it when drunk.

'Oh, it doesn't matter what he did! You saw the paper.'

'I never saw the paper. I heard about it from Harrap. And he never told me what he actually *did*.'

'Then why didn't you ask him?'

The answer was that his shame had prevented him. But he did not confess this to her, merely insisting, 'Mummy do tell me. What did he *do*?'

She got to her feet, rubbing first one of her knees and then the other. A soil-covered hand went to the hair that was sticking in damp wisps to her forehead. 'Well, if you must know,' she said, with what was almost hatred in her voice, 'it was what is called indecent exposure. You know what *that* means?'

He nodded slowly, horrified. The sunlight glinted on an edge of the trowel as she turned it in her hands, peeling off the soil that clung to it.

'Your dear father was loitering on the beach—and there, it seems, were these girls from the High School—and he—he just—'

She broke off; one muddy hand went to her lips to check the sudden tears and simultaneously her mouth widened as though to bite on it.

'Mummy! Please!' He caught her by the arm and shook her. *'Please!'*

'Your dear father—' she began again. 'Your dear father—' Then in sudden hysteria she shouted: 'I want to die, I want to die!'

'You must try to understand.' Jack's voice was at once haughty and quavering. 'You're no longer a little boy.' He drew on one of the Gauloise cigarettes with which the house now always reeked and then started to cough, the back of his small, freckled hand to his neat moustache. 'You must see these things as—as an adult.'

'But how could you? How *could* you?' Without realising it, Roger reproduced both his mother's words and her exact tone of voice. 'It's all so disgusting.'

'I agree it's not very—pretty.' The fingers that carried the cigarette to the slack, pink mouth trembled. 'But you really mustn't be such a little prig. You'll do worse things in your life, I'm willing to bet. Just you wait and see.'

'Poor Mummy. . . .'

'Your mother has been very understanding about the whole affair,' Jack said with an attempt at dignity. 'She's stuck by me. As any wife worth her salt *would* stick by her husband. As any son would stick by his father for the matter of that,' he added on a sudden vicious note. 'After all, what I did—though stupid—was hardly a crime. A temporary aberration.' He was quoting from Mr Bird, the solicitor. 'Could happen to anyone, as I said. These things—they—they just come over one. Just like that. Good God, Roger, you must at some time in that blameless life of yours have had some impulse you couldn't control!'

Roger merely stared at his father, who was now stubbing out his half-smoked cigarette in the saucer of his late morning cup of coffee.

'Why are you looking at me like that?' Jack demanded. 'As though I were an insect or something. Oh, you think yourself above all human failings, don't you, Mr Prig? Don't you? You make me sick!' He turned away petulantly on the sofa on which he was sitting, kicking out with his pyjamaed legs in the violence of his disgust.

'*You* make *me* sick,' Roger said quietly, as he left the room to his father's impotent shouting of 'How dare you speak to me like that? How dare you!'

At least his own room at the top of the house was quiet and orderly and clean. The books in the bookcase, which he himself had painted white, were arranged by subjects and by authors, and there was a catalogue to them as to the gramophone records—mostly of Bach and Byrd and Mozart and Haydn—that he had recently begun to collect. On the wall he had framed in black passepartout the four Dürer prints given to him by Harrap for Christmas. His work-table gleamed with jars and retorts and test-tubes.

It was such a hot day that even the white candlewick bedspread felt hot and sticky against his body as he threw himself upon it. No breeze came through the wide-open window.

Mess, mess, mess! There would never be any end to it; it would only get worse and worse, in the same way that the beautiful Regency house gathered more and more dust in its corners and crevices, more and more rubbish in its attics and more and more cockroaches and mice in its basement. The mess was self-perpetuating. And it was not even as if they were happy in their mess, like some of the boys at school. Mummy wanted to die, she had said so over and over again; and though Daddy was outwardly cocky his despair was really even deeper than hers. What future could there be for them? They would go on drinking and spending money until, in the end, they would have to sell up the house. Then, in some smaller, more squalid house, they would go on drinking and spending money until it, too, had to be sold. 'I'd be better dead.' Mummy had said that more than once. Daddy had never said it but it was even more true of him. Roger stared up at the light that trembled like a distant wave on the ceiling of the room and then the thought came to him, suddenly powerful and vicious: 'And Marje would be better dead too. And Mac. The pair of them.' He raised his head on an elbow and brooded darkly. Then he got up from the bed, put Byrd's *Ave Verum Corpus* on the gramophone turntable, returned to the bed and, half-listening half-thinking, continued to stare up at the quivering wave on the ceiling above his head.

The whole house was stinking of curry. The smell had even crept up to his room and wrapped itself around the curtains and the two drip-dry shirts he had hung in a corner, a towel spread beneath them.

'Won't you really have some lunch with us, darling?'

Roger shook his head. 'It'll make me too late.'

'I've made a lovely curry,' Myra pleaded with a pathos that for a moment made him want to rush to her and hold her in his arms. 'You know you love curry.'

'I'll be late. I'll buy myself some sausage rolls at Clark's.'

'Can't you keep your darling Harrap waiting for a little?' Marje asked. 'One would think you were meeting a girl-friend.'

Roger was about to turn on her; but then he told himself, 'It doesn't matter. Let her say what she likes.'

Jack, who was already half-drunk, his face covered in crimson blotches and his eyes dull, shouted, 'Let him go! If he doesn't want to have a civilised meal with us, he damn well doesn't have to! Does he?'

Mac drawled, 'I suppose this English passion for curry is a legacy of the Indian Em*pah*.'

'Aren't you going to kiss me goodbye, darling?'

But Roger had already gone.

For a while those last words of hers pursued him; he almost went back. Then he felt a strange, glacial calm spreading over his body; his nerves relaxed, his mouth ceased to feel dry, he no longer had to control the trembling of his hands and jaws. Gaily now he bicycled towards the sun and the King Alfred Baths and Harrap.

It would be all right. Of course there would be extensive enquiries; they would search through the dust and grime and disorder for a clue; they would wonder how the killing-bottle found itself on a shelf between a jar of demarara sugar and another of haricot beans; they might even question him with a mixture of suspicion for a potential murderer and pity for the only survivor of a terrible family tragedy. But they would be baffled by the lack both of motive and clues. They would decide in the end that somehow, inexplicably, a fatal mistake had occurred.

There were other ways he might have done it, of course; he had pondered them all. But the important thing was that with cyanide there would be no mess. On no account did he want any mess.

Their Night

It had been such a *nice* street in the years, oh, long before the war when she and Sandy had bought the cottage, one of the nicest streets in Brighton. There was the Cheltenham Hall Hotel opposite, a porticoed Regency building with Victorian additions, where only the best kind of people stayed—few of the 'long-nosed fraternity' as Sandy would call them; a row of large bow-fronted houses on the same side, going up the hill, and on the corner by the esplanade, the two darling cottages, the one which they bought and the one in which sweet Colonel Allen lived with his poor invalid wife.

Things were quiet then, one might almost have been in a village. Sandy used to say that the cottage was the only place in which he could be sure of a good night's rest. On tour and even in the Kensington flat he was a martyr to insomnia. When he spent that last six months in a coma, it was almost as though he were making up for all the sleep he had missed! Well, at least the poor dear had never seen what had happened to the street. He and the old Colonel had both been spared that. It had killed Mrs Allen.

Soon after the war the hotel had been sold, and the residents, many of whom had made their home in it for twenty years and more, were all given notice. Oh, it had been so sad, so many of them had been friends, so many of them had been kind to her during Sandy's last illness and after his death. Then there had followed the long period when the hotel had stood empty. There was talk that it was to be entirely done up, and talk that it was going to be pulled down to make room for a new block of flats. But there had been some kind of hitch. Someone had told her that the property was 'of historic interest' and that the new owners could not get permission to have it demolished. But then later she had read in the paper that there was some kind of legal trouble between all the different heirs of the man who had bought it and then, almost at once, had died. One could seldom get at the truth of that kind of thing.

The windows got broken, one by one, and thieves removed the lovely wrought-iron railings, lead from the roof and even the shrubs from the jungle-like garden. Then the first of the clubs opened. It was called The Regency Rooms and it was in the basement of the hotel. It was a quiet place and the people who went there, older men for the most part and never any women, seemed well-behaved, well-dressed and respectable. She thought that it must be some kind of bridge club but when she told this to Mr Lawrence, who had the paper shop at the corner, he gave a curious smirk and replied, 'Well, hardly.'

But the Regency Rooms moved or closed down, and the Lotus took its place. The Lotus was the beginning of the trouble. People would drive up to it at all hours of the night and the residents were always having to complain of nasty quarrels and the din of music and noisy talk and laughter. The Cave and La Siesta followed, and they, unlike the Lotus, seemed to be frequented entirely by teenagers. The cracked stucco of the ramshackle hotel, which had once looked so smart, was now covered with billboards advertising people with names like Screaming Lord Sutch or The Untamed. The teenagers seldom came in cars, but on scooters and motor-bicycles. The pandemonium on Friday and Saturday evenings was something unbearable !

One by one the big houses were sold up and their owners moved to the quiet of Hove and Rottingdean. That's what she ought to have done herself, of course she'd been a fool, but by the time she'd steeled herself to making the move, she would have got virtually nothing for the cottage. Why, Number Sixteen, which Sandy used to say was the most elegant house in Brighton, had only fetched five thousand! So she had decided to stick it out. After all, surely something would soon happen. Surely the police, if no one else, would take the whole situation in hand.

But the years passed. The grand houses became far from grand boarding-houses and lodging-houses, with the strangest of people in them—Irish labourers, and slatternly women who could be seen standing in the windows in their dressing-gowns in the middle of the day, and even a coloured couple or two. When she now got a taxi at the station and gave her address, the driver would often say 'The bad end or the good end?' It was so degrading. And yet when they had moved there, it was theirs that had been the good end and they had looked down on the people who had lived in the semi-detached bungalows up on the hill.

One became quite afraid of going out after dark, not only for oneself but also for Coco. Chihuahuas tend to be a bundle of nerves and the brutes seemed to know this. Youths and even sluttish girls coming out of that basement in which they congregated like rats, would shuffle the feet behind him or stamp on the pavement, so that he would jerk away in panic on the end of his leash, almost strangling himself. If she spoke to them, they would jeer at her or make rude noises. There was that awful occasion when one of them asked her . . . well, it was best not to think of that, it made one quite sick. Of course, he must have been joking.

Anyway that was not so bad as that time with the drunken Irish labourer. The man, quite a handsome man, had tripped over the lead and then over Coco, muttering to himself. But he had straightened to sway before her with the most gentlemanly of apologies. 'Did I hurt the poor little fellow then? You must forgive me, madam.' By then she had the whimpering Coco in her arms and the man put out a hand and stroked Coco's head. 'Ah, the poor little fellow! The poor dear little fellow! Did I hurt him then?'

'Oh, it's quite all right. Really it is. He's a fearful little fusser. Always likes to make the most of everything. You didn't hurt him. He just had a fright.'

The man kept on reiterating his apologies in a voice that was growing, yes, almost tearful. Well, she couldn't stay there all night with the dog in her arms. So, reassuring him for the last time that Coco was honestly not hurt, she turned away and continued down the street. It was then that he began to shout after her. Such words—and for no rhyme nor reason. Well, of course, he was drunk, and probably insane. But what on earth had she done—or what had Coco done—to deserve such filth to be shouted at them?

Many times she had been pushed off the pavement into the gutter by a gang of these strutting teenagers—boys or girls, it was hard to tell which!—and many times she had been woken, her heart thumping painfully while Coco crept shivering into her arms, by their raucous shouts and laughter. A lot of them were foreigners of course, and the French were the worst. They were supposed to attend schools of English in the town, but most of their time they spent making nuisances of themselves and doing damage for which the ratepayers footed the bill. Oh, yes, the French were the worst, but the Scandinavians ran them a good second.

Then poor Mrs Allen died and that nice doctor niece of hers came down to settle everything up. 'Are you going to keep the cottage?' And the girl replied 'Stay here? Not on your life! I'll sell the place just as soon as I can.' She had always been a bit tactless, there was never any harm in her. But how did she imagine that she would ever find a purchaser?

74

Month after month the board stayed outside the cottage, which, like the hotel before it, began to grow shabbier and shabbier, and more and more derelict. It would have broken the poor old Colonel's heart to see the garden, with its sagging fence and its rubbish and the couples who crept into it to carry on almost under the eyes of the passers-by. He had taken such a pride in that little garden. She told the police and the agents about the damage and the trespassing, but neither of them really seemed to care.

Then the summer came, and the crowds became worse, with more and more of those awful foreign students, guffawing and shouting incomprehensible things to each other and kissing in the street even as they walked along. It was then that the windows started to be broken. She would be woken by a crash and tinkle and Coco would start to yelp. The first time she thought that it was someone trying to get into her own cottage. Then she heard a burst of laughter and the clatter of feet scampering off.

The police said that they would put two men to watch the street, and the agents, after many days, had a carpenter replace the pane. But the police were often not there. The hooligans —or other hooligans—continued to return. Oh, that poor house! It was seldom that she now passed it on her walks with Coco without seeing at least one of the windows smashed.

Now she found that she could not sleep for waiting to hear that sound of breaking glass. Many nights she would lie awake into the early hours, until first the voices and then the sickening crash and tinkle, followed by howls of laughter, would bring her to the window. At once she would hurry to the telephone. But by the time a patrol car was on the spot the wretches had got away. Oh, she would like to see them caught! She would like to see them thrashed without any mercy! And the foreign ones should be put on a cattleboat and sent straight back home! It was not only the drink, of course, it was these pep pills and even things far worse. They had lost all sense of responsibility or decency.

So came *their* night—the night she and Coco would always remember. She heard the familiar voices in a foreign tongue— it was Swedish or at any rate one of those Scandinavian languages—but this time they went on for a long time outside the cottage, growing louder and louder and fiercer and fiercer, as though the people were quarrelling. She got slowly out of bed and, Coco in her arms, tiptoed to the window. Not that any of them would have heard her! She peered out from between the curtains. If she could remember their faces and they were to do any damage, then it might help those stupid, stupid police. Coco licked her ear, his muzzle soft and moist against its tingling warmth.

There were about seven of them—and what a crowd! One was in a skirt, with long, bedraggled blonde hair—she was just under the lamp-post so one could see her clearly. Probably some of the others were girls, too. One of the men had a jutting beard and hair which flopped in ringlets to his shoulders. It made one feel quite sick to look at him.

Suddenly one of the men lunged at the blonde girl, who was now leaning against the lamp-post with her eyes closed, as though in sleep, and her arms crossed under her stomach. He jerked her towards him and at once she struggled free. Again he caught her by the wrist, and as he did so, the youth with the beard brought up his hand, the fingers open, and then, closing the fingers, gave him a perfunctory jab in the face.

At that all hell was let loose! 'Oh, look, Coco, look! Just look!' As they swayed and grunted, boys and girls together, with occasional guttural shouts and shrill screams, trampling over the overgrown flower beds (the poor old Colonel's pride) scuffing up the gravel and tumbling over each other's legs only to rise again, her first horror changed to a marvellous exhilaration. There was something beastly and frightening and yet, oh so satisfying, about the dull thud when a fist met its mark. Thrilling, quite thrilling! Let them exterminate each other!

The bearded man, really a giant, had the other round the waist, and the two of them swayed together, their shadows huge on the peeling façade of the cottage. Coco gave a little whimper and squirmed in her grasp. But 'Watch, watch,' she told him, herself watching with eyes that glittered in the lamplight from the street.

The bearded man raised his assailant; then with a curious ejaculation, half grunt and half bellow of rage, he hurled him at the window. Glass showered outwards; and as though impelled by the force of the explosion, all of them—except that one boy straddled over the sill—began to race away in all directions.

The boy toppled and fell off the sill, with a thud on to the path. He lay there for a long time; she could hear his muffled groans. Then on hands and knees he dragged himself into the street, laboriously, taking many seconds between each movement.

When he was out on the pavement, under the lamplight, she saw the trail he was leaving behind him. Like a slug, just like a slug! He raised his face as though to look up towards her; but of course he could not really see her—not as she stood there behind the lace curtain with little Coco in her arms. Again he groaned. Then he gave a curious croak. Perhaps he was calling for help in his own language, who knows? His face was almost black with blood—not even his mother would have recognised him.

Slowly, inch by inch, he dragged himself on, and that trail followed after. Now he had reached her own front door. Oh, she hoped that he wasn't going to leave a mess on the doorstep. He lay there and with his raised hands began to beat a feeble tattoo on the door beside him. Then he tried to raise himself high enough to reach the bell or the knocker (such a pretty

77

one, shaped like a darling little rabbit, which Sandy had bought in that junk shop in Steyning) but at each effort he slumped back with a thud on to his knees.

She stroked Coco's head, letting his silky ears slip through her fingers in the way that he liked, and then put her face down to his muzzle. 'Oh, look what he's doing! Just look what the nasty man is doing!'

At last the boy managed to prop himself against the side of the door and to press a finger against the bell. His whole weight must now be upon it; the bell went on ringing and ringing through the darkened house. Then he whirled round, put out both hands as though to save himself, and went crashing down on to the pavement, to lie there motionless, his head in the gutter.

'Beddy-byes,' she whispered to Coco, and followed that with a sigh of satisfaction. She clambered back between the sheets, Coco in her arms, and then, as she snuggled against him she giggled into one of his tiny ears: 'We slept through it all. Don't forget, sweetest! We slept through it all.'

At the End of the Day

'Sitting with the curtains drawn on an afternoon like this!' the matron exclaimed as she tugged them apart. 'Whatever next! Why, you'd never know the sun was shining.'

'That's the whole point,' the old man told her. 'I don't want to know.'

'Isn't he *extraordinary*?' the matron appealed to the middle-aged visitor in the shining black elastic-sided boots and the overcoat with the velvet collar, who was perched on an arm of one of the two dilapidated easy chairs, a glass in a trembling hand.

'Incorrigible,' the visitor said, giving her a conspiratorial nod and wink. 'I tried to draw those curtains myself, but he wasn't having any.'

'Now would you please close them again?' the old man ordered in a thin, high-pitched voice that nonetheless carried undeniable authority. 'Since I have to pay such an exorbitant sum for this room, surely I may be allowed to decide whether to have my curtains drawn or not?'

The matron flushed in anger as she swept round to re-adjust the curtains; but she had managed to force a rigid smile before she turned back. 'Well, of course! If you *want* to sit in gloom, then why should we stop you? You know you're always free to do exactly as you wish.'

'I'd better be.'

The matron gave an unreal, tinkling laugh.

'When he bullies me like this,' she confided to the visitor, 'I know he's feeling at the top of his form. It's when he does what I tell him that I begin to worry.'

'Me too,' the visitor said, brushing some fluff off the sleeve of his coat with a limp-wristed hand.

'I saw you on the television the other night.'

'*Did* you?. . . Oh, in that awful cocoa ad! And it's one thing I just can't drink, it gives me a bilious attack at once, cocoa does!'

'Thank you, matron,' the old man dismissed her.

'Your tray will be along in a few minutes.'

'No, not in a few minutes. Not for at least half-an-hour. I don't want my visitor to see the kind of muck I have to put away.'

The matron and the visitor again exchanged ruefully amused glances, heads on one side and eyebrows raised.

'Silly bitch,' the visitor said, as soon as the matron had gone out.

'She's not a bad soul really. Quite kind.'

'You're the kind one. You put up with far too much.' The visitor peered into his glass, its rim touching his pointed chin. 'May I freshen this up a little?'

'Yes, go ahead, dear boy. Go ahead.' The old man drew his rug closer around him with hands that were blue and knobbly with arthritis.

'Cold?' The young man's method of freshening up his drink was to pour in another two inches of whisky from the bottle on the dressing-table.

'Not really.'

'Well, I am. Frozen.'

'Poor boy.'

'Poor you! You have to live in it. What's happened to the central heating?'

'It's on.' Suddenly the old man was doubtful. 'Isn't it?'

'You bet your life it isn't.' The visitor leaned over from his perch on the arm of the chair and ran his hand along the radiator. 'Stone cold.'

'Well, yes, of course, they always turn it off in May. I'd forgotten that.'

'May! It's only March now, ducks. The end of March.'

'So it is,' the old man said, confused. 'Well, I don't know what they're playing at.'

'Economising—as usual.'

'You're looking very smart this evening. Going somewhere?'

The visitor gulped some more of the whisky. The veins on his cheeks were growing more prominent. He nodded: 'Dinner with Gladys.'

'Gladys? Gladys?' The old man sounded suddenly agitated.

'It'll be one of her *white* meals again—macaroni cheese, mashed potato and cauliflower. Gladys Strout—you remember Gladys Strout.'

'Ah yes! Scandalous to feed you like that. These days she must be making a mint of money.'

'Poor old Gladys hasn't made any money in years. Not since she had that disastrous season on the West Pier. When the last G.I. left these shores, her last fan left with him.'

'Oh, yes, yes, of course. . . . Mind you, she's very good to me. Two weeks ago I found that I hadn't the—the wherewithal to —to settle my account. But she was perfectly prepared to wait until my next remittance came in. Damned decent of her, I must say. No, she's not really a bad sort.'

The visitor finally realised that the old man was speaking of the matron.

'I can't say that I'm exactly *mad* about her. But then I've never cared for butter-coloured teeth.'

'I suppose that Gladys Strout must live in high style. Some time ago she asked me round for a drink but I—'

'No, ducks, I *told* you—she's practically broke. Lives on the Old Age—and what help she can scrounge from others.' The visitor was beginning to get exasperated. 'Mind if I freshen this up?'

'Go ahead, dear boy, go ahead. You could put a splash into mine as well.' The old man extended his glass, his head shaking as though on a spring while his tongue worked round his mouth. 'This is one of the few pleasures left to me. And she'd like to take it away from me. Tries to get the doctor to say it's bad for me. Never did me any harm.'

'Never did anyone any harm. In moderation.' The visitor's face now looked as if the prominent veins on his cheeks had burst beneath the skin, spilling their purple.

'One has so few pleasures these days. A stroll on the front if the weather is good. That box over there. One's glass of scotch. And of course one's visits from you at the end of the day. You're such a faithful friend.'

The visitor had got up to examine the china arranged in a small display cabinet in one corner of the room. 'You've still got some lovely pieces,' he said. 'Just lovely.'

'Oh, you should have seen my collection in the old days!'

'Don't forget you promised to leave me this in your will.' He held out a Meissen tea-pot.

'Of course I won't forget. In fact—in fact it's in the will already.'

'Bless you! It's what I'd most like to remember you by.'

'Why don't you take it now?'

'Oh, I couldn't!'

'Take it, dear boy. Take it.'

'Have you any tissue paper?' the visitor asked eagerly, unable to conceal a smirk of self-congratulation at the success of his manoeuvre.

'Tissue paper?'

'To wrap it in. We don't want it broken.'

'Oh, I expect Miss What's-her-name can let you have some. You know—the matron of this place. She's not a bad soul really. The other day when I hadn't the wherewithal—'

The visitor drew in his breath with a sharp hiss. 'Something more in that glass, ducks?' he asked.

'Why not? One has so few pleasures these days. A stroll on the front if the weather is good. That box over—'

'I had an audition for the new Drury Lane musical last Friday,' the visitor quickly cut in. 'Did I tell you that?'

'How did it go?'

The other man pulled a face as though he had tasted something sour. 'I don't know what's happening to the theatre these days, honestly I don't. You were lucky to be born when you were.'

'As soon as I see Godfrey again I'll have a word with him about you.'

'Godfrey?'

'Godfrey Tearle.'

'Duckie—if you're going to have a word with Godfrey Tearle, it'll have to be in the next world.'

'Did I say Godfrey Tearle?' The old man plucked at the blanket in his confusion. 'I meant—you know—that chap in Royal Crescent.'

'Larry?'

'That's right. Larry What's-his-name. He's a decent young chap. I'll have a word with him. Might even ring him up. Yes, that's what I'll do. I'll ring him up.' He closed his eyes, putting his head far back on the cushion behind it, as though to impress this resolution deep. Then he opened the eyes again, smiled at the visitor and said: 'Well, I must say you're looking very smart this evening. Where are you bound?'

'To have dinner with Gladys Strout.'

'Well, you'll get a slap-up meal there. I envy you. These days she must be making a mint of money. Did I ever tell you the story of when she and Irene Vanburgh and I were all—'

'Yes, dear, you did. Now I'm just going to have a wee drop more in this glass and then I must be off. What about you?'

'Well, since it's one of the few pleasures left to me. . . .' The old man held out his glass; both his and the visitor's extended hands shook as though with palsy. 'I wonder what's happened to my dinner. It's nearly half-past seven.'

'You told her not to bring it at once. Remember?'

'So I did, so I did! . . . You know she's not really a bad soul. She's very good to me. Two weeks ago I found that I hadn't the—the wherewithal—'

'Duckie—I wonder if you'd do me a little favour? I must take poor old Gladys some flowers and I've come out without a sou. Do you—do you think you could possibly lend me a quid? Just until tomorrow.'

'Of course, dear boy. My wallet's over there—on the dressing-table. Help yourself.'

'Bless you.' The visitor went to the dressing-table and with his back turned to the old man abstracted a fiver. It was the only note in the wallet. 'I won't forget,' he said, knowing that he could rely on the old man to do so.

'I wish you could find a part worthy of you! I'm so out of touch these days. But when next I see Godfrey, I must really suggest that perhaps at Stratford—'

'Well, dear, I must be on my way. Take care.' The visitor first buttoned up his overcoat and then smoothed down his overlong, lank blond hair with both hands. 'God bless.' He stooped and kissed the old man on the forehead.

The old man put out a hand and gripped convulsively at his visitor's arm. 'You *are* good to me,' he said. 'One has so few pleasures left these days. One's glass of scotch. That box over there. And of course one's visits from you at the end of the day. Come again soon—won't you?'

'Bye then!' The visitor gave a wave with the hand that held the Meissen tea-pot and disappeared round the door.

The old man dozed, saliva trickling out of his mouth and slowly coursing down his chin on to the blanket.

'Well, there we are! Mary's off, so I've brought you your dinner myself.'

The old man stirred himself. 'About time too!' He peered at his watch. 'It's past half-past seven.'

'Well, you *did* say that you didn't want to eat until your visitor had gone.' The matron put on a cooing, breathless voice to conceal her exasperation.

'Visitor? What visitor?'

'What visitor?' She gave a jolly laugh. 'Your usual visitor.'

The old man frowned, as he played with the tassels of the rugs.

'Now do you want a little drink to go with your dinner?'

'Of course I do. I always do. You know that.'

The matron went across to the bottle on the dressing-table and picked it up. 'Heavens!' she exclaimed. 'You've managed to empty it. That's very, very naughty of you. You know that doctor said you were not to have more than two or three measures. And that bottle was almost full this morning.'

'It's my whisky, isn't it? I pay for it, don't I?'

The matron sighed. 'Well, that's that.'

'I want another bottle.'

'Another bottle?'

'Oh, come on, matron. Be a sport.' He now began to wheedle with all the charm that, fifty years ago, had made him a matinee idol. 'Send someone round the corner. Surely you can do that. One doesn't have many pleasures these days. A stroll along the front. That box over there. One's glass of—'

85

'Very well,' the matron conceded hastily, in order to cut him off.

'Take the money from my wallet. It's on the dressing-table over there.'

The matron looked into the wallet. 'There's nothing here,' she said.

'There must be. Don't be silly.'

'Look.' She held out the empty wallet before him.

'Well, that's odd. I went to the bank only two days ago. Remember?' He gave her an accusatory glare from under bushy eyebrows. 'How do you explain that?'

'I've no idea. Perhaps you bought something and don't remember.'

'I bought nothing, I remember perfectly well! Yes, it's odd, damned odd.'

'If you're trying to suggest that one of my staff—'

'I'm not suggesting anything. But there it is. Money gone. You've seen for yourself.'

The matron made an effort to get herself under control. Then she said: 'I can let you have a glass of my own sherry, if you'd like that. Would you?'

The old man muttered: 'Can't abide the stuff.' Then he looked up and flashed at her a brilliantly youthful smile. 'Well, that's handsome of you, matron. That's mighty handsome of you!'

When the matron returned with the glass of sherry the old man was again drowsing in the chair, his dinner untouched before him. He stared at her in momentary panic; then he again gave her that same brilliantly youthful smile.

'Thank you, my dear. Yes, over here—next to the tray.' He picked up the glass, raised it to her, muttering 'To your very good health,' and then took a sip. Smacking his lips with relish, he began to confide: 'She's not really a bad sort, you know. A bit rough and ready. She's had a tough life. But she's kind, really quite kind. Mind you, I don't know that I'd trust her very far. But running a place like this—well, it can't be any too easy—now can it? And I must say that—'

It was some time before the matron realised that he was talking about herself.

Cat People

The other Finnish boy, Vilho, who practised weight-lifting and collected ash-trays and cutlery filched from restaurants and hotels, shouted something to Erik as he raced down the staircase, two and three steps at a time. Erik, who was looking at Mrs Mackie's copy of the *Daily Mirror* while sipping at a late morning cup of coffee in the basement dining-room, shouted two or three words back with contemptuous indifference. The front door slammed, making the whole Regency cottage shudder.

'Aren't you going out with your friend?' Mrs Mackie asked, her broad face moist and red from the exertion of polishing the television-set. She was kneeling in front of it, as though in prayer.

Erik gave his small, sardonic smile. 'He is not my friend,' he said.

The answer pleased Mrs Mackie, who found the other boy noisy, clumsy and gauche. 'Well, considering that you both come from the same place,' she said.

Erik turned over a sheet of the newspaper in silence.

'Though one can see that you have such different backgrounds,' she went on. Erik put on a tie and changed either into a suit or grey flannels and a blazer every evening; his letters from home had the address heavily embossed at the top in Gothic lettering; after every meal he never failed to say thank you to Mrs Mackie. He was—as she would put it to her friends—every inch a gentleman. She got heavily to her feet, levering her saggy body up off the floor, palms pressed to the top of the television set and teeth clenched as though in pain. 'You like doing things on your own, don't you?' she said.

Erik merely smiled.

'Yes, I'm the same. We're loners, both of us. That's why my marriage never really lasted. I have to have my privacy. And you can't tell your husband to keep out of your way all the time, now can you?'

Erik rose lazily from the sofa, stretching his beautifully lithe and well-proportioned body, his arms above his head.

'We're cat people,' Mrs Mackie said.

'Please?'

'Cat people. We like to walk by ourselves. As soon as I saw you, I said to myself "Here's a cat person". I like cat people.'

'Now I shall go to the beach,' Erik announced. Hour after hour he lay out in the sunlight, in the briefest of briefs, with his golden head pillowed on his arms and his eyes shut against the dazzle.

'You have a lovely tan,' Mrs Mackie said. 'Your family won't know you on Monday.'

Erik moved vaguely towards the door.

'One day you should go to the beach,' he said. It was not an invitation.

'Oh dear, I'm far too busy. Three clients this morning—and I've still not done the shopping. If only you could persuade your friend to keep his room as tidy as you keep yours. That would take something off my hands.'

'He is not my friend, Mrs Mackie,' he reminded her with the same small, sardonic smile.

'Well, bye-bye then,' she called, as he began to make his way up the basement stairs.

'Bye-bye.' He had learned that colloquialism from her.

After he had gone, Mrs Mackie went up to his room to flick a duster pensively about its corners. Every morning she did this, though there was never any need for it. Erik kept his room scrupulously clean and tidy: his pyjamas folded and placed away in a drawer; two pairs of shoes and his slippers under the bed; a suit hanging in a polythene bag in the cupboard; and a number of tins and jars arranged symmetrically on the desk to contain pens, pencils, paper-clips, stamps and drawing-pins. A map of Brighton had been carefully attached to one wall with sellotape.

Mrs Mackie rarely went into the room of *the other one* (as she thought of Vilho), and when she did so she first pushed open the window in disgust, wrinkling up her nose at the smell of body-odour and unwashed feet, and then dashed round among the piles of clothes, books and newspapers, thrusting them from side to side and even kicking at them as she manipulated the ancient vacuum-cleaner. 'Pig,' she would often mutter to herself, noticing how his comb was clogged, how his shoes were scuffed and dirty and how the magazines littering the floor usually had on their covers photographs of women with bare breasts. She hated him.

But it was a pleasure to linger in Erik's room, which had the same smell of toilet-water—'lemony' was how she described it—that clung faintly to his presence. She would touch his ivory-backed brushes with the initials 'E.M.' inlaid in gold. She would stare at the envelopes of his letters and sometimes even draw one out surreptitiously, with beating heart, and examine it under the window, frowning as her lips moved in the effort of silently reading a language unknown to her. Then she would turn over his handkerchiefs, each of the finest linen, or run his ties through her fingers, thinking: 'Everything of his has *quality*. That's what I like about him. Quality.'

Her only disappointment was that the two suitcases were always locked. What did he keep in them? They were so heavy when she attempted to lift them, that she decided that they must be filled with either books or shoes. Probably he had also bought presents to take home with him. It was a little odd, always to lock them like that; but knowing that the other one pinched things from restaurants and pubs and trains, Erik was right to be careful. She often wondered if it was the other one who had made off with that dear little guardsman egg-timer that used to stand on the sitting-room mantelpiece—a grateful client had brought it for her and then, a day or two later, it had vanished.

Erik hadn't had any letters lately. But that of course was because he would soon be home again. She picked up the pile on the desk, fastened with a clip, and once again turned over the envelopes, one by one. She wished she knew whether Jorma was the name of a boy or a girl. He had a lot of letters from that Jorma. Probably it was a boy : Erik did not seem interested in girls like the other one, whom she had once even seen kissing some little tart in trousers on the sea-front in broad daylight. Erik was a sensible boy; he wasn't one to waste his money or to get himself into trouble with a shop-girl.

As she scouted round the wash-basin, she suddenly put down the cloth and reached for the bottle of toilet-water off the shelf. She removed the stopper and held it to her nose, breathing that lovely lemony smell deep into her lungs. It was a clean smell, that was what she liked about it. Clean, like him. Again she breathed and yet again, the perfume giving her a sensation of extraordinary euphoria, as though Erik were in the room close beside her.

Drat that bell!

'You're early, dear.'

'Am I?'

'Yes. I said ten-thirty, didn't I ? Well, never mind—no bones broken.' She opened the door into the room she called her study and switched on the light. She found it easier to get tuned in if she kept the curtains drawn.

The middle-aged woman in the square-toed lace-up shoes

and the pink blouse gave a little giggle. 'I don't know why—I feel kind of nervous. This is the first time,' she added.

'Well, there's no need to be nervous, dear. Sit down.' The woman sat, crossing one swollen ankle over the other and clasping her hands in her lap. She stared sideways and down at the empty grate as though unwilling to meet Mrs Mackie's gaze. 'That's better. Comfy? Now what was it you wanted?'

The woman again gave her curiously breathless giggle. 'Well I don't rightly know,' she said. 'I leave it to you. My friend— Mrs Aylward—said I should leave it to you.'

'Well, how about the crystal? Or would you prefer some psychometry.' (Mrs Mackie pronounced the word 'psychométry'.)

The woman's head jerked up and down. 'Just as you say, Mrs Mackie.'

Erik nearly always helped Mrs Mackie carry the things into the kitchen after supper was over: unlike the other one who usually bolted his food and rushed off, mouth still full, with the explanation that he was meeting this or that girl at the Starlight Room or the Regent Ball Room. On this occasion, however, Mrs Mackie told Erik: 'Now you run along. I can attend to all this. It's your last evening and I bet there's some girl-friend you want to say goodbye to.'

Erik neither confirmed nor denied the existence of this girl-friend. He merely continued to stack the dishes, saying: 'Oh, I have the whole evening.'

The other one, who had thrown himself down on the floor in front of the television set as soon as the meal was over, reluctantly rose to his feet to make desultory efforts to assist. After a while he said something to Erik in Finnish and Erik shook his head. Soon after that, the table still not wholly cleared, the other one looked at his watch, gave a sharp whistle and dashed up the stairs.

'Did he want you to go out with him?'

Erik did not answer as he pensively ran some hot water over a plate.

'I'm not surprised you said no. He's got in with a thoroughly bad set.'

Erik smiled down into the soap-suds.

Mrs Mackie fetched a long sigh. 'Pity me left alone with him in this house!' she said.

'Is it necessary for you to take lodgers?' Erik asked politely.

It was, in fact, necessary; but Mrs Mackie shook her head, as she answered: 'Well, I really do it for the fun of the thing, you know. I'm an observer of human nature, that's what I am. Now most people couldn't stand having one like that in the house for three weeks on end. But I get a kind of amusement out of it. Yes, really I do! I want to see just how far he'll go. Do you think that's strange of me? I like to see how far people will go.'

'So!' Erik had finished the washing-up for her. 'Now I will go out for a little walk.'

'Yes, you must say your last farewell to dear old Brighton.' She heaved an even deeper sigh. '. . . Well, we shall miss you. And you've never let me read your palm, you naughty boy. Don't you remember that you promised?'

Erik was fidgeting with the tea-cloth so that it should hang straight and exactly in the centre of the rail. She had often noticed his obsession with symmetry.

'I prefer not to know the future. Or the past,' he added with a last twitch at the towel.

'You *are* a funny boy.'

Mrs Mackie was a light sleeper; so that she was always having to nag at Vilho either to come home earlier or to make less noise when he came home late. Vilho would say he was sorry when she scolded him over breakfast, but the next night or the night after that he would do exactly the same again.

This time when the clicking shut of the front-door roused her from her sleep she was astonished to see that it was nearly five o'clock. She had never before known the other one to come home so late.

Furiously she jumped out of bed, thrust her arms into her dressing-gown, and rushed barefoot on to the landing. But with the speed and silence of a cat he had already disappeared into the darkness of the second floor above her.

Deciding not to pursue him now but to have it out with him in the morning, she was just about to re-enter her room when her nostrils pricked with that clean, lemony smell, faint on the still night air. With thumping heart, her flaccid arms clasped tight under her breast and her head cocked as though to hear some sound from the floor above her, she breathed it in again and yet again.

Perhaps it had not been the other one? Perhaps it had been Erik?

She clambered slowly back into bed and there stretched herself out on her side, her head supported on an elbow, the blankets thrown back. For a long time, delicious shivers running up and down her body, she continued to listen. But the house was wholly silent.

Erik left early, to catch the boat that would take him from Immingham to Gotenburg.

'You are kind to get up to make me breakfast,' Erik told her. She had never known him eat so much. Usually he only had a cup of coffee and a single piece of toast, but when she had urged him to have an egg in preparation for the long journey ahead of him, he had at once accepted. In the end he had eaten cornflakes, two eggs and four slices of toast spread thickly with butter and marmalade.

'You certainly have an appetite,' she said.

Erik began to whistle, something she had never heard him do before. The jaunty little tune must have been some Finnish folk-song.

'Well, you're not sorry to be getting home, that's obvious,' Mrs Mackie said. 'I've never seen you in such a gay mood at this hour of the morning.'

'I have enjoyed Brighton,' Erik said, smiling at her from under his luxuriant blond eyelashes.

'I hope you'll come again.'

'Certainly I will come again. I have enjoyed myself. Especially these last days.'

As she waved to him from the door—he strode off towards the bus-stop as though those two suitcases were no weight at all—Mrs Mackie all at once felt depressed. Vindictive thoughts of the other one came into her mind. She would have to tell him to go: with Erik as a buffer she had just been able to tolerate his presence but now she decided that she could no longer do so.

Mrs Mackie re-entered her bedroom and then, on an impulse, left it again and climbed upstairs to Erik's. He might never have been there—but for that faint smell of lemon! He had folded up the sheets and blankets; he had cleaned the wash-basin; he had opened both of the windows so that the damp, salt air could blow in. Thoughtful to the last! Oh, she would never find a lodger like him again!

She put a hand to the wardrobe and slowly opened the door, seeing her reflection in the mirror—an ageing woman with greasy locks of grey hair about a lined, disgruntled face —swing out to meet her. Then she gasped.

The whole of the base of the cupboard was full of bottles: gin bottles, whisky bottles, sherry bottles, bottles of the cheapest wines.

How did they get there?

Briefly she thought that the other one had played a malicious joke. Then she remembered the heaviness of the locked suit-cases and murmured to herself 'Of course, that's it, that's it.' She did not feel shocked. To have discovered something so intimate about Erik after the weeks of being gently repelled by the letters in a language strange to her, by the locked suitcases and above all by his smilingly impersonal courtesy, filled her with heady triumph. At last we're getting somewhere, she said to herself. What she meant was that at last she was getting near him.

She opened the drawer at the base of the cupboard and there too were bottles and, among them, a screwed-up ball of paper, evidently torn from a notebook or diary. At once she pounced. She thought at first that it must be his timetable from the school—there was a column of dates and then, horizontally, the twenty-four hours of the day, again divided off into columns. But the odd thing was that little asterisks had been set not against the hours when she knew him to have been at school but against hours like 2 a.m. or 6 a.m. or 7 p.m. What could it mean? Not every day had its asterisk, but some days had two or three.

Eventually she told herself that the asterisks denoted the times when he had started a drinking bout. But that explanation did not really satisfy her.

Oh, but there was the bottle of toilet-water! About a quarter-of-an inch of the greenish liquid gleamed at the bottom.

Mrs Mackie held the bottle up to the light; then she drew out the cork.

Deeply she breathed again and yet again; until, instead of the usual euphoria, she experienced a sensation of almost un-bearable foreboding and excitement. It was exactly as it used to be before one of her 'visions' when she was a girl: the visions that persuaded her and her widowed mother that she was psychic but which in recent years had come to her less and less

96

often and less and less intensely. 'Oh no!' she gasped. She swayed and shut her eyes, the bottle still clasped in both hands beneath her nose.

It was blood she smelled; and it was blood she now saw beneath her fluttering eyelids, first a vast, wavering curtain of it and then a localised jet spurting from the neck of someone who lay, unshaven and gross, on his side in a rumpled double bed. The blood saturated the sheet and dripped on to the floor, where it glistened on bare boards. She saw a huge frozen pupil and an open mouth, with a pink set of dentures fallen across the tongue that protruded from it.

Mrs Mackie replaced the cork in the bottle with wildly trembling hands as she heard Vilho calling to her: 'Mrs Mackie! Mrs Mackie!'

'Yes,' she answered; and then louder 'Yes! Yes, what is it?'

'Has Erik gone?'

'Yes, he's gone.'

'I wanted to say goodbye to him.'

'Well, you were too late.'

'Sorry, dear, I can't do anything for you today. . . . No, I'm not feeling too good. . . . No, just tiredness. . . . Sorry, dear. . . .'

Mrs Mackie put down the telephone and then once again read the piece in the *Argus*.

A middle-aged man had been murdered in a lodging-house near the station. The landlord had found the door still locked late in the morning and, getting no answer to his repeated knocking, had eventually broken in. The man had been stabbed over and over again in the neck and the chest. The police had established his identity—a name was given—and had already learned that the previous evening he had been seen in a number of bars frequented by homosexuals. The knife and the blood-stained key to the room had eventually been discovered on the floor of a cubicle in a public lavatory on the front.

Vilho was reading the papers from home, while munching a slice of toast.

'Listen to this,' he said. 'Here's a murder just like that one here last week. In Gotenburg.'

Mrs Mackie pushed two more slices of bread into the toaster. 'What murder?' she said.

Vilho explained. In Gotenburg, too, the victim had been a middle-aged homosexual; he, too, had been stabbed; and the blood-stained key of the lodging-house room and the knife had again both been recovered from the floor of a public lavatory.

'One crime is very much like another,' Mrs Mackie said. 'Can't you find something better to read than morbid stuff like that?'

'It might be Erik,' Vilho said as a joke. 'He was returning through Gotenburg just about that time.'

'Don't be silly.' But though she spoke crossly, Mrs Mackie was now glad that she had not given the other one notice after all. 'If you'd let me pour the tea for you, you wouldn't splash it all over the table.'

Vilho reached across her for the marmalade.

'Don't you ever ask people to pass things in Finland?' Mrs Mackie swept up to her feet, put her napkin in its ring and then climbed the stairs. Her forehead was burning and the skin around her eyes felt as though it had been pulled suddenly tight.

In her room she went to her dressing-table, opened one of its drawers and took out the bottle of toilet-water. She closed her eyes, her head thrown back and her legs wide apart, and held it beneath her nose. She sniffed and sniffed again.

The great curtain of blood swayed behind her eyelids, back and forth, back and forth. Now it was a wave, sweeping across a vast and desolate stretch of sand and she was being lifted up on it, arms outstretched and mouth gasping for air, while another crimson wave carried towards her a figure with similarly outstretched arms and similarly gasping mouth. 'Oh, Erik, Erik, Erik!' They met with ferocious impact and then went down, down, down, into the congealing darkness, clutching at each other in a mingling of triumph and despair as the waves closed above them. 'Oh, Erik!' she moaned.

An Evening by the Fire

There had been a time when, returning home from the shop in the winter, Frank Rowlands would say: 'Well, it's nice to get home to an evening by the fire.' But now his one thought was that it was nice to get away from it.

'You can't go out in this sort of weather.'

'Well, the dog must have his walk. Mustn't he?'

'That dog! It'll be the death of you.'

'I don't suppose he's been very far today, has he?'

'You know that I can't have him pulling on me. You know what it does to my back.'

Frank knew what many things did to Norah's back: stooping over the sink and carrying trays and picking up her ball of knitting-wool when it rolled under her chair and standing on trains or buses and using the vacuum-cleaner and actions of an even more intimate nature. But Norah was brave; everyone agreed that she was brave. If a thing had to be done, then she did it, no matter how much she suffered. 'You make me feel guilty,' Frank would say when she had performed any one of the many actions that made her back 'play up' and she would reply 'Silly! I can't afford to be an invalid.'

'That dog was a mistake. Whatever persuaded us to take him?'

But they both knew that it was he who had persuaded her.

'Oh, come, Norah! You know that you're fond of him.'

'The amount he eats! It's lucky we haven't children's mouths to feed as well. . . . Well, don't be long.'

She often said 'Don't be long;' and then when he returned

she would say 'Well, you *have* been a time!' His return was the signal for her to prepare his glass of bedtime malted milk. She herself never drank milk at night, she said it gave her acidity.

The dog, Bruce, was a huge black labrador and they had taken him over from neighbours who had had to move to a flat in London. 'I'm not surprised they couldn't do with him in a flat,' Norah said. 'Even this house is far too small for him.' He was always 'under her feet' (as she would put it), patiently moving somewhere else when she scolded him or kicked him aside. Strangely he seemed to be fonder of her than of Frank, sitting on his haunches to watch her with a rapt expression as she sipped at a cup of tea or knitted a pullover for Frank or frowned at the *Daily Telegraph* crossword. 'Oh, stop staring so!' she would often snap at him in exasperation.

Frank never stared at her : nowadays he would even deliberately avoid meeting her eyes.

'Now sit, boy! *Sit!*'

'You can go on saying that till kingdom come. He's too old to learn. Even with a biscuit.'

The air was damp and chill and except in the shelters, where a few couples huddled against each other, there was no one on the front. But that was how Frank liked it. After the noisy confinement of the shop and the silent confinement of the house, it was wonderful to stride out into the wide, icy darkness, with the wind squeezing the tears from under his lids and numbing his lips and making his forehead smart. During these winter months only every third lamp was illuminated, a luminous skirt of yellow swaying round its base.

Bruce ran from one of the wire litter-baskets to another. Supporting himself with his forepaws, he inserted an exploratory head and then began scattering the contents in all directions. During the day Frank would shout at him 'Bruce, stop that! Stop that at once!' He would be genuinely shocked at the mess the dog was making. But at night his attitude would suffer a curious change: let the poor brute get on with it, what did it matter? The paper that had wrapped up sandwiches or fish and chips would whirl down the wind; cartons would scrape along the railings; the dog would crunch and gulp. As Norah often remarked—'One would think he never got a square meal!' On this occasion Bruce scampered off with a polythene bag over his ears, stopping from time to time to scrabble at it with one of his paws, until at long last it went floating away from him.

It was at that moment that Frank became aware of a figure ahead, it too zigzagging back and forth like Bruce, but with none of Bruce's purpose. A young man it seemed, his hair long at the back under a flat cap and an overcoat, several sizes too large for him, draped over his slim shoulders to reach almost to his ankles. In one hand he was carrying a battered brief-case, which he would drag along the slatted seats of the benches as though it were too heavy for him.

Now they had neared the Hove end of the esplanade, where the trim little bathing-chalets, like so many miniature replicas of the trim little bungalows in which their owners lived, fronted the darkly plunging waves. 'It would be nice to have one of those chalets,' Frank would say to Norah on the occasions, usually on a Sunday afternoon in the summer, when they strolled past them together. 'What would be nice about it?' she would then reply. 'All those crowds! No thank you. And neither of us swims.' But Frank had sometimes thought that if he owned one of the chalets he might perhaps begin to swim again.

The figure approached one of the chalets, stopped and then rattled the handle. The chalet was locked. The figure then tried another door: not the door next to the one already tried but a door two or three chalets further on. The first handle he had rattled in the perfunctory manner of someone who is not really interested in getting inside; but with the second he made a determined effort, even putting a shoulder to the door. When he began to try a third handle, Frank shouted: 'Hey! What the hell d'you think you're doing?'

The figure turned; and Frank realised at once that it was not a boy but a girl. She said nothing, merely staring at him with curiously wide popping eyes.

'Those chalets are private property. You've no business to try to break in.'

'Do you think I'm going to steal something?' she asked in a voice at once whining and truculent, with a South London accent.

'I don't know what you're going to do. But those chalets are private property.'

'Oh, f—— off!'

Infuriated, Frank shouted after her: 'You just leave those doors alone or I'll have the police on your track.'

Bruce had begun to lope behind her in pursuit. The moment the girl noticed him, she cringed against the railings, as though expecting an attack. But when he merely jumped around her, wagging his tail, she put down the hand that was not carrying the brief-case and patted his head. 'Good dog. That's a good dog,' Frank heard her say.

'Bruce! Come here! Come here at once!'

The dog paid no attention.

'At once! *Bruce!*'

Emboldened, the girl began to snigger. Frank strode towards her.

'He seems to like my smell.' Bruce was now licking the lowered hand.

'That I can well believe,' Frank snapped in fury.

Eventually he managed to get the rearing dog on to the chain and began to drag him away, to the continuing laughter of the girl.

'Bad dog! Bad!' He hit out at him viciously with the end of the lead.

Two nights later it was Bruce who again found the girl.

Uneeringly he ran to one of the bathing-huts, seemingly as empty as all the others, put first his nose and then a paw to the door and levered it open. He disappeared inside.

Slowly Frank approached.

An almost full moon was shining low in an unclouded sky, and by its light Frank could see, as he peered into the hut, that the dog was snuffling at what appeared to be a rolled-up bundle of clothes on the floor. Then there was a little scream, followed by a giggle, and a tousled head appeared out of the folds.

'Christ! You didn't have give me a fright. Hello, boy!'

As the dog kept attempting to lick her face, the girl put out her hands alternately to push it away from her and then to drag its head back on to her breast. 'That's a nice feller! That's a nice old feller!'

'What are you doing here?'

'Oh, mind your own business!' The dog's muzzle was now somewhere in the recesses of her clothing.

'Bruce! Come here!'

'What's the matter? 'Fraid I'm going to corrupt him?'

"Bruce!"

'He likes me. You like me, don't you, feller?'

'These huts are private. You've no right to be in here. You must have broken in.'

'Too bad.'

Frank's eyes had now got used to the dim light filtering through the half-open door and he saw the half-eaten loaf of bread on the table, the bottle of cider with a paper mug beside it and the pile of tins, many of them open. At the same time he was aware of the appalling stench, which he guessed to come, in part at least, from the scuffed pair of suede bootees beside the door. Yet this stench, so far from sharpening his anger and disgust, filled him with a curious kind of palpitating excitement.

She was staring at him with those wide, protuberant eyes of hers as his own eyes moved about the hut.

'So what are you going to do about it?'

He did not answer. Only a second ago he had known very well what he was going to do about it: report it to the police. But now he was not sure.

'Stop that, Bruce!' he said feebly to the dog, who was still burrowing into the overcoat flung over her.

'Going to have me chucked into gaol?' Still he did not answer. 'Well, while you're thinking about it, you can give me a fag. Or don't you smoke because you're afraid of cancer?'

Staring at the bottle of cider with a bemused frown, he drew out a packet of cigarettes and held it out to her.

'Thanks. Match?'

He produced the match and even stooped to light the cigarette.

'Thank you, sir,' she drawled insolently. She drew deeply time and time again, resting on an elbow with her body still humped on the floor at his feet.

'How long have you been sleeping out?'

'Do you call this "out"? Try under the pier.' Suddenly she cleared her throat, gathered the spittle and, to his horror and disgust, spat into a corner of the hut.

'Run away from home?' he asked.

'What business is that of yours? . . . Oh, f—— off, beat it.' She now lay flat on her back, the dog straddled over her, and blew one ring of smoke after another up into the darkness.

He watched her in silence. Then he threw the packet of cigarettes down on to the ground beside her. 'Keep them,' he said, as he turned and left the hut.

Once more out in the clean, cutting air, he began to shout:
'Bruce! Come on, boy! Bruce! Bruce!'

He tried to whistle but his lips were trembling too much for him to do so.

He had wanted to forget the whole incident; he had certainly never intended to go back there again. But as he lay unsleeping beside Norah, her breath hissing gently between her closed lips so that they trembled at each exhalation, he all at once smelled that odour of perspiration and dirty clothes and shoes worn too long, with a terrible hallucinatory intensity. Was it on his hands? In panic he smelled them. Or had it clung to his hair? He got out of bed to go to the bathroom and wash. Norah stirred at once:

'What's the matter?' she murmured.

'Nothing.' He padded towards the door.

'You ought to do it last thing at night. I'm always telling you that.'

'Why don't you leave me alone?'

'Because I'm interested. I want to know what makes someone like you tick.'

'And what makes *you* tick? I suppose your wife has to wind you up each morning.' She gave a short, barking laugh and then began to cough on the cigarette that she had already demanded from him. The dog was sniffing at the shoes which once again stood near the door. Her rump in its blue jeans resting against the table, she crossed one leg over the other to reveal to him a sock so matted and dark that it seemed to have merged with the foot beneath it.

'How long can you go on living like this?'

'Forever.' She toyed with a lock of her straight blonde hair, twisting it around a finger. 'Why not? I've been living like this for almost a year.'

'What do you do for money?'

She shrugged, without answering. 'The winter's bad,' she said. 'Wait for the summer. Then it's easy.'

'How old are you?'

'Eighteen.'

'Come off it!'

She gave the curious barking laugh. 'All right. Seventeen. Do you like that better?' She patted the head of the dog, then looked up to say: 'Lend me a quid.' He stared at her. 'Well, give me one then. You know I'll never pay it back.'

He put his hand uncertainly to his inside breast-pocket. 'Why should I give you anything?'

'Do you want a *reason* for being generous? Is that it?' As she approached he backed, until in the end he felt the edge of the table digging into his buttocks. 'Is it?' Suddenly she had lowered a hand.

They stared at each other, he in fear and horror and she with a kind of dreamy contempt. Apart from her hand, their two bodies remained entirely motionless. Then he lunged clumsily at her, attempting to bury his head in the folds of her jersey.

'No. None of that.' She gave him a push. 'Just this.' He straightened, and as he did so, felt the dog's muzzle cold on his fingers. Rigidly he stood; until after a long, long time he was aware that the dog had begun to whimper—an intermittent keening sound like the one he made when Norah put his food to cool on top of the stove, too high for him to get at it.

'All right?'

Frank said nothing, drawing a handkerchief from his pocket. Then all at once he began to shout at the still whimpering dog: 'Shut up! Be quiet!' The dog sat on its haunches, looking up at him.

'Now give me the pound.'

He took out his wallet and extracted the note.

She began to shiver as she took it and tucked it in a pocket of her trousers. 'Christ, but it's cold!' She had said not a word of thanks.

'It's not that bad tonight.'

She hugged herself, lean arms over her breast and teeth chattering, so that the words jerked out between one spasm and the next. 'Go—up—for a—cup of coffee. That's what I'll do.'

She looked around for the dilapidated overcoat, hitched it off the floor and then thrust first one arm and then the other into the sleeves. 'I'm ice,' she said. 'Feel.' She put a hand to his cheek and quickly withdrew it with a giggle. 'Come on!' She was now addressing the dog not him, as she jumped off the ledge of the hut on to the esplanade. Bruce followed, clumsily leaping around her, his tail flailing from side to side and his back legs apart.

'He'll dirty you,' Frank said; and then thought, with a sudden access of loathing for the girl: 'Dirty you! More like, you'll dirty him.'

She walked always a step ahead of him, with the dog still prancing round her. If he quickened his pace in order to come abreast with her, she at once quickened her own. Near the place where the esplanade widened and was flooded with light, she turned, her chin on to her chest and her hands deep in the pockets of the ragged overcoat. 'This cold! Goes through you like a knife.' Again she was shuddering.

'It's not so cold tonight.'

'Not so cold! Are you out of your mind? . . . Well big boy, this is where I say a fond farewell.' All at once she had assumed a parody of an American accent.

'Which way are you going?'

'Thataway.' She gestured vaguely with her head.

'I'll walk a little further with you.'

'Nope. You go your way, I go mine.' She turned on her heel

108

and made to cross the road. On the edge of the pavement she turned: 'Bye!' She waved a hand. Then she shouted: 'You'd better call your dog. If you don't want 'im to meet with an 'orrible accident.' The jocularity with which she had previously assumed the stage American accent and now assumed this Cockney one filled him with a sudden loathing.

'Bruce!' he bawled.

The dog looked repeatedly now after her retreating figure and now at his master. Then at last he loped over to Frank.

Frank hit out at him with the lead. 'You come here when I call you,' he said. 'Understand?'

Together they walked back into the cold and darkness of the windswept esplanade. Now Frank too felt chilled and as he put his hands deep into the pockets of his coat, drawing it closer around him, his fingers touched the handkerchief.

He drew it out and clenched it in one fist as he walked faster and faster into the biting wind. Then at one of the litter-baskets he stopped beside the dog and hurriedly dropped it in.

'Bruce! Come here! Come away from that!'

'I wonder if you're sickening for the flu.'

'I'm not sickening for anything!'

'Feel your hands—they're frozen. That dog's going to be the death of you. . . . Well, sit down by the fire and I'll go and get your milk. D'you know what time it is?'

'Yes.' Frank looked at his watch. 'Thirteen minutes past ten. If you *must* know.'

'You've been out more than an hour.'

'Well, I needed the fresh air.'

'If you ask me, you need your head examined. In weather like this!'

As he took off his overcoat he guiltily put his hands deep into its pockets until he reminded himself: 'Idiot! You threw it away.'

'You missed such a good programme,' Norah's voice pursued him from the kitchen. 'You always miss the good programmes, going out like that.'

The next night when Bruce levered open the door of the hut for Frank to peer in, the girl was not there, even though her odour still filled the darkness. Frank hesitated on the doorstep; then he entered, lowering his head so as not to bang it on the lintel. He stood for a while, seeing nothing but a milky blur of the sea revealed through a crack in the door where it had failed to close entirely. His mind swivelled back to the previous night, when he had stood in exactly the same place and she had stood before him, one arm extended. Meanwhile he could hear the dog snuffling in the corners.

He took out his cigarette-lighter and extended it, now here, now there. The same half-devoured loaf of bread was on the table and beside it a packet of biscuits, some of them spilled across the dusty nylon cloth. There was now also a candle; this he stooped and lit. God, what a place to live! He sat down on one of the two canvas chairs, took out a cigarette and waited.

Suddenly the thought came to him: perhaps she had gone forever! He imagined her in another town—Eastbourne, Worthing, Bognor—walking another esplanade, trying the doors of other deserted bathing-huts and begging—or, worse, earning—a pound off some other respectable, middle-aged man like himself. Perhaps she was dossed down under the pier. Perhaps someone had offered her the home he himself could not offer her.

Then he saw the battered brief-case in the farthest corner and his panic at the thought of losing her forever was succeeded by a marvellous relief. He stared at the brief-case for a long time; the initials on its flap, E.G., almost worn away, reminded him that he still did not know her name. It was unlikely that those initials were hers. He imagined her picking up that brief-case in some junk-shop or at a market-stall; perhaps even stealing it. He thought of her carrying it as she wandered into coffee-bars or thumbed lifts from lorries late at night, and of her using it as a pillow as she slept on park benches. He crossed to the corner and picked it up; caressed it with his hands, astonished by the curiously greasy texture of the leather; and then, on an impulse, opened it.

He turned over the things that it contained: some stockings of a colour—blue, green?—that he could not make out in the feeble light of the candle; a suspender-belt, which momentarily he held against his cheek in a sudden access of desperate longing; two tattered paper-back novels; a blouse; a beret. . . . He felt nauseated by this pathetic flotsam of her life, and yet at the same time it filled him with a mounting excitement, since it seemed to bring him far nearer to her than she had been when, staring into his eyes with her own mocking ones, she had touched him with her hand.

Last of all he took out the tiny box. It was the kind of box in which old men keep tobacco and cigarette-paper and children keep geometrical instruments. The surface of it was rough —he assumed with rust—and an elastic band had been put round it to keep it together. Wanting to know everything about her, even to the extent of opening this box which no doubt contained hair-grips or safety pins or make-up, he slipped off the elastic band with a thumb-nail, so that it shot into the darkness. He would find it again in a moment he told himself, raising the lid.

For a long time he stared in incomprehension at the gleaming hypodermic. Then in his fundamental innocence he thought: poor girl, she must be a diabetic! Knowing that, he was even more appalled by this life of hers. Didn't one from time to time read in the papers of someone who had vanished from home and who would be in grave danger without a daily dose of insulin? She was crazy to lead this kind of life if she was ill in that way.

'Just what the bloody hell do you think you're doing?'

She was in the doorway and from her swaying he guessed that she was drunk.

'I—I—'

'You just give that to me!' Suddenly she had launched herself at him, clawing the box from his hands. 'Get out!' she screamed. 'Out! How dare you touch my things?'

'It's all right,' he conciliated. 'What's there to get so angry about? I'm sorry. I tell you, I'm sorry.'

But she continued to scream at him: 'Out, out, out! Get out! Do you hear me, get out! That's private! How dare you touch it!'

He edged out of the door. 'Are you crazy?' he asked. 'What's the matter with you?'

As she began to push the door shut, he hastily inserted a foot.

'I only came to give you this,' he said on an impulse. He pulled out his wallet and clumsily extracted a pound note.

'I don't want your bloody money!' she screamed in mounting hysteria. 'I don't want any part of you!'

He let the note fall from between his fingers, so that it drifted down into the darkness on her side of the door.

'Take it or leave it,' he said, hurrying off, with the dog pattering along beside him.

Of course he went back: not the next night nor even the night after but the night after that. By then he had made all sorts of plans for her: to persuade her to go home or to find her a job or to give her the money to rent herself a room. In all these schemes he saw himself partly as a benevolent and protective father and partly as her lover. The squalor and shame of that one fumbling encounter would somehow be redeemed.

112

It was a misty night, each lamp a blurred smudge receding down an esplanade that all at once seemed endless. Bruce kept disappearing and then reappearing, his reappearances heralded by the curiously loud patter of his feet. Frank coughed repeatedly, and each time the cough echoed on and on ahead of him. He drew out a handkerchief and held it to his mouth; and then all at once he remembered that other handkerchief, abandoned in the very basket into which Bruce was now inserting his head.

Was that a light coming from the hut? Then Frank realised that what he had thought was a light was, in fact, the headlights of a car. It was odd; no cars were allowed on the esplanade. As he was still staring incredulously into the fog, Bruce all at once dashed off.

Yes, it was a car: a police-car. Two men were dragging something out of the hut, and because the something appeared to be on the ground it was not until he was less than thirty yards away that Frank realised that it was the girl. Now she was screaming: 'You lay your hands off me, you f—ing bastards! Let go! Leave me be!' and together with these shrill, obscene screams Frank could also hear swearing and grunting from the two men on either side of her. Curiously a third man, Frank could now see, was seated impassively at the wheel.

Bruce halted about ten paces away from the mêlée, his ears pricked, his head thrown back and his hackles bristling along his spine. Then he began to bark.

At the sound the girl's resistance immediately ended. She scrambled to her feet, swayed and then, a policeman at either elbow, began to walk towards the car.

She looked up; momentarily her eyes met Frank's, with exactly the same derisory gaze with which she had stared at him when they had stood so near in the hut. But now, in some curious way, what passed between them seemed even more intimate, shameful and humiliating. One of the policemen

113

pushed her into the car; the other gave Frank a curt glance, said sharply, 'All right, the circus's over,' and then climbed in beside her.

'I've never heard of anything so silly. Going out in a fog like this. Walking along the front! Here—you'd better sit by the fire. You look as if you were sickening for something.'

Still in his overcoat, his hair damp across his forehead, Frank lowered himself into the armchair in which Norah had previously been knitting, hunched himself forward and stared into the flames. His whole body was shivering.

'I'd better put a drop of brandy in your milk!' He did not answer. 'Would you like that?'

'Fine. Fine.' It was only with an effort that he could control the chattering of his teeth; only by gripping his hands between his knees that he could stop them trembling.

'You'll have to give up these walks until the warmer weather comes. Even if I have to take out Bruce myself in the afternoon.'

'Well,' he said. It was almost a groan. 'Well.' He gripped his hands tighter between his knees. 'Anyway, it's nice to get home to an evening by the fire. That's something. Yes, that's something. To get home to an evening by the fire.'

But his teeth went on chattering, his body went on shaking.

The Containers

The doctor gave Brooks three containers. Made of a waxed paper that had the appearance of parchment, they seemed far too small and fragile for their intended purpose. 'Disposable,' he explained. 'Everything we use is disposable these days. The trouble is'—he scratched ineffectively with his ball-point pen on the shiny surface—'one has the greatest of difficulty in writing on them. . . . Hell!' At that he began to search in the top drawer of his desk for some labels, eventually managing to collect three. On the first he inscribed 'Mr Brooks—1', on the second 'Mr Brooks—2', on the third 'Mr Brooks—3'.

The doctor walked to the garden gate with Brooks, who now had charge of the three containers in a carrier-bag with 'Pontings—The House for Value' printed on it. 'Now I want *everything*,' he said. 'Don't forget—everything.' He patted Brooks on the shoulder : 'All right?'

'All right.'

Unused, the containers smelled of celluloid. The lids did not screw on without a certain amount of careful adjustment and, once they were on, the containers themselves tended to be top-heavy. In the doctor's gleaming surgery it had seemed to be simple enough to use them as instructed, but even on the walk home Brooks had started to worry.

Each of the three containers was intended for a period of twenty-four hours, and curiously on each of the three nights that they remained in his possession, a different dream connected with them—recurrent, confused and clogged with anxiety and even terror—was to keep Brooks tossing and sweating. Since the start of his mysterious illness Brooks had grown used to the way in which all the events of the day, like the food which he had so much difficulty in digesting, were regurgitated over and over again during the hours of darkness. But these particular nightmares—even though, when he had awoken from them he could tell himself how ridiculous they had been —seemed far more terrible than any that had preceded them.

The first was concerned with his housekeeper, a woman in her sixties like himself, who had been with him, ever since the death of his wife, for a period of almost twenty years, without a single moment of intimacy ever having passed between them. Brooks had told her little about his illness and nothing at all about the containers, which he had hidden from her in the box-room, knowing that if he put them in the bathroom cup-board as at first planned, she would certainly find them there and wonder about their purpose. In this dream—which was really an intricate spider's web of dreams—the housekeeper went up to the box-room on some errand, found the containers and opened one. Horrified, she rushed screaming down the steep stairs, as once, long ago, when she had found a rat there on the window-sill. Another variation of this dream was that she decided to play a diabolical practical-joke on him so that there, on his breakfast-tray the following morning, was not his usual jar of honey, shaped like a pineapple of opalescent glass, but one of the containers. In yet another variation, she removed the containers without saying a word to him, so that when he went to collect them from the box-room in order to take them back to the doctor, he found in panic that they had completely disappeared. How was he to explain their loss to the doctor? It was, of course, out of the question that he should ask the housekeeper about them.

The second night was the night of the dream of the police-man. Brooks was walking to the doctor's house with the con-tainers in the Pontings bag when he became aware that a tall policeman was eyeing him with suspicion. Suddenly the policeman turned about and began to follow him from behind. Brooks knew that he must not hurry, since to do so would only confirm the policeman in his surmise that he was up to something dishonest. But involuntarily he quickened his pace, the arm carrying the bag growing all at once rigid and painful. 'Excuse me, sir. *Just* a moment, sir.' A hand rested on his shoulder. 'Might I take a peep into that bag of yours?' Sometimes Brooks shouted 'No, no! Certainly not!' Sometimes he made off at the run, with the policeman in pursuit. Sometimes he submitted in docile horror as the policeman gravely took one of the containers out of the bag, unscrewed its lid and then peered inside, to look up and ask in a tone of brutish bullying, 'Now what's all this about?'

The third night was the night of the accidents. As Brooks came out of the house, he suddenly slipped on a patch of mud by the porch and the bag shot from his hand. A container rolled out, tumbled down the path and burst open as it somersaulted on to the pavement. Or someone hurrying past him jogged his arm and a container bounced from the bag. Or, worst of all, he was crossing a road when a car swerved round a corner and knocked him flat. A crowd gathered round, a woman screamed, someone pointed: 'Look at that blood!' But it was not blood; it was the contents of the squashed containers. Faces blurred in fascinated horror, as he managed to faint or even die from the embarrassment.

When he eventually set off for the doctor's house, his housekeeper noticed that he looked even paler than usual and, worried, asked him if he ought not to take a taxi. But remembering that in the third dream there had been the occasion when the taxi had given a sudden jolt and one of the containers had splashed its contents on to the floor ('What's that god-awful pong?' growled the driver) Brooks retorted pettishly that it was absurd to waste the money when the walk was one of less than a quarter of an hour. The housekeeper, who was used to his stinginess, shrugged her shoulders and returned to her dusting. An inquisitive woman, she had discovered that Brooks had been consulting a specialist, but she had no idea what was contained in the Pontings bag.

In fact, the journey proved to be simple and uneventful. The path was dry and so were the pavements; no one jostled him; and there was so little traffic that he was able to cross the road without a vehicle in sight in either direction. He passed one policeman, standing in a doorway, but the man seemed more interested in watching three Scandinavian girl students emerging from the Morocco Coffee Bar than in watching an old man scurrying past with a creased bag with 'Pontings—The House for Value' printed on it.

The doctor was at his hospital and it was therefore to the doctor's wife that Brooks had to entrust the containers. 'Some —er—specimens,' he stuttered. But she was used to such cargoes being brought to the door and took the bag from him as though he were a postman delivering a parcel.

'Would you like the bag back?' she asked.

'Well, actually, your husband gave it to me.'

'Oh, *did* he?' She laughed. 'I was wondering what had happened to it.'

'I'm so sorry.'

'Never mind.'

'Then he'll let me know?'

'He'll let your doctor know.'

'When would that be?'

'Oh, just as soon as possible.'

Brooks experienced a marvellous euphoria when, rid of the containers, he began to walk jauntily back to his house. While in his possession they had seemed to be merely a source of embarrassment, disaster and panic. Now he was finished with them.

What he did not realise was that they still contained, as they waited in the doctor's laboratory, something far more embarrassing and disastrous and far more productive of panic than any of the mishaps he had sweated and groaned at in his dreams.

But of that he was yet to hear—'just as soon as possible.'

The Doll

In three separate shop-windows he had seen that photograph
—with above it the question 'HAVE YOU EVER SEEN
THIS GIRL?' and below it the admonition 'IF YOU HAVE
SPEAK NOW!' But one did not want to be observed study-
ing a notice like that, did one? People might suspect one of
being in some way involved oneself. So each time he gave no
more than a shying glance, to be followed by that curious
gesture of first lowering his pointed chin down on to his collar
and then pushing it outward, which indicated to those who
knew him that he was feeling self-conscious or embarrassed.

'Morning, Mr Reynolds!'

'Morning Eunice.'

'*Good* morning, Mr Reynolds. Quite a nip in the air, isn't
there?'

'Yes, quite a nip.'

'Now what else for you, Mr Reynolds? We have some nice
chicory in.'

'My gentleman's off chicory.'

But the chatty exchanges which he usually enjoyed so much
now were a burden to him. He wanted to gaze at that photograph somewhere where no one could watch him doing so.

'Oh, Mr Reynolds!'

That woman who had been recommended for the loose-
covers and who had made them so badly was barring his
path.

'Good morning.' He nodded and tried to hurry round
her.

'I wanted to explain. About those loose-covers. It was a question of cutting the cloth on the bias. Sir Malcolm just didn't seem to understand. You should have heard him on the phone! It was the bias. And then that finicky floral pattern he chose. . . .'

Reynolds, a shopping bag in either hand, shifted from one foot to another, his eyes not on the moist, pale blue eyes in the quivering face opposite to him but darting among the passers-by in an agony of restlessness.

'Is it his custom to talk in that kind of tone to a lady? I must say he gave me quite a shock. One doesn't look for a man of his refinement—'

Silly bitch!

At last he got away from her; and there, as he entered St. Ann's Well Gardens, loomed up another of the mammoth photographs. Hurriedly he glanced in all directions; then he gave himself up, with an almost voluptuous sigh, to a long contemplation.

Oh, it was a shame, a terrible shame, to think of a poor little thing like that lying out somewhere dead. If she *was* dead. They were not sure of that of course, there was only the evidence of what they had called 'a bloodstained article of clothing'. What could that have been? Knickers most like. Her mother had recognised them as hers together with that comic she had been carrying the day she had disappeared. On the beach that elderly woman with the dog had found them—they said the woman kept that shop called Dog's Den.

It was a shame, a real shame to think of anything happening to such a pretty little thing, with that lovely long hair like silk and that little turned-up nose and that gay little smile. Well, if she hadn't been such a dainty little darling no one would have been interested in her. They said in the paper that, though she was twelve, her mental age had been that of a girl of five, but to look at the photograph you'd never think that she wasn't just as bright as a new pin. Oh, that face looked just brimful of intelligence.

She was a doll, a real little doll. But dolls were dead things, whereas the one thing the photograph told one was that here was a kiddy who was really *alive*, full of *joie de vivre*, with that lovely smile of hers and those laughing eyes of hers, and that, oh, so fun-loving expression of hers, as though she were telling one that the world was a marvellous place. Poor kid, poor little kiddy! Because of course it wasn't a marvellous place, not for her any more than for anyone else, with that awful bloodstained 'article of clothing' and who knows what ghastly tortures she must have suffered before it was over.

He put his head on one side, musingly oblivious of the weight of the two shopping-bags full of the groceries for which Mrs Evans was waiting. He couldn't rightly remember ever having seen her with the other children from that special school and that was odd, because it was the kind of face, so gentle and trusting and well, yes, beautiful that would stick in the memory. He had talked to some of the children on his way back through the gardens after shopping in the mornings but he had never seen anyone like her, of that he was sure. With most of them you could tell that something was wrong as soon as you clapped eyes on them: there was this curious way in which all their features seemed to have been drawn together to the front of their faces and the features themselves were tiny. But everything about that poor little mite's features was perfect. Oh yes, he would certainly have noticed her if she had been playing on the swings with the others. Unless, of course, he hadn't realised that she was one of them and had imagined that she was one of the normal children who also played there. But the normal children were usually much younger—one didn't play on swings when one was twelve; and in any case when the children from that special school arrived the other children would usually drift off. He thought it cruel the way that mothers of the normal children would begin to wheel away their prams, shouting over their shoulders 'Come along, Fiona—time we moved on!' or 'Rex! *Rex!* Come *on!*' Often he himself brought some sweets with him and the children would remember this—oh, they could be bright enough if they wanted to be —and then two or three would spot him on the bench on which he always sat and they would at once run over, to be followed by a whole jostling, gabbling pack of them. The two women in charge would go on knitting and chatting. Once he had tried to engage them in conversation but he understood at once, from the way in which neither looked up as the larger of them answered, that they didn't want any company except each other's.

'What a pretty little thing!'

Reynolds started at the sound of the croaking voice behind him.

It was the old man with the tottering, grey muzzled labrador bitch on the end of a piece of string. Reynold always tried to avoid him.

'Shocking,' he said, swallowing on the word.

'And yet they do away with capital punishment. The world's going stark, staring bonkers.'

The labrador bitch was now straddled, back legs wide apart and an expression of patient suffering on her face as her whole body strained and strained again.

'I gave her some paraffin last night,' the old man said. 'I thought it might ease her, like.'

But Reynolds was hurrying off.

'Well, you certainly took your time,' Mrs Evans said. She banged the fish down on the table as though she wished to hurt it. 'It's me that gets the blame if his lordship's lunch is late. "I think that a little Sole Véronique might perhaps tempt my invalid's appetite".' The far from exact imitation of Sir Malcolm's 'posh' voice voided, on this occasion as on many others, the accumulated venom which her small, neat person could no longer contain. ' "And don't forget the mousseline potatoes, now will you, Mrs Evans?" How does he imagine that I'm to cook that kind of meal for him if you don't bring me the fish until nearly twelve o'clock?' As she spoke these last words, she picked up the sole and began to sniff at it.

'It's quite fresh,' Reynolds said.

She sniffed at it again, a look of scepticism on her yellow face.

'He's in a fine old mood,' she said. 'One of his best.'

'Why? What's the matter?'

'If he tells anyone it will be you, now won't it?' she said. 'I'm not the one who gets his little confidences.' She began to move him away from the refrigerator, the flat of one hand patting at his ribs. 'Two men called to see him,' she said.

'Two men? What men?'

'Police. They *said*. Didn't look like it to me.'

'Police!'

'Scruffy like, one of them was. Just a boy really. They were with him quite a time. Oh, I knew he was upset from the way he started up again about that noise of the next-door radio. As soon as they had left him. It's not as though the radio's on at night-time. Not late, that is.'

'What would the police want here?'

'Your guess is as good as mine.'

At once, Reynolds did not know why, there had come into his mind that photograph of that poor little thing with her pretty doll-like face and blue, blue eyes and long hair like silk. Perhaps they were making a house-to-house check like the one they made when that woman had been murdered in the off-licence in the Lanes. Two such polite men they had been—'just a routine check' they had called it. It had been the night when he had been attending the Whist Drive at St. Barnabas's, so he

124

had had no difficulty in giving them an alibi. But in an odd way, for all their courtesy and for all the certainty of that alibi, they had made him feel somehow furtive and guilty, so that even as he talked to them he was conscious of his face beginning to redden, of his hands beginning to tremble and of the words emerging from between his lips with the parched, laborious preciseness of someone nervously repeating a lesson learned by rote.

'It might be something to do with the car.'

Mrs Evans shrugged.

'Or perhaps he complained to the police about that radio.'

This time Mrs Evans made no response at all, as she continued to busy herself with removing the skins and pips from some grapes.

'What a footling job!' she muttered to herself at last.

Sir Malcolm did not mention the visit of the police all that day and Reynolds knew better than to ask him.

'Oh, dear, oh dear, oh dear!' he exclaimed as Reynolds carefully eased the luncheon tray across his knees. 'I see that our good Mrs E. has again been digging into that confounded deep-freeze.'

'Sir?'

'These beans look more than a little jaded.'

'There were no fresh beans in the shops this morning, sir.'

'Well, there must have been *something* fresh. What about chicory?'

'But I thought that you said that you didn't like—'

'I've nothing against chicory. Nothing at all. In moderation, that is.' Sir Malcolm suddenly gave Reynolds one of his piercing glances from under the loosely wrinkled, pale-grey skin of his eyelids. 'Are you all right, Reynolds?'

'Perfectly, sir.'

'Your hands are shaking.'

Reynolds had just drawn Sir Malcom's napkin out of its ring and had unfurled it with a single downward flick.

'My hands, sir?'

'You look as if something had upset you.'

'Oh, no, sir. Not at all.'

Sir Malcolm picked up a single grape on the end of his fork and peered at it from every angle. Then he popped it into his mouth and sucking on it said: 'All right, Reynolds.'

It was only when Reynolds was preparing Sir Malcolm for bed, holding out the tray with a tumbler of water and the two sleeping-pills on it, that the old man at last mentioned the visit.

Having gulped first one pill and then the other, he went through his habitual gesture of stroking the wattles of his throat with a palsied right hand, presumably to coax the pills on their downward passage, before he said: 'Oh, I had an enquiry about you today, Reynolds.'

'An enquiry, sir?'

'Yes, an enquiry.' The old man paused as though maliciously eager to prolong the other's anxiety. 'A police enquiry.'

'A police enquiry, sir?' Reynolds was conscious that his hands holding the tray had again begun to tremble and knew that it would be only a matter of time before Sir Malcolm again commented on the fact.

'No need for alarm. It was about this—er—this squalid case of the vanishing girl. How her parents allowed her to consort with a total stranger—or strangers—is quite beyond my understanding. It would be odd enough if she had been in full possession of her faculties but in the case of a child who was actually simple—*subnormal*, I think was the word used by our two friends—well, such irresponsibility is little short of criminal. Wouldn't you agree?'

'Yes, indeed, sir.'

'Now don't look so worried! I—er—got you off the hook. I can promise you that. Fortunately I had only to look at my diary in order to satisfy them that on the two—or was it three? —days at issue, you were with me in London. It was when I was having those confounded tests at the London Clinic. Remember? Oh, you have nothing to fear, my dear Reynolds! I'd have lied for you, if need be, that goes without saying. After all it's no easy matter to find a good servant in times like these. But in fact no lie was necessary.'

'But why—why did they pick on me?'

'You may well ask. It was because—as they put it—they could not leave a single avenue unexplored. Or was it that they could not leave a single stone unturned? I forget. Anyway—it seems that some busybody had telephoned them to suggest that they might—er—investigate you.'

Reynolds was appalled. 'But who would want to do such a thing?'

'Oh, someone who wished to be *public-spirited*, I expect. I do hate public spirit, don't you?' Sir Malcolm turned to slap at the pillows against which he was propped. 'It seems, you see, that this little girl—this Veronica or Valerie or Vivienne or whatever it was—numbered among her friends a middle-aged gentlemen who was known to her parents merely as Ray.'

'Ray!'

'Yes, Ray. Not a name for which I care. I could never call *you* Ray, for example. But the anonymous caller suggested that Ray might have been a—um—diminutive for Reynolds.'

'But that's slander, that's nothing but slander!'

'Now don't get so agitated. As I told you, I at once got you —er—off the hook. The police informed me—something of which I am bound to say I had always been ignorant—that it is often your way to sit in St. Ann's Well Gardens and talk to the children from the same school to which this unfortunate little Vera or Violet or whatever it was used to go. No, no'—

Sir Malcolm raised a purple-veined hand as Reynolds's mouth was about to open in expostulation—'I think such an interest in the afflicted to be entirely to your credit. Entirely. And I told our two gentlemen that.'

'Thank you, sir.'

'No, obviously you could not have been this Ray. And so'—Sir Malcolm leant far back on the pillows, smiling—'it seems most unlikely that you will be summoned for an identification parade!' He drew the sheet up to his pointed chin: 'Do you know,' he asked, 'how this Ray first met the child Victoria?'

'I've no idea, sir.'

'No, of course you wouldn't. Well, believe it or not, he just walked up to her parents on the front, said, "What a pretty little girl you have there!" and offered to take her to the Aquarium. Now just think of that!'

'It's incredible, sir.'

'As you say—incredible.' The creased eyelids fluttered and descended. 'Well, now I must turn in. Now don't worry, Reynolds. I've no intention of losing you. You're far too valuable to me.'

'Thank you, sir.'

Mrs Evans was still in the kitchen, though it was long after the hour when she usually left for home. When Reynolds came in with the tray, she reached for her crocheted brindle beret and began to tug it over her close-cropped grey curls. 'Has our lord and master turned in?'

Reynolds nodded.

'Did he say anything about those visitors?'

'What visitors?'

'Those visitors this morning. Those so-called detectives.'

It suddenly came to Reynolds that perhaps it had been Mrs Evans who had telephoned to the police. He knew that she disliked him.

'Oh, those.'

'Yes. Did he say anything about them?'

Reynolds shook his head.

'Perhaps he'll tell you tomorrow.'

'Maybe.'

'He tells you everything. In the end. Doesn't he?'

Sir Malcolm told Mrs Evans nothing and this infuriated her.

When Reynolds did not answer, she went on: 'Yes, you'll know about it soon enough.'

There was something in her tone which was not merely vindictive, as so often in the past, but even grimly menacing. Or had he imagined that? He stared after her, eyes wide and hands trembling as he clutched them together over his stomach as though in some sudden attack of abdominal cramp. Meanwhile she gave a last tug to the beret, and called out, 'Bye for now!' and strode out into the darkness.

Reynolds lay in bed, trying to think of the date when he and Sir Malcolm had gone up to London. He had no memory for that kind of thing. No, his memory had never been good; it had always been a worry to him. He could memorise a long shopping-list or all the items sent in a week to the laundry, but whole blocks of events had a way of slipping imperceptibly into oblivion. Once when he had complained of the vagaries of his memory to Mrs Evans she had fixed him with that sardonically appraising gaze of hers and had commented, 'Oh, you can always remember what it suits you to remember.'

'What do you mean by that, Mrs E.?' he had demanded, nettled.

'Oh, I don't mean you in particular. I mean you in the general sense. People. Everyone.'

If Sir Malcolm said that they had been in London at the time, then they must have been there. Sir Malcolm never failed to fill in his diary every evening after dinner, however bad his health. But there had been something *queer*—almost as though he were making game of him—in the way he had said that about getting him off the hook and being prepared to lie for him. In fact, Sir Malcolm never told lies; in all his twenty-two years with him Reynolds had never known him to tell a lie —not a lie that mattered. But in this case had there not been some vague hint of conspiracy between them?

Reynolds turned over on to his back and stared up at the shadowy ceiling, his head cradled on his skinny arms. He hoped he wasn't going to have another of his spells of sleeplessness, like the one he had when Mrs Evans had first come to work for them and Sir Malcolm had seemed to take a malicious pleasure in favouring her, although she was the newcomer. He had those pills from the doctor but after the first, which had made him feel giddy and light-headed all the next day, he had never taken another.

He would *know* if he had ever had anything to do with her. Wouldn't he? Surely? That was not the kind of thing one could forget. It was true that he could not remember—well, not properly—the death of his mother or of Iris in the air-raid. But his mother had died when he was only six; and in the case of Iris he himself had been half-buried under all that masonry beside her, so that was not really so surprising. Shock could do things like that to your memory, that was well known.

Such a pretty little thing, like a doll, with those blue eyes of hers (yes, he was sure they must have been blue) and that long, silk-like hair and that sweet, upturned nose. Who would want to hurt her? He certainly wouldn't. She was the kind of little girl he would like to have had for his own—the sort of girl Iris might have been when she was small, the sort of girl she might have had—and if he had met her all he would want to have done would have been to stroke her hair and talk to her and sit her on his knee and buy her some sweeties. It was terrible to think of those blue eyes shut forever and those chubby arms and legs sprawled out on that lonely stretch of beach and sand in the hair and sand on that lovely little mouth of hers. . . .

All at once he remembered the doll and his whole body went rigid as though in a sudden spasm. He had forgotten the doll, he hadn't thought about it once for, well, going on forty years. Mimsie—that was the name he gave her because he couldn't bring himself to call her Mummy whatever his father said— had often scolded him about it—'A big boy like you, going round with a doll! You should be ashamed of yourself.' He was seven at the time. Mummy, his real Mummy, had given him the doll for Christmas and it had this lovely flaxen hair and these blue eyes that opened and shut and this peaches-and-cream complexion. He would carry it around with him and even trail it by one arm through the dank weeds that overgrew the bottom of the garden, so that the dainty, frilly little skirt would get all soggy and the legs would be scratched by the brambles and stung by the nettles, just like his own. 'I'll give it to the dustman the next time they call,' Mimsie threatened. 'You'll see if I don't.' It was then that he buried the doll, before tea on a cold winter's evening, his whole body trembling and the gulping sobs rising in his throat as he first scrabbled away at the mouldering leaves from under the beech-tree and then began to dig, dig, dig ferociously with a trowel while the breath wreathed out from between his clenched teeth. 'Dust to dust, ashes to ashes,' he muttered, because he remembered those words from Mummy's burial; and then he scattered the first earth over that dainty little frilly pale blue skirt and on to the shut eyes and over the rose-bud mouth.

Once it was over he felt an extraordinary exhilaration, so that having raced back to the house, he burst into the cramped sitting-room with so much violence that everything in it shook and Mimsie looked up from painting her finger-nails to tell him to quieten down.

He forgot about the doll; yes, that was odd—he completely forgot about her, she might never have existed. Until one day, when Daddy and Mimsie had gone into Colchester for the day, leaving him behind all alone, he had wandered, disconsolate and bored, down into the undergrowth at the bottom of the narrow strip of garden. Suddenly, with a curious mingling of terror and excitement, he had remembered that she lay somewhere here near his feet and, stooping, he had begun to burrow away with his bare hands, breaking some of his finger-nails and clogging others with dirt and mould. There at last she was, her dainty dress all rotted and in tatters and her eyelashes and her mouth and her delicate nostrils filled with mud. He ran with her up into the house and placed her in the kitchen sink with some soap-flakes in warm water. Gently he began to wash her, running his hands over the smoothness of her arms and legs and body, until bit by bit she came back to life for him.

The dress of course could never be the same; so he wrapped her up in an old vest of his that Mimsie had put in the shoebox to use on the shoes.

After that she often died for him, was buried and was brought back to life. Daddy and Mimsie never knew anything about it; it was a secret not to be told them. Slowly, however, from the long stays in the earth and the scrubbings at the sink, the hair began to fall out, the silken eyelashes and then even the eyes themselves to disappear and the fingers and toes to crumble. Each such change he would watch with a fatalistic curiosity, pierced at times with a sudden brief pang of grief; until the time came when he knew that the burial would be the last and that he would never again disturb the grave of leaf-mould.

Yet how odd, he thought now, that between each death and resurrection he should completely have forgotten her! Involuntarily the memory of her would erase itself from his mind until, no less involuntarily, it would flash back with stabbing vividness, making him long for the first moment when he would be alone for long enough to dig her up again.

Reynolds sat up in the bed, clutching at his bony knees with hands equally bony. If he could so easily forget about *her*, might he not have forgotten about the other one too? Perhaps in the case of that poor little kiddy no less than in the case of the doll the sleeping memory would one day—perhaps soon—rouse itself to glide back, snake-like, into his conscious mind. *Could* he have known her? *Could* he have done such a thing?

He jumped out of bed and scrabbled in a drawer for the bottle of sleeping-pills. He put one on his tongue and then, while beginning to savour its bitterness, put another and another. He had to obliterate that fear as soon as possible.

'You're half asleep, man! What's the matter with you?'

'Sorry, sir.' Reynolds fumbled to insert in the razor the blade he had forgotten.

'Aren't you feeling well?'

'Perfectly well, thank you, sir.'

'You look pale. And I shouldn't be surprised if you weren't about to get a stye in that right eye of yours. Well, I hope you're not sickening for anything. That would be a fine kettle of fish.'

A middle-aged woman sat on a swing and screamed each time that it rose higher and higher. She had on a shapeless, belted raincoat and a plastic sou'wester. Reynolds watched, his body hunched forward on the bench, with the two laden shopping bags resting against his shins.

Perhaps the woman was not really middle-aged; many of them had a prematurely grown-up look, some who were only sixteen or seventeen one could mistake for thirty or forty.

. . . On that afternoon he might have been sitting here like this and she might have slowly, dreamily detached herself from that group of them playing some prolonged, meaningless game in the bushes, and wandered over in his direction. He might have smiled at her and felt in his pocket for a sweet and then held it out. That was what he usually did with them—it was like coaxing a nervous dog to come nearer and nearer to one. She might have sidled up and put out her hand and then he might have smiled at her, reassuringly, and she might have smiled back. 'What's your name, dear?' 'Vivienne.' 'That's a pretty name.' Then one of the two women in charge might have called to her, looking up over her clicking needles, and Vivienne would have wandered off, with a whispered thank-you.

But he would see her again. He was strolling along the pier (was now, not might be) and there she was walking between two grown-ups, each of whom held one of her hands. It was a Saturday (Sunday?) and that was when those children were allowed out with their parents. The two grown-ups and the doll-like child paused to look down at the fishermen below and he paused behind them. They turned and, courage coming to him in some miraculous fashion, he found himself saying 'What a pretty little girl you have there!' Of course she did not recognise him and he was not going to let on that he had met her before.

'Yes,' said the mother, running a plump hand through that silk-soft hair. 'But we mustn't tell her that or we'll make her vain, won't we?' The mother wore glasses so thick that her eyes bulged like hard-boiled eggs behind them. Her voice was cooing and falsely genteel.

It was all so easy : they seemed to *want* him to take Vivienne off their hands.

'Wouldn't you like to see the Aquarium with your Uncle Ray?' he asked after some minutes of desultory conversation.

'Yes, you'd love that, wouldn't you, pet?'

134

'That's right,' chimed in the father, sucking on his pipe. 'You run along with your Uncle Ray.'

Reynolds retched for a long time uselessly in the ammonia-smelling lavatory in one corner of the gardens. Then he pressed his ice-cold forehead against the ice-cold tiles. Yes, that was how it had been! That was it! He remembered how he had taken the car from the garage, slipping the key off Sir Malcolm's ring when he had shuffled from the bedroom to the lavatory, and how he had driven the poor, dear little thing out to that lonely stretch of beach, with the plastic sheet and the thermos and the beach-ball in the back. He had not meant to do anything, of course he hadn't. But the screams, a magnified echo of the gulls circling above their sprawling bodies, and the sight of the blood and the scratch she had given him on the inside of his thigh—well, how could anyone be expected to keep his head with all that going on?

Poor dolly, poor broken little dolly! He had bundled her into the car—oh, gently, gently, of course—and had thrown the plastic sheet over her and had driven back through a narrow cleft in the Downs with the sky a blue as pale and serene as the blue of those darling eyes. He would have to bury her somewhere secret under a tree; and then later, when no one knew that he had gone up there again, he would go back and find her once more. Yes, that was what he would do. That was it.

The leaves had a curious sweetish smell on them, like the mouldering leaves at the bottom of the narrow garden. The eyes were shut in the same way and the long, silk-soft hair lay in the same way on its bed of earth. The frilly skirt stuck out stiffly; there was a patch of blood on it, like a scab. 'I'll come back for you,' he whispered. 'I'll come back.' He put his lips to the porcelain forehead, his hands in the hair. 'I'll come back, my darling.'

*

'Well, surely *I* should know!' he cried out in exasperation at them. But they shook their heads and yet again exchanged those glances, at once amused, annoyed and pitying, with which they had greeted each fresh protestation of his guilt.

'Where does he live?' one of them asked.

'We ought to telephone to someone to fetch him.'

'Maybe an ambulance would be the best plan.'

'Look, old chap, we know that it just *can't* be you. For all kinds of reasons. So stop pulling our legs, eh?'

'Where does he live?'

'Who *is* the old boy?'

'Look, old chap, you'd better cut along and forget all about it.'

'Where does he *live*? Just get him off my hands.'

So it took a long time of patient and persistent arguing to persuade them that he could show them the place on the Downs where he had buried her. He could see it so well, out there before him, even while he was gazing into their red, stupid faces and shouting at them 'Let me show you! Just let me show you!' He could see the stile, over which he had had such difficulty in carrying her in the dark, and the moonlit path, a vast silvery-skinned snake slithering away from him, and then the three trees, with the interlaced branches that made a curious pattering noise against each other as the wind blew through them. The plastic sheet felt oddly warm, as though it were no more than a living skin to what lay beneath it. But of course that must have been his imagination, because when he unwrapped her she was as cold as the doll.

Unerringly he found the way for them through the bright February sunshine, a scurrying figure with bowed shoulders and a curiously tripping gait among the burly men with shovels and spades and the camera-man and the other man with the tripod and the lamps.

They still didn't believe him, he could see that. This was just part of leaving no avenue unexplored, of leaving no stone unturned.

'There!' he pointed.

Again they exchanged those glances, at once amused, annoyed and pitying.

'All right, boys. Get to work!'

They dug, not knowing what they would find. But he knew, oh he knew all right. There she would be, with her dainty little frock all damp and rotted about her, and the mud in her beautiful silk-soft blonde hair and in her nostrils and over her mouth. But one only had to wash her a little, wash her gently, gently, and the pink porcelain flesh would brighten again under the frilly skirt and the eyes would click open and the pretty little, winsome little smile would appear.

How had he *known*? they asked him over and over again; and when he screamed 'Because I put her there, you fools!' they shrugged shoulders or looked angry or asked him if he was right off his rocker. How had he *known*? they next asked that middle-aged bus-conductor with a limp, father of three children and a member of the Baptist Church, when eventually they had caught him. But the bus-conductor could not give them the answer they sought. No, he had never seen Reynolds in his life; Reynolds had never followed him, as far as he knew, on that fateful winter evening; no, of course they were not accomplices—he always had those turns of his alone.

'But how did you *know*?' Sir Malcolm would often ask Reynolds in the months and years that followed.

But Reynolds could not tell him; he himself did not know how he had known.

The Performance of a Lifetime

It was the Italian barman at the hotel who had first put the idea into Igor Servin's head. With his long, slicked-down hair, his narrow shoulders and his dainty feet in their pointed black patent-leather shoes, he did not look the sort of boy who would be used to taking country walks. 'Such a lovely weather,' he said. 'This is not usual for England in January. You should visit the Downs.' Igor had half-heartedly suggested that the boy might accompany him; but with his curious twitching smile the Italian had explained that he would have to attend an English class that afternoon. Then he drew Igor a sketchy map on the back of a beer-mat and wrote on it 'Devil's Dyke' and 'Patcham' and the numbers of the buses. 'You get off the bus *here*,' he said, 'and then you take a path, *here*—very easy to find, see—and then you. . . .'

Igor now took the beer-mat out of the pocket of his rain-coat and peered at it before again staring down into the valley below. What the Italian boy had forgotten was that, at this point, there were two paths branching off in totally different directions.

It was curious: even at that moment Igor knew that the correct path was the one to the right but nonetheless he took the one to the left. It was a half-conscious action similar to other half-conscious actions on this long and tedious tour: forgetting, for example, to wind his watch in Bournemouth, so that as he lay on his bed in the hotel, blowing smoke up at the ceiling, he was suddenly summoned by the buzz of the telephone to hear an anxiously shrill woman's voice demand of

138

him, 'What's *become* of you, Mr Servin? Are you still in your hotel?'; or all but failing to get off the train at Birmingham, leaping from the moving carriage, with his umbrella abandoned on the rack behind him. Mishaps of this kind always tended to happen when he was both bored and without his wife. Well, after Brighton and then Eastbourne, he would have that long holiday. He certainly needed it.

Igor Servin was a short, heavily-set man in his early fifties, with thick red hair on the backs of his sinewy pianist's hands and a round head that was almost bald. Although he was dressed in the garb of an English country-gentleman—a well-worn but well-cut tweed suit, brown brogue shoes and an expensively drab raincoat—no one would have assumed him to be anything other than a foreigner as he picked his way down the steep, muddy path with continual glances at the watch on his hirsute wrist.

It was years since he had suffered from nerves before a concert; but this boredom was really far more dangerous. Except for the rare occasion—the inauguration of a new concert hall, a programme which taxed his technical resources to the limit, or the first performance of some work, the acceptance of which he had to impose on the audience—each recital had the monotonous inevitability of scrubbing a floor; and the fact that he could scrub that particular floor better than all but a handful of other people was no consolation to him. Horowitz had abandoned the concert platform for many years because he found the excess of tension intolerable. Could one not then make the excess of tedium one's own excuse?

As he slithered down the rain-soaked incline, clutching from time to time at a branch or a tuft of grass, he went over the programme ahead of him in his mind. The organisers of the concert had jibbed at both Bartok's Fifteen Hungarian Peasant Songs and Messiaen's Cantéyodjáya: they did not feel, as they put it in their letter, that either work was 'ideally suited to the architectural character of the place in which the recital was to be given.' Idiots! Did they imagine that only Mendelssohn, Saint-Saens and Berlioz should be played in the Albert Hall? And in what way were the Debussy Preludes, substituted at their request, more in keeping with the opulent vulgarity of the Prince Regent's Music Room? What he dreaded most of all was the inevitable Chopin Sonata in B flat minor as a conclusion—not, of course, that there would not be a number of encores after it: provincial English audiences were even greedier about getting their money's worth than those in London. After he had played the Chopin in Cardiff a little old woman in a crocheted beret had clutched at his arm as he was about to enter his taxi and had hissed at him through ill-fitting teeth that the way he had played 'that Funeral March piece' had been 'a miracle, a veritable miracle.' 'Thank you, madam,' he had replied and had then added with grave irony: 'I feel as if I were dying myself each time I play it.' At that the seamed, vaguely disappointed face had at once been illuminated in an extraordinary fashion—yes, that too had been 'a miracle, a veritable miracle'—as she had again gripped his arm and exclaimed: 'Oh, how you must suffer! How you artists must suffer!' He bowed: 'Yes, madam. We suffer.'

The Italian boy had said that the path descended into a village: but this path, zigzagging down a shoulder of the hill, merely petered out in a ploughed morass. Far off to the left there was a solitary square stone farmhouse, set down askew in a field and apparently untenanted; no road was in sight. Again Igor looked at his watch, with mounting anxiety. He had exactly two-and-a-half hours before the recital was due to begin; obviously he was lost.

It was some forty minutes later that, muddy, sweating and with clothes stuck with burrs, he at last burst out through a gap in a straggling hawthorn hedge on to a narrow lane. But which way to go? In vain he looked for the sea as a guide: he was isolated in a curious beige-coloured basin of land, at the bottom of which vague wisps of mist were beginning to coagulate. He began to stride down the lane in one direction, until he all at once decided on a wholly illogical impulse that it was in fact in the other direction that he ought to be tending. His clothes felt disagreeably tacky and tight and one of his heels was blistered.

A small van came jolting towards him and he attempted to flag it down; but the driver either did not or would not notice him. Minutes passed as he continued to toil up towards the horizon. Then from far off, he heard the put-putting of what he thought must be a motor-bicycle. This time he took up his position in the centre of the lane.

It was not a motor-bicycle but an ancient Austin Seven, painted a gleaming black and yellow, with a flapping hood and wheels almost as attenuated as those of a bath-chair. A young man was perched high up at the wheel, the hood seeming to brush the top of his head, with a huge dog of indeterminate breed sitting gravely beside him. When he saw Igor frantically waving, there was a screech and hiss of brakes and the whole car bounced up and down three or four times before finally coming to rest.

'Brighton?'

'That's right.' The boy had some kind of college scarf wrapped round his muscular neck with the ends reaching almost to his waist. 'Hop in.'

Igor looked at the dog.

'Jake can go on the back seat. He's quite safe.' The young man tugged at the dog's collar and pushed at its rump until, grunting, the vast animal clumsily flopped down on top of a mound of newspapers, books and clothes.

'Lucky for me,' Igor said, as the boy restarted the car. 'I was lost. And I have to be in Brighton by seven at the very latest.'

141

'Don't be so sure that it *was* lucky,' the boy said. His hands, gripping the wheel, were large and strong, the nails heavily grimed. 'This car has been known to break down. In fact, I had to change one of the tyres only five miles back.'

Igor began to explain the circumstances of his walk : how he had never been in Brighton before; how the Italian waiter had drawn a map for him; and how there had been the two paths and he had taken the wrong one.

The boy grunted from time to time in response. 'What a clot,' he exclaimed at the end, of the Italian not of Igor. 'No wonder you lost your way.'

The sun, low in the sky, all at once filtered through some trees to glisten on the boy's curiously fine, ash-blond hair, his cheek-bone and one of the large hands on the wheel. Glancing sideways at him, Igor realised with a pang, not unlike the first onset of an illness, that he was astonishingly handsome. But not merely that : in some way, God knows how or where, Igor felt that he had seen him already.

'And what have you been doing?' Igor asked. 'Exercising your dog?'

'Well, it's not really *my* dog, you know. But I exercise dogs for people. This one belongs to an elderly couple who live in a two-roomed penthouse flat in Hove. It's cruel keeping a dog in circumstances like that, don't you think?'

He went on to explain that until he was fifteen he had lived on his father's farm in Rhodesia. Here in England he missed the open countryside and the animals—'I suppose I'm what you'd call an outdoors type. Rugged.' He gave a small smile, as though of self-congratulation, as he said the last word.

'Are you a student?' Igor asked.

The boy nodded and then swore as he had to swerve to avoid a cat that whisked across the road. 'The College of Education. I'm training to become a teacher.'

'And where will you teach? Here or in Rhodesia?'

The boy shrugged his shoulders. 'What are you?' he asked bluntly. 'You're not English, are you?'

'No. I'm not English. I was born in Russia but I have American nationality.'

The sleeves of the boy's jacket had been bound in leather; the corduroy of his trousers, tight over his muscular thighs, had acquired a glistening patina; his collar was too small for his neck—evidently the Oxford cloth must have shrunk—so that he had left the button unfastened, relying on his tie to keep the ends together.

'Could you push back that strut of the hood? It often works loose.'

'This?'

'Yes, give it a push. Just a push. Upwards.'

Igor had to lean back and over the boy. His arm was on his shoulder.

Then there followed one of those moments of madness to which even the sanest of people will sometimes succumb. With luck, the moment of madness goes unnoticed or is ignored; and in that case the individual who has suffered the aberration may himself forget that it ever took place. But if luck is not with him, the penalty may last a lifetime.

Instead of withdrawing entirely once he had pushed the strut back, Igor let his arm remain along the other's shoulder, gently touching the firm flesh through the shaggy tweed.

The boy gave no indication of noticing the pressure, which Igor now increased.

Curling the fingers of his hand so that their tips brushed the firm line of the other's jawbone, Igor then moved them slowly up to the cheek. The boy said nothing; the car put-putted on.

Emboldened, his breath now catching uncomfortably in his throat, Igor placed his other hand along the boy's thigh.

The boy went on driving. Then all at once he began to whistle softly between his closed teeth. The tune was, curiously,

'Land of Hope and Glory'.

'Where do you want me to drop you?' he asked as they neared the outskirts of the town.

Igor swallowed: 'Well, I'm staying at the Metropole. But anywhere here will do. I can find a taxi.'

'I'll take you to the Metropole.'

'You're very kind.'

Outside the Metropole, Igor said: 'Won't you come in and have a quick drink? I've got half-an-hour before my—my next engagement.'

The boy stared at him with eyes that had become frighteningly implacable. He put a hand across Igor's body and held the door which the older man had just begun to open. 'That'll be a fiver,' he said.

'What?'

'You heard me. A fiver. You don't imagine you can get away with that kind of thing for nothing, do you? A fiver.'

With trembling hands Igor took out his wallet and drew forth the note.

'Make it ten.'

'*Ten?*'

'Yes, ten. Why not?'

Igor withdrew another note, half-expecting the boy to say in the same grimly quiet tone: 'Make it fifteen.'

'Ta.' The genteel monosyllable, spoken in a deliberately mincing tone, was obviously an insult.

As their hands met over the money, Igor thought again, with a mixture of bewilderment and a pain that was almost physical: I've met you before.

He found himself saying idiotically, 'Thanks for the lift.'

Without another glance the boy put the two notes on the seat beside him, clashed the gate-gears, and then drove off, the car backfiring spurts of blue smoke.

*

144

It was the adrenalin of course. There was that actor at the Comédie Française who had once told him that, unless he was shaking with terror before going on the stage, he knew that his performance would be a failure.

All his senses seemed to have become extraordinarily acute: so that when a late-comer crept into the room he noticed, as he adjusted the piano-stool, that momentarily a chill breath of air had entered with him. He was conscious of the touch of the keys, smooth except for the B flat, which had an almost imperceptible roughness on one side; of the smells of wax-polish and of dust and of mouldering vegetation from the fern in a pot at the other side of the dais; even of the ticking of the watch on his wrist. Well, it had been a narrow shave; a very narrow shave. What had come over him?

As he started to play the Bach Chaconne he knew that, though neither the middle-aged women in their ugly hats and the corpulent dark-suited men seated in the front of the hall nor the bedraggled young people massed standing at the rear would probably be aware of it, they were going to hear the performance of a lifetime: a lifetime of experience; a lifetime of labouring to perfect a miraculous technique; but above all a lifetime, seemingly serene, secure and successful, but in fact darkened by a perpetual if unacknowledged agony. Unacknowledged or acknowledged only now.

But I've met him somewhere before, he told himself in that same restless bewilderment. Where, where?

In the interval he sat on a straightbacked chair and took sips of icy water, while a young man with the profile of a rapacious bird told him, 'Well, we've had a surprisingly good turn-out,' and from the hall next door he could hear the shuffle of feet and murmur of voices. 'People actually standing', the young man said, preening himself, his thumbs tucked into the tops of the pockets of his Edwardian-cut jacket, as though the fact that that crowd had been wedged in at the rear was due entirely to himself.

But where have I met him?

Then, at last, as he began to play the Chopin Sonata, a long, ghostly wave seemed to sweep back over a waste of more than thirty years and he remembered, yes, how he had given his first English recital—at, yes, the Aeolian Hall—and he had played this same sonata, with a terror so acute that he had feared at first that he would not be able to control his hands sufficiently even to strike the right notes. It had been his first success— even though the audience had been pitifully sparse and cough- ing had spattered over his immaculate phrasing until he had wanted to scream at them from his overwrought nerves, 'For God's sake, shut up! Shut up!'

After the performance, as he had emerged elated into the street, a hand had touched his sleeve. 'I wanted to say—that was really super.' The young man was the same age as him- self, with high cheek-bones, large capable hands and pale hair above a sunburned forehead. They had had dinner together and the next day Igor had left for Rome—or was it Madrid? —and they had never met again.

At the back some people were shouting 'Bravo' and 'Encore'; but he told himself cynically that this was not because they had heard the work played as they might never hear it played again—they merely wanted to ensure that he earned every penny that the tickets had cost them. There was a pain between his eyes and a pain at the back of his neck; he could feel the sweat trickling between his shoulder-blades, he could even smell it from under his arms.

Well, he told himself resignedly, he'd have to give them what they wanted. One of the Goyescas, a Chopin Étude or even that piffling little piece by Percy Grainger which he always included on his English tours.

It was as he was taking the last of a number of bows that,

146

far at the back of the hall, he suddenly saw the face of the boy among innumerable other youthful faces. He felt a curious lurch within himself, as though in prelude to a prolonged attack of retching. The pain between the eyes and at the back of his neck became an insistent stabbing.

'I'll come with you to your hotel,' the young man in charge of him half-heartedly proposed.

'No, really, there's no need. Thank you.'

The bird-like profile was turned now to left and now to right, as though acknowledging an invisible host of subjects, while the two of them made their way to the door.

'You're sure you wouldn't like to have dinner with me?'

'You are very kind. But after a performance. . . . Thank you all the same.'

'A drink then?' The young man, certain now that Servin would continue to refuse, became more insistent.

'You are very kind. But—I'd rather rest.'

At last he was alone in the back of the taxi, to say over and over to himself: 'Now he knows who I am. A celebrity! I'm really at his mercy.'

And there, already, was the boy standing at the entrance of the hotel, the scarf thrown round his muscular neck to flutter its ends in the wind that blew icily off the sea.

Igor pretended not to see him, but he called out in a loud voice: 'Mr Servin!' so that for fear of the burly doorman, squinting curiously in their direction, Igor had to stop.

'Yes?' he said sharply.

'I—I—wanted to say—' The boy was inexplicably embarrassed, almost bashful, as he came slowly over, his eyes turned sideways and down. 'You were magnificent!' he got out in a sudden burst. 'I never knew it could sound like that. I—I feel so ashamed.'

'Ashamed?' Igor's attempt at a smile became a grimace,

as of someone who has bitten on something sour. 'How do you think *I* feel?'

'I'd always thought from your records that you were one of the greats. But that—that performance of the Chopin! It was out of this world.'

'Thank you.'

The boy held out his hand. 'Will you take this back? . . . Please?'

Two notes fluttered in the wind that was making the tears sting in Igor's eyes.

'No, no.'

'*Please!*'

'But if it hadn't been for you, the performance would never have *been* like that. . . .' He broke off: it was too laborious to explain. 'You earned it,' he said. But that might be interpreted in quite another way; indeed, the deep flush that mounted up that splendid neck to the cheeks showed that it had.

'I ought never—' the boy began to stammer.

Suddenly Igor both knew the solution and found the right touch to carry it off. He tweaked one of the notes out of the boy's hand, with the smile that invariably charmed his audiences. 'Like this,' he said. 'All right?'

The boy looked doubtful and bewildered.

'Really,' Igor said. 'One doesn't often give the performance of a lifetime. And I owed that to you.'

'Well all right,' the boy said, still doubtful, as he tucked the note carelessly into one of the bulging pockets of his jacket. Then suddenly he looked up at Igor and gave him a small, embarrassed but radiant smile. 'Yes, it *was* the performance of a lifetime,' he said. 'It really was.'

Good Neighbours

Soon after the Blyths had moved into their house, they had been sitting down to breakfast in their dank basement dining-room when, in spite of the sunshine outside, they had become aware that the high narrow windows, as of a cell, were streaming with water. Fred Blyth went out to investigate and found one of their two spinster neighbours, the Miss Barman whose name was Lise, leaning over the railings between their two front gardens with a hose in her hand. She was wearing a man's shirt, the sleeves rolled up to her elbows, and grey flannel trousers bunched together by a wide leather belt not far below her armpits.

As soon as she saw Fred peering up at her from the base-ment steps, Miss Lise at once withdrew both the hose and her head.

'I hope you don't mind,' she said apologetically, now re-directing the jet at the base of one of her own rose-bushes. Fred was surprised by the sineweness of the old woman's arms; in one of her jerseys or a jacket she always looked so frail. (Later Miss Lotte was to confide in Mrs Blyth that her sister had almost died in the concentration camp in which she herself had also been confined.) 'I used to water the flowers for the two Miss Clarks and I noticed that after this lovely weather we've been having, they're looking rather dry.'

Coral Blyth had been nagging at Fred to water the flowers for several days and Fred had in turn been nagging at Jack, their fourteen-year-old son, to do so.

'How very kind of you!'

'Well, you see, I used to do it for the two Miss Clarks,' the old woman repeated.

From that morning, Miss Lise never failed to water the neighbouring garden during a dry spell.

Miss Lotte, who was obviously much younger than her sister and whose thick, artificially blonde hair seemed to have been sculptured in heavy whorls about her flat, damp face, had been equally kind to Coral. 'Just tell them that you're a friend of Miss Lotte,' she would say when recommending the Viennese Patisserie at which one could find *real* Sacher Torte or the little delicatessen only a step round the corner or the hairdresser's shop at which they gave a reduction to clients on Mondays. 'Everyone knows Miss Lotte.'

Coral tried it out, dubiously at first: 'Miss Lotte sent me,' she said to the butcher. But to her surprise, the joint that week was far better than the one the same butcher had given to her the previous Friday.

'If you'd like to let me have those net curtains I'll wash them out for you,' Miss Lotte volunteered; and Coral, like Fred in the matter of watering the garden, felt both grateful and guilty. She had been meaning to wash out the grimy curtains for several weeks. 'That woman notices everything,' she said to Fred.

At the back of the houses two narrow gardens ran side by side, but the Blyths, not without reason, preferred to call their garden a yard. Some previous owners—perhaps the two Miss Clarks—had had the whole area paved with concrete, with the exception of a strip of flower-bed that snaked beneath the walls. The concrete had cracked and weeds and moss had pushed up betwen the fissures. Coral had hung a pink nylon washing-line from one wall to another, the children had used the space to dump their bicycles and toys and Fred himself had erected an untidy mountain of packing-cases in one corner. 'Oh, do get

150

rid of those packing-cases,' Coral would scold him from time to time, and he would then retort : 'You know perfectly well that the dustmen won't take away things like that without a lavish tip.' 'Well, tip them then!' But the tip was never given, not because of stinginess, but because of Fred's inherent unwillingness ever to do anything that could be postponed to a later date.

In contrast, the Barman garden really was a garden. There was crazy-paving, a bird-bath, a herbaceous border, a Victorian wrought-iron bench to which Miss Lise appeared to add a fresh coat of glossy yellow paint almost weekly, and even a tiny greenhouse : all these in an area not much larger than the kitchen. Morning and afternoon Miss Lotte would feed the birds, and it was Jack Blyth who first noticed, peering out from his attic window, that before she did so, she always laid out a sheet of newspaper on the crazy-paving, weighting it down at the corners with four stones—always the same four stones, kept beside the greenhouse—before scattering the crumbs upon it. She never waited to see the birds eat but would at once waddle back into the recesses of the house, dusting off her hands on her floral apron. Sometimes Miss Lise would offer Fred some plants—'I've got these over, see,' she would tell him. 'I've no real use for them.' Fred would then say, 'Well, that's mighty kind of you,' and then go on to explain that for the moment he was so busy at the university that the garden would have to wait.

It would not be entirely true to say that neither family ever saw the inside of the other's family's house, because the Blyth house, as crammed with possessions as with people, always seemed to be spilling its contents out into the street : the front door ajar; bathing-costumes or carpets flung over the windowsills; the french windows at the rear usually open even when everyone was out; the curtains—in the rooms where there were curtains—seldom drawn. If the Barman sisters wanted to know

151

what went on in the Blyth household, they had only to look and listen.

But the life of the sisters was cocooned from the rest of the world and even from the Blyths in folds of damask and velvet and net. There was even a striped canvas curtain over their front-door and the windows of their kitchen, like those of their bathroom, had frosted leaded panes. The only sound that ever came out of their house was that of Miss Lotte calling to Miss Lise at work in the garden: 'Lise! Li—i—ise!'; and even that was not so much a shout as an amplified stage whisper.

When discussing the sisters with their friends, the Blyths would say that they were 'odd', 'quaint', and even 'weird'; but having characterised them in this fashion they would never fail to add, 'But of course they're *such* good neighbours.'

The cat changed all that.

It was a tortoiseshell cat, with head and feet out of all proportion to its emaciated, fine-boned body, and a curious white marking along its upper lip that gave it the appearance of constantly sneering. Cathy, the younger of the two Blyth daughters, had found it miaowing outside the house, as it high-stepped back and forth over a small area of the pavement, and had finally succeeded in coaxing it down the area steps by holding out for it a saucer of the top of the milk.

'What on earth is this doing here?' Coral had demanded when she had found the cat asleep on the bread board.

'It's lost. So I brought it in and fed it.'

'Of course it isn't lost. Cats don't get lost. They find their way home.'

'It can't have been fed for days,' the other daughter, Iris, put in. 'Look at the way its bones all stick out.'

'It looks perfectly all right to me,' Coral said, knowing that it didn't. 'Anyway, we can't keep it, this house is full enough as it is.'

152

'We can't push it out in to the street again,' Iris pleaded. 'It'll only get run over. Don't you understand, Mummy—it's lost !'

'Nonsense !'

Coral put a notice on the low railings that separated the front garden from the street; then, when that failed, Fred was persuaded—after several days of procrastination—to go to the offices of the *Evening Argus* and insert an advertisement. But to that, too, there came no response. The children then bought flea-powder, a brush and comb and a feeding-bowl, and gave the cat the name of Cilla.

It was at that point that the trouble started.

Coral met Miss Lotte at the supermarket, from which the older woman would each day return lugging two mammoth baskets piled high with groceries. (The Blyths often wondered who ate all that food, since the sisters appeared never to entertain.) On this occasion Miss Lotte had blocked one of the aisles with her laden trolley while chatting to the girl at the cheese-counter. 'Just say that Miss Lotte sent you,' she was saying as Coral approached. Then she noticed Coral.

'Good morning, Mrs Blyth.'

Miss Lotte's greeting was as jolly as usual. She held out a packet from her trolley. 'Just take a look at this smoked salmon. Much better than you get round the corner. Just look at it. You get some.'

Coral, who would not have dreamed of buying such a luxury, smiled and said : 'Yes, it does look lovely.'

'Don't let him give you anything off that old piece he has on the counter. I made him start on a new piece for me. You ask him for the new piece. Say that Miss Lotte told you about it.'

'I'll do that,' said Coral, who had no intention of doing it at all. 'Thank you.'

As Coral was about to squeeze past the trolley, Miss Lotte checked her : 'Is that your cat we see?'

'What cat?'

'That tortoiseshell cat—sometimes in your garden, sometimes in ours.'

'Oh, it's a stray,' Coral explained, wondering how Miss Lotte, usually so observant, had failed to read their notice on the railings. 'We're trying to find its owner.'

'There are so many cats,' Miss Lotte said with a deep sigh, as she removed a jar of mango chutney from the shelves. 'And all the cats seem to like our garden. Don't ask me why!'

That was all. Coral thought no more about it.

The second event was the appearance of Cilla one morning with a large patch of bare, pink skin on one of her flanks. The Blyths asked each other what could have happened to her and Coral said that as soon as she had a moment she would have to take her to the vet. But the moment never seemed to offer itself and gradually the skin healed. 'It looks as though someone had thrown some boiling water over her,' Catherine declared; at which Fred asked who on earth would want to do a thing like that and told her not to be so silly.

At eleven o'clock the next Sunday morning Fred, still in his pyjamas, was blearily making a pot of tea to take upstairs for himself and Coral when he noticed, through the window of the kitchen, that Miss Lise's head of bobbed grey hair was intermittently popping up above the garden wall. The old woman was wearing trousers as usual, a huge pair of gardening gloves and the battered straw hat she always put on when working behind the house but never when in front of it.

Fred thrust his head out of the window and said with all the brightness that he could muster on a Sunday morning before a drink: 'Good morning, Miss Lise. And what a lovely morning too!'

Miss Lise seemed unaccountably nervous. 'I hope you don't

mind that I put up this wire. I've planted a rambler rose and I wish to train it here.'

'Fine, fine! Just go ahead.'

As Fred snuggled back between the sheets, he said to Coral: 'Even on a Sunday morning old Lise is at work in that garden of hers. Beats me!' Then, like Coral after her encounter with Miss Lotte in the supermarket, he gave the matter no more thought.

The wire for the rose, when finally erected, turned out not merely to be barbed but to be festooned over the top of the wall in a murderous tangle. 'I do think that she might make that trellis a little less conspicuous!' Fred exclaimed when at last he became aware of it, several days after its erection.

'It won't look so bad once the rambler has covered it.'

'That'll take some time! That yard has become an eye-sore.'

But both of them knew that the yard had been an eyesore ever since they had moved into the house.

It was on another Sunday, several weeks later, that the Blyths at last came to understand the real reason for the wire.

The whole family had gone down to the beach for a bathe and a picnic lunch, but Fred and Coral had begun to bicker, as they so often did on Sundays—Fred's 'Well, good grief, surely you could have done better than sardine sandwiches,' had started them off—and Coral had rushed home. Going into the kitchen to make herself an omelette (she herself also hated sardines) she all at once became aware that the shadow of what appeared to be a man was falling across the concrete of the yard. Fearfully she peered out from around a curtain to discover, at first with no more than relief, that the man was only dear old Miss Lise. But what was she doing there?

Miss Lise was plainly embarrassed when confronted. Indeed,

as Coral came out of the kitchen door, she began hastily to scrabble together the tools and barbed wire she had littered about the yard.

'Good heavens, Miss Lise! You gave me such a fright. I thought for a moment that someone had broken in.'

'I—I. . . . Didn't you go out?. . . I saw you. . . .' Her usually grey face, with its puffily heavy eyelids and sagging jowls, was suddenly suffused with crimson. 'I rang the bell,' she went on, obviously making an effort to steady herself. 'I felt sure you wouldn't mind.'

'But what are you doing?'

It was only then that Coral noticed that the barbed wire rampart had now risen to twice its original size, to reach the first floor. 'This is *hideous*,' she exclaimed.

'It's the only way,' Miss Lise said with melancholy finality.

'What do you mean—the only way?'

'This cat keeps coming back. There are other cats too. What am I to do? Maybe it's the horse-manure I put down. Maybe they like the horse-manure. Why doesn't the cat stay here? Here is nice.'

'Well, I'm very sorry if the cat has been bothering you. But this is just *awful*. We can't live with all this around us. Think of the view from our sitting-room window.'

Miss Lise appeared not to take this in. She merely continued : 'Then the birds. My sister is very fond of birds. Two nights ago we find a dead bird on the greenhouse roof. What are we to do? Maybe it's the horse-manure. I put half a ton of horse-manure under my rose-bushes.'

'Lise! Li—i—ise!'

'Coming.'

'Lise!'

'Yes, yes, I am coming. Coming!' She smiled at Coral, batting her heavy eyelids and running her tongue around her perpetually chapped lips. 'Excuse me,' she said, hurrying up the ladder with the agility of a boy. Astride the wall, she began to drag the ladder up after her.

Foolishly, Carol found herself assisting her in this task.

'We shall just have to keep Cilla indoors. That's all. We'll have to get her a tray and keep her indoors.'

'Oh, Mummy! We can't do that! We can't! It's cruel.'

'It must have been Miss Lise—or Miss Lotte—who threw that boiling water on Cilla,' Jack said.

'They wouldn't do a thing like that,' Carol protested. But she was no longer sure that they wouldn't.

'Cilla is to go out,' Fred said. 'She has every right to go out. In any case, it's not only Cilla, it's the other neighbourhood cats.'

'That ginger tom,' said Cynthia.

'Mrs Price's Siamese. It often jumps from one garden to another.'

'The tabby with only one eye,' said Jack.

'Exactly,' said Fred.

'Perhaps *they* put out its eye,' Cynthia suggested.

'Cilla is to go out. And I shall have to see a solicitor about that monstrous barricade round the yard.'

Fred postponed seeing a solicitor as he postponed everything that was capable of postponement; but the next morning, when the water began to splash against the basement windows, he hurried up the area steps to have a word with Miss Lise.

'That's a horribly unsightly erection you've put up,' he began.

Miss Lise retreated, the hose now spluttering water over her neat garden path instead of over the Blyth's weeds. 'I'm sorry,' she said. 'But the cats—always the cats— Even last night she came over. How does she manage it? There is a hole—this

157

small—' she made a round with her blunt forefinger and thumb—'and she comes through. How does she come through? It seems impossible. But she comes through.'

'Lise! Li—i—ise!'

'Excuse me, please.'

'Don't you think that at least you might have asked my—'

'I rang the bell but there is not any answer. I saw you all going down the hill to the front.'

'It—it makes one feel as though one were living in a damned concentration camp!'

Perhaps his subconscious had prompted the words; having spoken them, Fred at once realised that, in the circumstances, they were unforgiveable. Now he, no less than Miss Lise, was grateful for an unusually strident '*Lise!*' followed by: 'What *is* the matter?' from Miss Lotte in the house.

Miss Lise bolted down the steps into her basement. It was the last time she was ever to water the Blyth's front-garden, so that from then on it was slowly to degenerate into the same state of barren disorder as the yard.

'We really must do something about it!'

Every few days some fresh strand or fuzz of wire appeared on the rampart. Sometimes a whole sheet of corrugated iron would be added and on one occasion Fred looked out of the kitchen window in the morning to find what appeared to be part of an iron bedstead suspended far up in the air. But neither Coral nor Fred was the type of person to make a decisive move. Jack suggested that he should pull down the whole monstrous erection while the sisters slept, but Fred and Coral both deprecated that—it might be illegal, it would only make more trouble, it was best to let sleeping dogs lie.

It was therefore left to Cilla to vindicate their honour. Night after night she made her forays, with Jack announcing excitedly, after watching her from his attic window: 'She's made it! She's made it!' and Catherine joining in to add the information, 'She's digging by the rose-bushes. And the one-eyed tabby has joined her.' The perseverance of the cats was matched only by the perseverance with which Miss Lise would each morning get to work with her ladder, her pliers and hammer and her huge rolls of wire-mesh and barbed wire. Often Cilla would be cruelly cut in this war she was fighting as much on their behalf as on her own. Tufts of her hair now decorated the ramparts like the bodies of slain soldiers in the carnage of a civil war.

By ten o'clock in the evening all lights were usually extinguished in the next-door house. The Barman sisters were unique in the terrace in having a gate with a lock, a post-box inset into it, and this Miss Lise would invariably fasten before night had fallen. Evidently they never expected any callers after that hour.

Fred and Coral on the other hand habitually went to bed long after midnight: not because they had anything of importance to occupy them but because the decision to retire was one which, like all other decisions, they preferred to defer for as long as possible. They would yawn at the television set until it went blank and then they would either drowse over books and magazines or actually fall asleep while listening to music on the hi-fi equipment that trailed wires all over the sitting-room.

'Darling—are you sure that you've got nothing cooking on the stove?'

'I've already told you—nothing. Now do let me listen to this in peace.' But Coral had been sleeping, not listening to the Bruckner Fourth. Again she closed her eyes.

Several minutes later Jack rushed in, in his pyjamas, to rouse both his parents:

'I think the house must be on fire!'

'Don't be silly,' Fred told him crossly, rubbing his eyes. 'Go back to bed.'

'There's an awful smell of burning. Don't you get it?'

'Nonsense.'

'But, darling—you know—he's *right*,' Coral yawned. 'There *is*.'

'When I told you that ten minutes ago, you wouldn't believe me.'

'I only said that I'd left nothing on the stove.'

Fred ran down into the kitchen, followed by Jack. Coral turned off the Bruckner Fourth, did up the press-studs at the side of her skirt, and then put her head out of the sitting-room door and sniffed. There certainly *was* a smell of burning; there was no doubt about it.

Several minutes later Fred wandered out into the yard, to discover that it was not their house, but the sisters', that had caught fire. Smoke was pouring out of an upstairs window; and as he watched it in stupefied amazement, he all at once saw the first ugly flames lapping at the heavy damask curtains. At that he began to shout 'Miss Lise! Miss Lotte!' Coral joined him and was at once despatched to telephone for the fire-brigade.

Miss Lotte's head at last appeared, not at the blazing window, but at the one next door to it. The head was almost unrecognisable now that the heavily sculptured whorls of hair were pressed flat under an old-fashioned net that fastened beneath her chin.

'Fire!' Fred shouted.

'Oh, my heavens!'

Miss Lise's head now appeared beside hers.

'Fire!'

'Oh, my heavens!'

Both heads were withdrawn.

A moment later Fred could hear the sound of innumerable

bolts being drawn and keys being turned on the other side of the wall, followed by the scrape and patter of feet on crazy-paving. 'Save us! Help! Help! Save us!'

'It's all right!' Fred shouted. 'Stay in the garden. My wife has phoned for the fire-brigade.'

'We are trapped—trapped!' Both first-floor windows were now vomiting flames. 'Help, help, *help*!' Miss Lotte's voice rose to a crescendo.

'Help!' Miss Lise's took up; but her croak was a feeble thing in comparison with the screams of her sister.

Jack was at the upstairs window by this time and so it was he, not Fred, who saw the sisters as they struggled to climb the wall, now jagged and now slithery, of corrugated iron, barbed wire and wire-mesh. Miss Lise repeatedly attempted to push her sister up before her but each time Miss Lotte tumbled back into her arms. Miss Lotte's screams became yet more piercing: 'Help! Help! *Help!*' Windows were thrown up in the houses all round to reveal horrified faces illuminated by the shuddering glare of the flames.

'Will no one help us?'

Something soft fell at Fred's feet; then, a moment later, he felt a gentle, rhythmic brushing against his calf. Looking down he saw the pinpoints of Cilla's eyes reflecting the flames above her.

Fred picked the cat up in his arms and at once she began to purr.

She was still purring there when the fire-brigade rushed out into the yard with their ladders and axes and hoses; still purring when the two sisters sat gulping tea in the kitchen next door to their devastated house, while Coral dabbed at their lacerations with iodine-soaked cotton-wool and asked them if it hurt.

Late the following morning—it was again a Sunday—Fred tottered out of bed and went to the window. He had driven the sisters to a hotel, after they had said that thank you, no, they could not possibly impose on the Blyths any more by accepting their invitation to stay the night; and then he and Coral had made yet another pot of tea and had argued as to whether they should wash up the cups used by the firemen at once or in the morning. Needless to say, they finally agreed to leave them till the morning.

'What a mess! God, what a mess!' The firemen had hacked and tugged at the barricade, so that now the whole yard and the garden next to it were littered with coils of wire and sheets of corrugated iron.

Coral grunted: 'What d'you say?' from under the blankets. But Fred had not really been addressing her.

'That's put paid to our back garden.' It was the first time Fred had ever thought of it as a back garden and not as a yard.

Among the debris on the other side of the wall were charred fragments of curtains, shattered tables, a half-devastated mattress and a single armchair, plump in its lemon yellow velvet jacket except where one of its arms had been shrivelled by the flames. Behind, the whole house, once so carefully sealed and muffled from the world, now lay as open and desecrated as a bombed synagogue.

Cilla sat in the armchair, her inordinately large front paws doubled under her and her inordinately large head turned up to look at Fred with a still, unwinking gaze. Two other cats, the Siamese and the one-eyed tabby, were stalking each other through a jungle of wire.

A Beautiful Old Man

Diana Broughton waited alone in the lounge, all mirrors and white pottery urns containing elaborate flower-arrangements and shimmering grey silks which had darkened where the bodies of the clients of the Adelaide Crescent Hotel had had repeated contact with them. She was waiting, as she waited every night, for the night porter, Les, to bring her tea in a silver pot, around the handle of which she would have to wrap a frilly, heavily-scented handkerchief before she could touch it. There would be a jug of milk, though she never took milk in her tea, and two Marie biscuits, which she never ate. If there was no one else in the lounge then Les would talk to her.

Tonight, after the two whiskies she had been given before her appearance before the television cameras and the three whiskies she had drunk in the Pullman with that young actor whose name she could never remember, she would have preferred another drink to a pot of tea. But Les, who never drank or smoked himself, obviously disapproved of other people doing so. Later, when she had said a blurred good night to him and was alone in her bedroom with the knocking and gurgling of the plumbing and the faces of dead people in silver frames all around her, she would go to the secret place where she hid the bottles and have a little nightcap.

'Good evening, madam.'

'Ah, there you are, Les!' She uncrossed her legs, still shapely except for their swollen ankles, lowered them from the other end of the sofa on which she reclined, and then began to struggle out of her mink coat. 'I was wondering what had happened to you.'

'Nothing has happened to me, madam. Nothing ever does.' A man in his sixties with a pink-and-white complexion, a silvery quiff of upbrushed hair and a hard, athletic body, he placed the tray on the table in front of her, and then hastened to help her off with the coat. 'It's only three minutes past, you know.'

'Is it? It seems so much later.' She put a trembling hand to her forehead. 'It's been a long day.'

'Mrs Hartley tells me you were great on the telly.' Les spoke with a trace of a Tyneside accent. 'I wish I could have seen you. It's a pity the time didn't fit.'

'Didn't fit with what?' Diana wanted to ask him. But instead she said, 'Oh, I don't know. He asked me such absolutely *fatuous* questions. A mere child, he was. With this extraordinary Beatle-style hair-cut and a maddening habit of interrupting one as soon as one was about to say something remotely interesting.'

'They all do that,' Les said. 'All those interviewers.'

'Those lights give one such a head. Not like footlights at all.'

'Would you like me to fetch you an aspirin, madam?'

'Have you got one handy? It'll save a journey up to my room.'

'I always keep a bottle,' Les said, rummaging in his own special drawer beneath the reception desk. 'Just in case. Never take them myself, mind you.' He produced the bottle and came over to place it on the tray in front of her. 'Would you believe me if I told you that in my whole life I had never had a headache?'

Of no one else would she have believed it, but of him she did.

Her charm-bracelet jangled on her shrunken wrist as she shook out first two aspirins and then, after some deliberation, yet another.

'*Three*, madam?'

'Yes, three, Les,' she sighed. 'I'm afraid so. If it's less than that they seem to have no effect. I suppose I've built up what they call a resistance.' She began to gulp down the aspirins one after another, her head thrown back so that the slack, wrinkled skin of her throat was suddenly pulled taut.

'Those things don't do you any good. That's what I'm always telling my sister with whom I live.'

'Yes, I know, Les, I know!' she wailed, luxuriating in this respectful scolding, as she always did. 'You don't have to tell me. If only I had *your* health.'

'I was a sickly child. You may not believe this now but they thought that I'd never pass my teens. And now look at me!'

Diana looked. The pale blue eyes under the bushy white eyebrows were lambent with health; the expression of the face had a childish serenity. 'You're lucky,' she said with a sigh.

'Lucky?'

What she meant was that he was lucky to be one of those people whom the world could neither jar nor bruise; and if the price of such immunity was simple-mindedness—Mrs Hartley was always saying that Les was simple-minded—then was it not worth the price?

'No, it's not luck,' he went on confidentially. 'You've got to take care of your body, see. Exercise—that's the first thing, madam. Daily exercise. Now as soon as I get out of bed, I have my twenty minutes of physical jerks before the open window. Then I always walk to work—all the way here from beyond the gas-works. And then of course—winter and summer—I have my dip. And the right mental attitude is important. I always say the world is how you find it.'

Diana had heard all this many times in the past; but unlike Mrs Hartley, the manageress, or a number of the 'regulars', who would hurriedly cut Les off, she derived from the long-familiar recital the same kind of comfort that the religious derive from a well-known prayer.

165

'Oh, how I do envy you, Les!'

'Envy me, madam? But what have I got for you to envy?'

She might have answered, as she had often been tempted to answer in the past: 'Health. Innocence. Beauty.' But now, as then, she merely shook her head, around which the dyed red curls tightly clustered, and continued to stare down into her cup of tea.

'Here am I,' Les went on, 'a man of sixty-three and what have I done? You're a name, you have all your friends, you have enough money to do as you please. But I—well, I've knocked around the world of course, but what have I to show for it? That's what I ask myself, madam.'

It was what she had also asked herself—often. What had he to show for it? And the only answer was that answer she could never make: Health. Innocence. Beauty.

Mrs Hartley would give a curious shying movement of the head, sniffing sharply at the same time so that the nostrils of her beaky nose dilated, when Diana used the word 'beauty' of Les. Beauty was a word applicable to the sunsets outside the bow-fronted windows of the lounge, to the pallid niece that Mrs Hartley was educating at an expensive convent or even to her dachshund, Mr Smith. To use it of a man—any man and especially of a man in his sixties—showed what a silly woman that Diana Broughton really was.

All that was now said between Diana and Les as she gulped the black, bitter tea had been said over and over again in the past, she reclining on the sofa and he standing respectfully by the hearth in the winter, and by the window in summer; and it was this very familiarity that brought her the calm that would eventually enable her to go upstairs and face the solitary horrors of the night.

'Well, I suppose I ought to be turning in,' Diana announced at last.

'Yes, it's getting on, madam.'

'I hope I'll be able to sleep better than I did last night.'

'I'm sure you will, madam. You must be tired after your performance.'

'Well, good night, Les.'

'Good night, madam. Happy dreams.'

Were dreams ever happy? she wondered, as Les snapped shut the gilded doors of the little cushioned box that served as a lift. *His* must be. It was impossible to imagine him waking up in the middle of the night and fighting his way out of the tangled blankets to lurch across to the secret hiding-place for burning gulp on gulp of oblivion. Impossible to imagine him sweating, his gaze fixed on the reflection of the sea shimmering across the ceiling, or moaning against a clenched fist or lost, panting and wide-eyed, in a brief and frenzied act of self-placation.

'He's such a beautiful old man,' she had said so often to Mrs Hartley; and I, she now thought as she stood in her slip before her bedroom mirror, am such an ugly old woman. She shivered and then yawned, one hand scratching like the claw of a predatory bird at the silk over her bosom. Slowly her thoughts began to return with sour disgust to the Beatle-haired child who had put his kind but clumsy questions to her. Of course, in *your* day. . . . How does it feel to see a remake of the film in which a generation ago you scored your greatest triumph? . . . In *your* day. . . . Actors of *your* generation. . . . Looking back over the years, what advice would you give to an actress at the outset of her career?

What advice? Still in her slip, she threw herself across the bed and, chin on hand, stared at the curtains at a point where the shadows lurking in the heavily sculptured folds seemed to form the shape of a hooded presence. Well, what advice? First, my dear, don't marry an actor of genius in the mistaken belief that he can impregnate you with that genius as easily as with the child who turns out to be a moron. Secondly, if you must

167

marry an actor of genius, then be faithful to him. Thirdly, when the marriage breaks up and your beauty grows puffy and creased and your child is relegated to a home, then don't take to the bottle. Because the bottle will only accelerate your slide down into that abyss of fear and loneliness and humiliation.

The bottle, the bottle! She jumped off the bed, scrabbled in the secret place and eventually jerked it out. Had she really drunk all that the night before? Or had that Irish maid—the new one with the ill-fitting false-teeth who had had the impertinence to call her 'Love'—had a swig at it? Well, here goes.

As she gulped the burning whisky, head thrown back and legs wide apart, she thought: If Les could see me. And then: It's so unfair. Some people, like herself, blundered through life as though they were traversing an unknown room in the darkness. They ricocheted from one piece of furniture to another, bruising and cutting their flesh and breaking their bones. But other people, like Les, either had the ability to see in the darkness or else remained miraculously impervious to the repeated collisions. They were the untouchables. Les had never been touched. He was like a sheet of glass on which not a single fingerprint, not a single mote of dust, had ever alighted. One looked through him and he was clear, transparently clear.

Again she gulped and yet again. Then she threw herself on the bed and, knees drawn up in a foetal position and arms over tousled head, she began to mutter: 'Les, Les, Les.' The repetition of the name was as consoling as the liquor that still burned her tongue and throat.

Les lay out alone on the oil-spotted, abrasive shingle, with a khaki-coloured towel under his muscled body and a leaden sky above him. His pale blue eyes were open, the fingers of his hands were splayed wide apart. A transistor set near his cheek played 'Tales from the Vienna Woods'. He was humming to the tune.

His nipples were pink, the same colour as his lips, against the hoary grey of the hair on his chest. Under his arms and in a narrowing line from his sternum to his navel the hair was completely white, as on his outstretched limbs. The cold wind that blew through the silvery quiff had dried the salt on his body so that the skin felt dry and scaly—a sensation he always liked. The only signs of old age were a slight swelling of the diaphragm, even when he was lying like this on his back, a creasing at the throat and a boniness of knees and elbows.

Above him the late afternoon people hurried along the promenade, dragging their dogs or thrusting their perambulators before them or clutching at their coats or hats. Few looked over the rail at the old man lying out in his faded blue bathing-trunks on the khaki-coloured towel; and because of the rasp and thud of the sea, exploding in an icy spume, few heard the 'Tales from the Vienna Woods'.

A French girl and an English boy scurried zigzagging along the promenade, so closely linked by the arms flung around each other's shoulders that from time to time their legs would get entangled and they would have to cling even more tightly to each other in order not to fall. At one point the girl, Anne-Marie, let out a shrill scream as the wind jerked at her skirt and then lifted it above her head. She was conventionally pretty, with black hair that scraped in stiff, jagged prongs across an overwide forehead, slender hips and a mouth that was seldom properly closed. The boy, Michael, had a carefully arranged bouffant orange coiffeur, falling over his small, pointed ears, which contrasted with the general untidiness of the rest of his appearance. His chin, as pointed as his ears, was tucked into his duffel-coat and the tattered ends of his blue jeans flapped around grubbily naked ankles beneath which he wore a pair of scuffed suede shoes.

M

Two skinny girls of seven or eight were tossing a red rubber ball to each other. One of them threw under-arm with a balletic twirl as the ball spun feebly from her hand; the other, tomboyish in shorts and polo-necked sweater, threw over-arm with a wriggle and shake that made her straggly blonde hair bounce on her shoulders. As Anne-Marie and Michael approached, a violent gust of wind caught at the ball and whirled it in their direction in a wide loop. The boy put out a suede shoe, sidestepped, put the shoe out again and then gave a kick, lifting the ball back into the wind and sending it over towards a bench on which two elderly women, all muffled in furs and with a swollen black labrador outstretched as though dead at their feet, were shouting at each other. The ball thudded on the back of the bench between them, making them cringe; one of them even let out a little squawk. Then it bounced, bounced again and plopped on the body of the recumbent dog, who jumped up, shook himself and gazed all around him with eyes misty with cataract. The boy and his companion went off into peals of laughter, as one of the two women reprimanded the two little girls: 'Can't you be a little more careful? You might do some real damage. Go somewhere else to play.' 'Yes, go somewhere else. Not here,' her friend took up, her face swollen and frosty under a swirl of reddish fur.

'You are naughty!' Anne-Marie giggled.

'I didn't mean to do it. It was the wind.' Michael's spidery, feminine fingers touched her breast under her jacket. 'Honestly it was. I meant to kick the ball back to those children. Honest.'

'Naughty boy!'

He put his lips first to her icy cheeks and then to her lips with the soft, nuzzling movement of a new-born child feeling its way to the nipple. His kiss tasted sour.

Suddenly Anne-Marie broke free from him, jerking first her body and then her hand out of his grasp, to scamper to the railings. Her eyelashes, as spiky as the jagged prongs of hair across her forehead, batted in the wind. 'The waves, the waves!' she turned back to scream. 'B—ee—g! So beeg!'

Michael joined her, his hands now deep in the pockets of his duffel-coat and his feet executing a small shuffling dance.

'And look! Someone sunbathing! But there *is* no sun! Crazy!'

Les's eyes were now closed and the once wide-splayed fingers had moved to behind his head. The transistor set still played at his cheek, but the music had become 'The Teddy Bear's Picnic', sung by a jaunty baritone at the back of his throat.

'Idiot!' the boy exclaimed. 'That's one way to catch one's death.'

'He has a beautiful body,' Anne-Marie murmured, staring down at it. 'Maybe he made that body for himself.'

The boy propped himself sideways against the rail so that he was now gazing not downwards at Les but at Anne-Marie's averted face. 'Christ!' he exclaimed. 'I never knew you were a gerontophile.'

She turned. *'Quoi?'*

'Beautiful! If that's your idea of beauty!' He put out a hand and snatched at the tips of her fingers; but she quickly withdrew them.

'Yes,' she cried. 'But yes!' She now leant far over the railings. 'And to swim in this weather—he must be tough.'

'Out of his mind, you mean.'

Then, when she seemed not to hear him, her face still averted and her gaze still fixed on the sleeping man below, the boy stooped and picked up a handful of the pebbles with which the high seas had strewn the promenade. Balancing one on a thumb-nail sharpened to a miniature lance, he flicked it down. 'Not so good!' The pebble had fallen beyond the transistor-set. He tried again and this time, managing to get the pebble to fall between Les's legs, he emitted a little whoop of delight. 'That's more like it!'

He continued to flick the pebbles and Les continued to sleep; until, at long last, one actually fell on the outstretched body, bouncing from shoulder to chest and then trickling to the navel. 'Holed in one!'

Les opened his eyes and scrabbled vaguely with a hand to brush the pebble away. Then, staring at it where it nestled in a fold of the faded pale blue slip, he turned over on his stomach, to reveal heavy shoulders that from their long contact with the shingle had the appearance of having been scarred with shrapnel. He yawned, scratched his chin, retrieved the pebble from his towel and then looked up.

The boy made a simian grimace at him; the girl continued to stare.

'Hi! Les grinned and waved. Then he held out the pebble on his palm: 'This yours?'

The boy squinted angrily downwards, making no move either to return the greeting or to answer the question. But Anne-Marie slowly raised her hand: 'Hi!' she called. 'Hi there!' She smiled and Les smiled again. 'It must be cold!'

'What's that?'

'Cold!' she screamed into the wind. 'It must be cold! You must be cold!'

Les laughed, now sitting up and hugging his knees in his arms. 'Marvellous!' he shouted back. 'Not cold at all.'

'Oh, come on!' Michael urged her peevishly. 'Come *on*! We'll be late for the film.'

'Let's have a swim too!'

Ignoring what seemed to him a fatuous suggestion, the boy strode off alone along the promenade; and after a moment, with another wave to Les, the girl scampered after him.

Weeks later, when the summer had come and the beaches were crowded with screaming children and damp-faced women and men whose shoulders were raw with sunburn, Anne-Marie lay out among a debris of newspapers, wrappings, empty bottles, towels and clothes, in a new two-piece bathing costume that cut uncomfortably into the brown flesh of her thighs and made her feel as though her breasts were completely bare. Michael lay near to her, face downwards, freckles spattering his narrow shoulder-blades and the pale hair down the ridge of his spine glittering silvery in the sunlight. His ankles were still grubby and the upturned soles of his feet were stained orange from the scuffed suede shoes. He had gulped more of the sour Spanish wine than anyone else in the party and now his head ached and every movement seemed an effort. A plain girl, who had refused to undress—first making the excuse that she had forgotten to bring a costume and then saying 'Oh, I really can't be bothered' when Anne-Marie had offered to lend her one—was talking in a high-pitched nasal voice to a young man, head also buried in arms, who did no more than grunt from time to time. 'It was all so old hat,' she was saying, a bead of sweat trickling down the side of one cheek to her wobbling chin. 'Slow-motion. Silent-movie captions. Stopping a frame from time to time.' As she talked, one little paw with bitten nails scrabbled in her canvas bag and eventually pulled out a squashed packet of cigarettes. 'Fag?' she asked.

Again her friend grunted.

'Give us one,' Michael said. 'Light it for me.'

The plain girl emitted a little laugh that made her choke on her own cigarette. 'What bloody cheek! Light it for yourself! Or get Anne-Marie to light it for you. Did you hear him, Donald? Asking me to light his bloody cigarette for him!'

'Light me a cigarette, Anne-Marie.'

The French girl was staring into the distance.

'Anne-Marie!'

Anne-Marie took the cigarette from the other girl, put it to her glistening, pale pink lips and then reached out for the

173

matches. Unconsciously her other hand moved to the flimsy top of her bathing-costume to make sure that it was still in place, while her eyes held their far-off gaze.

'This cigarette's all smeared with lipstick,' Michael muttered in disgust as he plugged it into his mouth. 'For Christ's sake!'

When Anne-Marie did not answer he sat up, both hands to his head, the slender fingers pushing up through the bouffant orange hair. 'What are you looking at?' he asked.

'Nothing.'

But she continued to stare; until, turning in the direction of her gaze, Michael at last found her target.

Les, his burly body propped against a stanchion of the break-water, was smiling at her.

'Does he remember me?' Anne-Marie asked. 'He must do.'

In fact Les had no recollection of the girl at all; but he had seen her glancing in his direction and, being a man naturally friendly to everyone, had at once responded.

'Stop it! Stop it now!'

Anne-Marie looked again at Les, brown fingers lazily scratching at her bare shin. Once more he smiled; and this time she raised a hand to make a waving gesture, as though polishing a window.

Michael gripped her wrist and jerked the hand down. 'What the hell do you think you're doing?'

'Being friendly. Can't one be friendly?'

'Now they're at it again!' the plain girl groaned to her companion. 'Nothing but bicker!'

'Would you mind!' Michael turned on her. Then: 'Anne-Marie—that's enough!'

'I look where I wish to look. That is my affair.'

Michael jumped to his feet, his eyes bloodshot under the nest of orange hair, and began to stride away, an elongated silhouette, as though made of wire, against the glare of afternoon. Anne-Marie raised a hand to shade her eyes; the plain girl got slowly to her feet, smoothing down her creased floral skirt. One of the other girls turned over lazily to watch.

'What a clot!' said one of the boys. 'He'll get himself bashed.'

Michael stood over Les. The gold crucifix on his skinny chest fell forward.

'*Do* you mind?' he said thickly.

'Do I mind what?' Smiling up at him, Les suspected nothing.

'I'd rather you didn't stare like that at my girl. If you don't mind, that is.'

Still Les smiled, crossing his arms so that the biceps swelled. 'Fine,' he said. 'She smiled at me, I smiled back. Friendly. That's all.'

'Well, don't smile.'

'Fine.'

The repetition of that word 'fine' and the perpetually good-natured grin both infuriated Michael. 'Just leave us alone!' he said. 'You'd better watch it.'

The level gaze of the pale blue eyes did not falter. Then: 'I'm going in for another dip,' Les said in a pleasant, conversational voice. He rose to his feet, did a couple of knee-bends and began to canter towards the sea.

'What did you say to him?' the plain girl asked, when Michael returned to the group. 'You were *brave*!'

'Oh, mind your own bloody business.'

He kicked his beach-bag to one side and then flung himself down beside it, burying his face in its folds.

From then on it was curious how often Michael and Les were to meet each other.

Once, as Michael was about to take a wire basket from the pile at the entrance to the supermarket, another hand reached down ahead of him, and without looking round he knew to whom it belonged. But when he glared at the older man, Les merely looked back with a vague tranquillity as though he had no idea who Michael might be.

Reeling out of a pub with some friends at closing-time, one hand raised to stifle a sour belch, the boy collided with a passer-by and again, without having to look into the broad, tanned face, he knew its identity.

'Can't you look out where you're going?' he shouted on that occasion.

'Sorry, mate.'

'I'm not *your* fucking mate!'

But he had passed on.

Three times Michael was with Anne-Marie when they ran into the old man on the front.

On the first of these occasions, Les would have walked by without giving either of them a glance, if Anne-Marie had not deliberately forced his eyes to meet hers. She smiled, inclining not merely her head but her whole body, until, when he was almost past her, Les gave her a genial but impersonal smile in return.

On the second occasion, Michael felt her fingers tighten in his long before he himself had been aware that the old man was striding towards them, under his arm the rolled towel that contained his faded blue slip. ' 'Ullo,' she said in a voice so soft that it was almost a whisper, and Les, startled, halted a moment in his tracks, then smiled and said, 'Good evening. How are things?'

On that last occasion the encounter was the cause of a quarrel.

Michael demanded what the hell she thought she was do-ing and she replied that she would do as she pleased.

'Not when you're out with me.'

'Too bad.'

'What the hell do you mean—too bad?'

'If I cannot do what I wish to do when I am out with you, then I do not go out with you. Understand?'

On the final occasion when the two of them saw Les, their affair, which had started in the spring, was already petering out in rancour and tedium. They would savage each other verbally, he with profanity and abuse and she with sarcasm, because it was only during their inevitable reconciliations that they were now able to make satisfactory love. Anne-Marie was about to return to France where a fiancé was awaiting her; and Michael, who had dreaded that moment, was now half-glad of its coming, as a mortally sick man is half-glad of the approach of death.

The two of them, in one of their increasingly rare periods of total accord, had stopped to be photographed arm-in-arm by the lame beach-photographer who dragged himself along the front, the sweat glistening on his pale, horse-like face. Her head was on Michael's shoulder and his arm was around her waist. Then, just as the photographer was saying, 'All right, love! Now don't move your head!' Les walked towards them.

This time he recognized who they were, paused until the shutter had clicked and then said, 'Well, that'll make a nice souvenir of Brighton!'

Anne-Marie released herself from Michael: 'Yes, I need a souvenir,' she said, her face which all that day had irritated Michael with its expression of apathy, suddenly illuminated. 'I leave the day after tomorrow.'

'You're leaving Brighton?'

She nodded. 'I return to Paris.'

'Well, good luck then.'

Les walked on.

Michael remained silent for a long time, his arm no longer around her waist as they continued to stroll.

Then he began to mutter thickly: 'Oh, yes, he's beautiful all right. A real beauty. A beautiful old man.'

Michael was usually late for his dates with Anne-Marie, explaining either that his little three-wheeler had broken down, that someone had called at his digs just as he was about to go out or that there had been something urgent—usually un-specified—that he had simply *had* to finish off. It was no sur-prise to her, therefore, when on their last meeting she had been wandering up and down in front of the Palace Pier for almost quarter of an hour and he had still failed to appear. As the evening crowds of trippers surged round her on their way to the performance of Old Fashioned Music Hall on the Pier, she all at once decided that she did not really want to see him at all and that in his lateness she had a pretext to make off. All that afternoon, as she had been packing her suitcases, she had been telling herself how deeply she would miss him; but as she moved aside to allow two elderly people, muffled in spite of the heat of the summer evening, in overcoats and scarves, to push an even older person, of indeterminate sex and even more muffled, on to the pier in a wheel-chair, she realised that so far from being sad at the imminent separation she was about to experience a liberating joy. The dream had seemed only a dream while she was experiencing it; now that she was in the process of waking she knew it to have been a nightmare. Well, she would go. The clock outside the jeweller's shop opposite showed that he was twenty minutes late; and if he telephoned or called at her lodgings she would merely tell him that she thought twenty minutes long enough to wait for any-one.

She pulled down her short white linen jacket, adjusted her handbag on her arm and began to wander off.

Already the summer was almost over; dusk was seeping down through the narrow streets, like a clogging vapour, to thin to a

178

yellowish transparency when it reached the wide front. The air was parched and thundery.

As she strolled westwards towards Hove, she heard the melancholy sounds of male voices singing from one of the bars on the esplanade below her:

'I know 'cos I've seen them,

'I know 'cos I've been between them. . . .'

She had been happy in Brighton in spite of the discomfort of having to share a bathroom with three other girls, the nauseating food and the perpetual rows with Michael. But she was glad now to get away from the squalor which clung to every nook and cranny of the elegant city like the years-old grime and dust in the crevices of the battered old Regency staircase that soared up in the centre of the rooming-house in which she had lived. The only gaiety was the off-pitch gaiety of those lugubrious voices bawling out their solemn obscenities over a counter awash with lukewarm beer; or of the students who now scuffled in front of her, one with the head of another under his arm while the third kicked at the victim's bottom with a plimsoled foot. 'Oops! Sorry!' All three had collided with her.

Then, suddenly she was face to face with Les.

'Hello,' he said, smiled at her, and then was about to walk on.

But she stopped in front of him, saying ' 'Ullo' and giving that little bow of hers from the waist. 'Have you been swimming?'

'That's right. I swim every day on my way to my work.'

'On your *way* to your work?'

'That's right. I work at a hotel. Adelaide Crescent Hotel, up there.' He pointed with the roll of his towel.

'I once met a lady who lived at the Adelaide Crescent Hotel. She asked me to go and see her but I never did. An actress she said she was. We met in the train.'

'Our Miss Broughton—Diana Broughton?'

Anne-Marie was staring at the splendidly muscled neck that soared like a pillar out of his white aertex shirt. 'Maybe.'

'Yes, I expect it was our Miss Broughton. We've two other theatre ladies but they neither of them go out all that much, I expect it was Miss Broughton.'

Beyond him and across the road, she became aware that Michael had drawn up in his silly little open three-wheeler, picked out clumsily with red and green paint and its back window dotted with comic stickers. 'Where are you going?' she asked in sudden panic, forgetting that he had told her. She did not want to meet Michael; on no account did she want to meet him.

'Well, as I said, I've got to get to my job. Night porter in the Adelaide Crescent Hotel.' He looked at the old-fashioned watch on his hairy wrist. 'Wouldn't do to be late or I'll get a wigging from our manageress. Not that I ever *am* late,' he added, thinking that the expression of alarm on her face meant that she had not realised he was joking. 'Well, goodbye, miss. Nice to have seen you.'

He turned away; and a moment later Michael gripped Anne-Marie's arm, so hard that she gave a little cry.

'What the *hell* do you think you're doing?'

'Waiting for you.'

'*Here?*'

'I was on my way home. Twenty minutes is long enough.'

'And why the hell were you talking to that imbecile?'

'I'll talk to whom I like.'

He tightened his grip, putting his narrow face close to hers as he said, 'Watch it! Just watch it!'

She pulled free with a laugh. 'Watch it? What is this "watch it"? What do you mean—watch it? What am I to watch? . . . Now I go!' She jerked away from him and then ran across the road.

Looking after her, Michael realised from then that he had lost her forever.

Michael and some friends, all male, had been making a pub-crawl from one to another of the bars of the Lower Esplanade.

Tunneled under the busy road above, the bars had been crowded all through the summer with trippers, Irish labourers, students and male and female prostitutes; but now that the autumn had come, with peevish gusts of wind flapping at the canvas awnings and making the gaily-coloured signs creak and squeak, each of the long counters, stretching away from the arched entrance to the dim recesses beyond, had the forlorn air of a deserted Underground platform late at night. People no longer screamed at each other or bawled out songs or rammed fists into each other's faces; and the only prostitutes were a few of the Brighton regulars, women with hoarse, confidential voices, sturdy legs and fur coats that seemed too small for their ample frames.

It was Michael's birthday : something he had forgotten until, coming out of a lecture, he had glanced at the evening paper and realised the date.

'No, not in there! Not in there! That's where Scottie trod on that woman's handbag and there was all hell to pay from her gentleman friend. Don't you remember? "Don't you never come back no more," Mine Host politely told him.'

'Politely!' the boy called Scottie shouted. 'Politely! He twisted my arm behind my back and the next thing I knew I was face down in someone else's vomit outside.'

'Let's have some music. Let's go to Flanigan's.'

'We can make our own music.' A gangling youth in horn-rimmed glasses adjusted the scarf that circled his scrawny neck to reach almost to his buttocks, before he began to sing in a shrill falsetto :

' "Oh, no John, no John, no John, no!" '

'You're pissed,' Michael said.

'Who said I'm pissed? But I *want* a piss. That's another matter. Another matter altogether.'

'Who else wants a piss?'

'Hands up for a piss!'

Swaying, laughing and pushing each other, they began to crowd into a public lavatory, little different from the bars on either side of it except that the tunnel in which it was sited was even lower and narrower and the stench was of urine instead of beer.

'Christ, what a pong!'

'Do I really look like that?' The gangling youth was staring at himself, wide-eyed, in a blotched mirror.

'You look far worse.'

' "Oh, no John, no John, no John, no!" ' the youth sang out again, this time *basso profondo*.

Michael's hand was at his flies; but he was so drunk that to undo each button seemed to require immense thought and effort. Then slowly he became aware that someone not of their party was just about to finish using the stall on his right. He turned his head; his eyes met Les's.

All at once he began to shout: 'What the hell do you think you're staring at? Haven't you got one of your own?'

Les, astonished, asked, 'What's the matter, chum?' but he had hardly got out the last word before Michael's fist landed in his face. 'Bloody poove!' Again Michael hit out ineffectually; then all the others were crowding in, with shouts of 'What goes on here?' and 'Give it to the filthy bastard!' and a falsetto parody cry, from the gangling youth in the scarf, of 'Oh, my *dear*!' The largest of the party, who played in the university rugby team, had caught Les by the shirt, while another youth gave him a sideways blow on the cheek; until, in a moment, they were all of them on top of him and he was slipping down, one arm trailing in urine and his knees cracking, first one and then the other, against the side of the stall with the noise of revolver shots. Les raised his arms in an attempt to ward off the kicks and blows, squirming and drawing his knees up to his chin; he even shouted.

At first his assailants were all yelling abuse, bawling encouragement to each other, and even laughing; then in a moment silence fell, no sound coming from them except an occasional grunt and the thuds of blows and kicks and the clatter of shoes on concrete.

Mutely they stared down at the old man, writhing bloodstained and sodden, half in and half out of the turbid trough of urine. Then, still mute, they crept away, to race up the stairs into the light and din of the street above.

Les was late; Diana Broughton had never known him be so late. She had finished reading her novel, there was nothing to watch on television except three school-teachers being interviewed about Comprehensive Schools and she was growing increasingly restless as she stared at herself in one of the elaborate Edwardian gilt-mirrors and thought of the secret place.

That afternoon she had been to see her former husband, at his own invitation.

His young wife had greeted her in the tiny but exquisite Campden Hill house and had told her, although it was ten minutes past the hour they had arranged, that 'poor dear Godfrey' had been delayed and would not be able to be there for a while. 'A while' had been forty minutes; and meanwhile the two women had played with the small, pertly pretty three-year-old girl who was on the floor of the drawing-room, with her toys scattered around her. They had found it difficult to talk to each other.

Godfrey had rushed in, worn-looking but boisterous, had cried out 'Diana darling!', arms extended, and had then kissed her on both cheeks. She had noticed, appalled, that he had taken to wearing a toupée and that his front teeth had been capped.

Putting the child on his knee, he had immediately begun to explain why he had wanted to see her. ('I'd better talk business at once—we're supposed to be attending the Royal Academy Dinner.') He had been invited by the British Council to form a company to take on a world tour and he had at once thought —how could he not think?—of his beloved Diana. Did the idea appeal to her? After all, they had always remained *friends* through every temporary—er—difficulty, and she knew what a terrific admiration he had for her talent. So what about it?

'But Godfrey, darling—what a *sweet* thought!'

It was only later that he slowly got it through to her that the 'sweet thought' was not, as she had imagined, that she should repeat her Cleopatra or her Lady Macbeth or her Madame Ranevsky, but that she should merely take on Lady Capulet in *Romeo and Juliet* and Lady Sneerwell in *The School for Scandal*. Attempting to conceal her chagrin, she had repeated, 'Well, I must think about it, my dear,' until, nettled, he had made it plain to her that if she wished to think about it, she had two days in which to do so.

When the door of the house had closed on her—'No, my dear, I don't want a taxi, I need a little stroll'—she could hear him and the little minx laughing together. Of course, she told herself, they were not laughing at her: but the sound of the girl's mirth, pouring crystalline out of the open window to spill in the street below, had intensified the depression and rage induced in her by the insulting offer of those two parts.

. . . Where *was* Les? Now, curiously, it was with him, instead of with Godfrey, that she felt angry and aggrieved. It was too bad of him; he knew that she liked to have her late-night cup of tea before turning in. She had already knocked on the door of Mrs Hartley's private sitting-room to ask what had become of him; but Mrs Hartley, absorbed in a game of bridge with three other of the 'regulars'—that common couple who had once run a greengrocery business in Knightsbridge and the retired military man she called 'The Mad Major'—had merely shrugged her shoulders, contemptuously unconcerned, before she murmured, 'Oh, I expect something has held him up.'

If he didn't bring her that cup of tea, then she wouldn't be able to sleep. She would just have to wait on and on in the deserted lounge, staring at her reflection as she was doing now, until the dawn pushed grey under the heavy damask curtains and the cleaning women arrived. She couldn't *face* that room upstairs until she had seen him; no, honestly she couldn't.

All at once the memory come back to her of lying in bed, a child of seven, in an Earls Court boarding-house, and of her actor father, a widower, tiptoeing in to find her still awake. 'Aren't you asleep?' he asked; and she had shouted back at him through her tears, 'How *can* I sleep until you kiss me good night?'

Mrs Hartley was turning out the lights.

'Not going to bed, Miss Broughton?'

'Not for the moment.'

'Well, I'll leave this one on for you. Will that be all right?'

'Yes, yes, thank you.'

'Good night then.'

'Good night.'

Mrs Hartley had more than once intimated to her favourites among the 'regulars' that she wouldn't be surprised if there were not something 'up' between Miss Broughton and Les. 'Well, good luck to her,' she would add, wishing to live up to her chosen role of broad-minded, cynical but sympathetic woman of the world.

'Oh, there you are, Les! At last!'

Diana had been woken by the sound of the night porter crossing the marble floor of the vestibule. She spoke crossly, as she rubbed at one eye with the back of her hand. Then she stared at him in growing horror: 'What's *happened* to you?' she asked.

'Nothing, madam. A little accident, that's all.' Les could hardly speak through lips that were purple and swollen.

'An accident!' Slowly she took in the half-closed eye; the lacerated forehead; the blood-soaked bandages on a hand; the abrasions and bruises.

'Yes, madam.' The 'yes' came out as 'yeth' and, hearing it, she realised that a front tooth was missing. 'A fall,' he said. 'I had a fall down some steps on the Esplanade.'

'But ought you to be working?'

'Never had a day off,' he said, with some of the old pride. 'At the hospital they told me to go home and to bed, but there was no need for that. It takes more than a fall like this to lay me off work.'

'But you look—' she was going to say 'ghastly' and then restrained herself. 'Poor Les! Does it hurt?'

He shook his head, his tongue making its way over the blubber-lips while the eye-lid of the half-closed eye fluttered oddly. 'A bit. Only to be expected. . . . Now how about your tea? Or is it too late for you?'

Still staring at him, she rose to her feet: 'No. Not now, thank you, Les. It's getting on. I'd have turned in long ago but I dropped off on this sofa.' Then involuntarily she repeated, 'Oh, poor Les.'

He followed her to the padded cell of a lift and opened the door. Their eyes met as she was about to close the door again, and looking into his, usually so serene and jolly in their simple optimism, she was horrified to see reflected in them nothing but her own despair and misery and hatred of existence.

'Happy dreams!' he called. The words came out mechanically; still the haunted eyes held hers.

'Thank you, Les.'

Upstairs, she pulled the bottle from the secret place and gulped from it repeatedly, in order to forget that hideously lacerated face and that battered body and above all that expression in the eyes.

It was the last time she was ever to think of Les as a beautiful old man, or to wait for him to bring her a late-night cup of tea.

Loss

Dr Nakamura was waiting for Eithne, as he usually waited for her but she never waited for him, on the platform of Falmer Station. She had often asked him why he did not choose some place more comfortable—he could, after all, far more conveniently pick her up outside her office—but the only answer was a hurried drawing in of the breath on the monosyllable 'Sa . . .' and a shrug of his shoulders. 'Perhaps you're ashamed of me,' she would sometimes add bitterly, when the day had been a particularly tiring one or when she was suffering from one of her migraines. For some reason, this suggestion always agitated the Japanese. 'Ashamed of you?' he would cry out. 'Why should I be ashamed of you? Why? I am *proud* of our friendship.' If she then still persisted, 'Then why do you hang about for me *here*?' he would mutter something about gossip and her reputation and the fact that he was a foreigner in England on a scholarship. The discretion that was so deeply a part of his nature always filled her with exasperation and, on occasions, even with rage.

This time, approaching him where he sat alone on his usual bench at the farthest and, as she often pointed out, the draughtiest end of the platform, Eithne had adopted the slightly knock-kneed, slouching walk, head lowered and hands deep in the pockets of her overcoat, that showed that the day had not gone well for her. 'Cold!' she called out, as though it were a greeting, when she was still several yards away.

Nakamura got up, hugging his scuffed black brief-case over

a chest that Eithne knew to be far more muscular than his slight, even fragile, appearance in his clothes might suggest. 'You are cold?' he asked.

'Yes, I am cold.' She had a habit of imitating, not the accent, but the rhythms of his speech. 'Either that heating is turned up so high that one becomes a steamed pudding or else it's turned down so low that one becomes an ice-cream.'

Nakamura looked into her handsome, cross face for several seconds before he gave a delighted giggle. 'Ah, Eithne, I like the way you say things! So original,' he added.

Before she had met Nakamura she had never been conscious that she had any gift for self-expression. It was he, a foreigner, who had first discerned it in her, and taking confidence from his discernment Eithne had then set about developing the gift. As a result, suddenly, in her mid-thirties, she had found that she was able to make people listen to her and laugh at her.

The cold air, swept along the platform by the incoming train, brushed against them like a tangible presence. Eithne clung to Nakamura's arm, her other hand struggling with the hem of her skirt. 'Christ!' she muttered through clenched teeth. Nakamura, always polite, opened the door for her, held out a hand, saying 'Please,' and then gave a little bobbing bow as she stepped in.

Once she was settled in one corner of the long, open compartment, Eithne looked around her. Even when she was with Nakamura, she could not stop herself from looking around, so ineradicably engrained was the habit. Well, I wouldn't mind him, she told herself, glancing at the profile of an obvious student, with the kind of large hands and wide mouth and coarse black hair that she liked; but she recognised, now as on other similar occasions, with a perennial astonishment, that though she would not mind him—or, indeed, any of the other young men like him—it was Nakamura that she would always prefer. 'I suppose I'm in love with him really,' she would say to Rose, the girl with whom she shared; and Rose would then squeal, 'Oh, Eithne, *no*!'

'I have made progress today,' Nakamura announced, using a rotating movement of his forefinger and middle-finger to make a little peephole through the misted glass of the window. 'You have probably heard it said that the first Christian book to be published in Japan was *Sanctos Nogosagveono* in 1591, but I have always suspected that maybe—' At that point the train entered a tunnel and Eithne was glad that his precise, beautifully modulated voice should be lost in the whoosh and roar. If he were mad about classical music, like Clive, or about politics, like Keith, she might be able to keep up with him. But religion had never interested her and the history of Christianity in the Far East just bored the pants off her.

'. . . Though the first work of *Western* literature introduced to Japan was of course "Esopono Fabulas"—better known to you as "Aesop's Fables",' Nakamura was ending as the train again emerged into the dimming light of evening.

'Now fancy that!' Eithne exclaimed, cuddling up to him, her hand drawing his own hand into the pocket of his overcoat. She got a secret pleasure out of using on him a gentle irony the existence of which he never even suspected.

'Yes, it is interesting,' Nakamura agreed solemnly, squeezing her hand in the pocket. 'And surprising.'

Eithne was staring at the young man in the corner. His face was averted from them; but she knew, as she always knew such things, that he was looking not out of the window but at her reflection in the glass. Probably, she thought, he was saying to himself, 'Now why should an attractive girl like that want to take up with a middle-aged coloured?' (To Eithne Japanese were 'coloureds'; and she herself, though now in her thirties, was 'a girl'.) That people should put that question whether silently to themselves or, as in the case of Rose, audibly, excited Eithne, she could not have said why. 'Yes, I suppose it *is* rather kinky of me,' she would sometimes admit to Rose. 'But honestly I go for him in a way I've never gone for anyone else. And that includes Jim.' Jim was the merchant-seaman husband that Eithne had not seen for almost six years

Nakamura went on talking about his research; but Eithne, as usual, did not listen to him. It was enough to feel his muscular body so close to hers through the overcoat that muffled it, to press his hand and at the same time to dart an occasional glance at the face of the student, who had a curious way of sucking on his full lower lip as he frowned at her reflection in the window.

Nakamura was now explaining how, with the persecution of the Christians, people in Japan had come to fear that if they were seen with a foreign book, they might be thought to be converts and that, in consequence *Aesop's Fables*, once so popular, had ceased to be read. He gave his dissertation without looking at her, his eyes on the spot, just above a framed sepia-coloured photograph of Littlehampton, where someone had scratched with a penknife 'J. Wright is a tart'; and all through it his hand never ceased to massage hers, sometimes so fiercely that she all but cried out in mingled pain and pleasure.

'That boy was watching us,' she said, as they got out at Brighton Station and hurried for the barrier.

'What boy?'

'That boy in the corner.'

It was typical of Naka (this was Eithne's nickname for him) that he should at once say in alarm, 'I hope he does not know me. I hope he is not in my department.'

'Silly!'

'But why should he stare at us?' Nakamura pursued.

'I expect he was wondering how I managed to pick up such a handsome man.'

Again the irony was lost on Nakamura.

'Do we go to my place or do we go to yours?'

'Let's go to yours,' Eithne said. 'We can call in at Food Fayre and get some stuff. We don't want to eat out, do we? Not in this perishing weather.'

'After supper I must work,' Nakamura said.

Arm-in-arm they were scurrying into the wind that swept up from the front.

'Work! But you're always working these days.'

'I must, I have only two more months in England. Once I return to Tokyo, I will have no time. Busy, busy, busy. At last, after ten years—no, eleven years—I am in sight of finishing my book. I wish to finish it before I leave England. That is my plan.'

'Will you dedicate it to me?' Eithne asked in joke.

Nakamura stopped in his tracks, the arm that was linked with Eithne's anchoring her to the pavement beside him. 'Ah, Eithne,' he said with genuine regret, 'that is what I should *wish* to do. Without your interest and encouragement. . . . But unfortunately—I regret—such a thing is not possible. I must dedicate my work to Professor Oda. Professor Oda is now eighty-seven, he is my former *sensei*. I owe the dedication to him. . . . Do you understand?' he finished anxiously.

Eithne laughed. 'I was only joking! What would your wife say if she saw my name at the beginning of your book?'

Still serious, Nakamura replied, 'That would be no problem. I would tell her that Mrs Eithne Morrow was my research helper—that she gave me great assistance.'

Evidently, Eithne realised, he had already worked that out.

'Besides my wife is not interested in my work,' Nakamura went on. 'She is not like you. She is a typical Japanese house-wife. Children, home, cooking. You would say that she is an ignorant and uneducated woman. Though of course,' he added quickly, 'she comes of a good family. Her father was a baron.

192

Not that there are now barons in Japan, but her father was a baron.'

Eithne had heard this often; but daughter of a baron or not, she had never felt jealous of Nakamura's wife—except at the beginning. During those first weeks, when she and the Japanese lay uncomfortably on the single bed—if one or other of them fell off it, Eithne would giggle but Nakamura would always seem genuinely distressed—there on the mantelpiece were the photographs of the woman in kimono, of the little boy with the overlarge head and the overlarge girl with the little head; and when Eithne glanced at them, over Nakamura's naked shoulder or past his flushed cheek, she would experience a pang of dismay or exasperation. But after her fifth or sixth visit the photographs had suddenly gone and in their place was another photograph, cut from a newspaper or magazine, of an elderly and sombre-looking gentleman with an ill-knotted tie.

'Who's that?' Eithne asked.

'Arthur Waley,' Nakamura had answered.

'And who's he when he's at home?' Eithne pursued, between one bite at Nakamura's shoulder and another.

'Arthur Waley? You know who Arthur Waley is. He is a great man. A great scholar.'

'Oh,' said Eithne. And then in a different tone 'Oh, oh, oh!', as she felt the weight of Nakamura's body settling on top of her.

Now, as soon as they had let themselves into the cramped little flatlet that had been fitted into what had once been the huge reception-room of a Brunswick Square mansion—the elegant sweep of the bow had been barbarously severed by a flimsy partition and, all proportions having thus been destroyed, the ceiling now gaped cavernously—Eithne at once put a match to the gas-fire and then set about changing into what she always called 'something comfortable'. This was the heavy silk kimono that Nakamura had given to her, saying,

o   193

'This is really man's kimono.' Its shade was that of pewter and it smelled of the Turkish cigarettes he had smoked in the days when he himself had worn it. At first Nakamura had been nervous of her removing any of her clothing in his flat, though, oddly, he never showed the same circumspection about removing his own clothing in hers. But now he had got used to the fact that neither his landlady nor the other tenants of the house had any interest whatever in what went on behind his locked door.

The kimono suited Eithne's monumental build. When she wore it she ceased to slouch: throwing back her shoulders and arching her spine, so that she all at once acquired a dignity and presence lacking in her day-to-day appearance as typist in a pool of nine girls. She would release her thick auburn hair from its bun at the nape of her neck, allowing it to cascade down her shoulders. Nakamura liked her hair; most men did, she found.

Usually, as on this evening, it was she who did the cooking, while Nakamura, content to leave to her a household task with which throughout his life in Japan he had never to concern himself, squatted cross-legged on the bed, reading. But sometimes, in a sudden craving for the food of his own country, the Japanese would take over. On those occasions Eithne would balance this or that titbit on the ends of her lacquer chopsticks, would put her head on one side as she peered down in a miming of horror or amazement and would then scream out something like 'Raw fish! Revolting!' or 'This rice is *slimy*!' before she popped the object into her mouth.

'Would you like a drink while the potatoes are boiling?'

Nakamura shook his head, putting an arm round her waist as she leant slackly against him. 'No. I must keep my head clear,' he said.

'Clear? What for?'

'For my book.'

'Oh, you and that precious book of yours! You're like husband and wife. I believe you care more for that wretched book of yours than you do for me.'

Nakamura wriggled his toes uncomfortably; he had slipped off his shoes without undoing the laces before squatting on the bed. 'My book is very important to me,' he said. 'Though maybe to no one else,' he added with a small, self-satisfied smile.

'Of course it's important to you. I understand that. After all, I came into your life far later than that book. Ten years later. You've lived with it far longer than with me.'

Nakamura squeezed her waist. 'You are so understanding,' he said.

Although Nakamura would drink nothing, Eithne herself drank, both before supper and during the meal. Since even a single martini would make Nakamura go red in the face, he never ceased to be astonished by her ability to swallow one after another without any observable effect other than the voluptuous langour, so at odds with her brisk everyday behaviour, with which she would recline on his bed, gorged with food, and then reach out for the cigarette she insisted that he lit for her.

'This soup is good,' Nakamura said, sucking at it with the noisy relish that she had never been able to teach him to abandon.

'Out of a tin,' she said. 'One day I'll make you a *real* soup.'

'The days are getting few.'

She put out a hand, her plump forearm rosy in the light of the lamp as the sleeve of the kimono fell away from it, to rest the backs of the fingers momentarily on his cheek. 'I shall miss you,' she said. 'What'll I do without you? No more of these cosy evenings, no more journeys back from Falmer.'

Nakamura continued to suck loudly at the soup, his head lowered. Eithne realised that she had embarrassed him, as she usually embarrassed him with too vehement a demonstration of her love; and with that realisation came, for the first time in their relationship, a sudden annoyance.

'You don't care,' she found herself saying in a loud voice.

Nakamura looked up now, startled. 'Eithne! Of course I care. But what are we to do?'

She shrugged. 'Nothing.'

The meal over, she stacked the dishes by the tiny, cracked sink and then threw herself across the bed, lying on her stomach with her head supported on her hands. 'I'll deal with the washing-up later.'

Nakamura, standing by the folding card-table at which they had eaten, was staring at her while excavating one of his beautifully strong, white teeth with a tooth-pick. There was a curious expression, at once remote and embarrassed, on his handsome face.

'Cigarette,' she said, extending a hand.

Slowly Nakamura took a cigarette from the case she had given to him—it had belonged to Jim and she had found it at the back of one of her drawers—and put it to his lips; equally slowly, as though he were deliberating some problem, he fumbled for a match.

'Come on, slow coach!'

He handed it to her. Gulping greedily at it—most of her actions seemed to have that same brisk rapacity—she said between puffs, patting the eiderdown: 'Come.' Nakamura hesitated. 'Come,' she repeated.

The Japanese withdrew his feet slowly from their slippers, approached the bed and then placed himself beside her. She held out the cigarette and he sucked at it, both of them watching as the smoke curled up towards the ceiling and then, strand by strand, disintegrated.

'I wish I could go to Japan with you,' Eithne sighed.

Nakamura drew in his breath with a sharp hiss. 'Alas, that is not possible.'

196

'Of course it isn't possible,' she retorted fretfully. 'But one can wish, can't one? I'm sick of England.'

'England is a nice place to live.'

'You've said it—*nice*! Too nice! Too bloody nice!' She tossed and wriggled briefly on the bed as though she were uncomfortable.

Nakamura continued to stare silently at the ceiling, his arms to his sides and his jaw clamped together with what appeared to be the rigidity of conscious effort.

Eithne went on: 'What a hole this is!'

'What is?'

'This room, this flat. Like the whole of this awful country. Look at these houses from outside—you'd think they were full of rich people with butlers and chauffeurs and antique furniture. But behind their splendid fronts—did you know that the owners are made to paint them once every three years?—what do you find? Slums, just slums.'

'This is not a slum,' Nakamura said, so shocked that he jerked up to a half-sitting position beside her recumbent body.

'Of course it is. A *nice* slum. All England's a nice slum.'

'You should see a real slum in my country.'

'I wish I could. Oh, I do! I'd like to see a real slum. At least there'd be some life in it.'

'A terrible kind of life. No, Eithne, you should not say such things.'

Suddenly Eithne began to laugh, the sound gurgling in the back of her throat as she gripped the bed-head with her plump hands. 'Have I shocked you then?'

Nakamura did not reply; in fact, she had.

'I'd just love to go to Japan,' Eithne went on. 'Do you think I could find a job there? Would they have any use for me?'

'Maybe an American or English firm—' Nakamura began, anxiously slow.

'But I wouldn't want to be there unless I was with you, Naka. Unless you could meet me each day at some station in Tokyo and we could come back together to some horrid little flat like this and I could cook you a meal or you could give me some raw fish and sticky rice.'

'Alas, that is not possible,' Nakamura said, dejectedly.

'No, alas, that is not possible,' Eithne concurred, again imitating not his accent but his intonation. 'Never mind. Forget it.'

She turned towards him, took his hand and guided it into the opening of her kimono.

But on this occasion, instead of dexterously unfastening her brassière as he always liked to do, Nakamura left his hand cold on her warm flesh, merely giving a little sigh.

'What's the matter?' Eithne asked.

Again Nakamura sighed, the merest puff.

'Well?'

Nakamura swung his legs off the bed, cradling his head in his hands, while his stockinged feet turned inwards, one on top of the other in a pigeon-toed stance. 'Eithne, I must work,' he said. 'I told you.'

'Work! At this hour?'

'Yes. Alas, yes.' He got up, feet still turned inwards, and made for the brief-case he had abandoned on the table when he had come in. Pulling up one flap and then another, he took out a pile of crumpled papers. 'All this.' He waved the papers in the air. 'Only two months. I must get them all in order.'

'But not *now*.'

'Yes. Now. Time is running short. Time and tide wait for no man. Unfortunately.'

Eithne got slowly off the bed, first kneeling on it and then lowering one leg to the floor, to be followed by the other. 'So you want me to go?' she said.

Nakamura stared unhappily at the papers in his hand. Then

he looked up with an astonishingly sweet smile: 'Of course I do not *want* you to go. You can stay, Eithne, of course you can stay. But I must work and maybe that will be boring for you. And distracting for me,' he added.

'I'll go,' Eithne murmured, stripping the kimono off. Standing there in nothing but her brassière and pants she all at once felt chilled; her teeth began to chatter, her body to shake. Hurriedly she began to struggle back into her clothes.

Nakamura, watching her, asked: 'Are you angry with me, Eithne?'

'Of course not,' she muttered, her head diving into her jumper.

'You do understand?'

'Oh, yes, I do understand.'

'It's my book. That's what I came to England *for*. I must complete it. Ten years now I have worked on this book. Too long, Eithne.'

'Yes, too long,' she said, hitching at a stocking without once meeting his gaze.

'I owe it to my university—to finish this book. And to the foundation. All that money, Eithne!'

'Yes, yes!' Suddenly she was shouting at him in exasperation. 'Don't go on explaining! I understand! Of course I understand! It's the book, the bloody book, that counts!'

'Eithne!' Nakamura was appalled by her sudden violence.

But at that, surprisingly, Eithne began to laugh, going to him and putting her arms round his shoulders and her head on his chest. 'Don't worry, Naka,' she said. 'I'm a little disappointed, of course. But I understand, of course I understand.'

Nakamura, relieved, gave her a little squeeze and a kiss on the forehead. 'I should *like* you to stay,' he began, but Eithne cut him off.

'No, no! No more of those explanations!' She broke free

and began to finish dressing with the embarrassed speed of a patient before a hard-pressed doctor. 'There we are! Now where the hell did I put my bag?' Nakamura retrieved it from under the eiderdown and handed it to her. 'Thanks. . . . Well, work hard, Naka. Work hard.'

'I will try, Eithne. Hard work is my programme for the rest of my stay in England.'

She patted him on one cheek with mocking playfulness: 'That was interesting—all that about Aesop's Fables. Don't forget to put it in your book, will you?'

Taking her seriously, as he always did when she was teasing him, Nakamura gave a grin of pleasure: 'Of course I shall put it in my book. Thank you, Eithne.'

'Well, same time, same place.'

'Same time, same place.'

Briefly they kissed; but there was something perfunctory about the way in which Nakamura rapidly inserted his tongue into her mouth and then withdrew it, so that it did not surprise her that, as soon as they had separated, even as she opened the door and turned to say a last goodbye, his gaze had moved sideways and away from her to the pile of crumpled sheets of paper of varying size that lay on the table.

After he had closed the door on Eithne, Nakamura leant against it for several seconds as though in fear that she would return to attempt to carry it by storm. His thick, glossy eyebrows were drawn together, his mouth pursed. Then, with a sigh, he crossed to the table, picked up his manuscript and carried it to the desk. His eyes were on one of the closely-written pages as his hand reached out, fumbled and eventually switched on the reading-lamp. Jumping up, he then turned off the overhead light and returned to the desk. The brilliant circle of illumination in which he sat isolated, with the washing-up (Eithne had forgotten it), the bed and the card-table all excluded, brought him a curious sense of stability and peace.

In the same way, as a small boy, the youngest of a family of nine children, he would isolate himself in some corner, crouching with a book on the floor before him, while older voices argued and bickered above his head. In the same way, later, as a student, sharing a room with three of his fellows, he would escape from their incessant badinage about girls by concentrating in a small circle of light on some academic problem. In the same way, on his way to England, he would lie on his bunk in the cabin he shared with two Australians, and slowly slip away from them, their crude voices growing fainter and fainter and their gross presences in sweat-stained underclothes growing more and more insubstantial. 'Well, what do you say to that, eh, Prof?' One or other of the Australians would nudge him. But he had nothing to say to it, since he had heard nothing.

The tiny characters made his eyes burn and swim; but their very smallness was part of the magic that enabled him to escape. He drew a pen from out of the pocket of the jacket draped over the chair behind him and made one meticulous annotation in the margin and then another. On an impulse he jumped up and turned off the gas. When absorbed like this, he did not notice the cold; so why waste money?

Soon he had forgotten about Eithne: both about the brief pang of regret he had felt when deliberately denying himself the pleasures of her plump, ardent body, and about his subsequent guilt as dejectedly she had reached for the handle of the door before he could get to it, had slipped through with a mumbled 'Good night' and had pulled it shut behind her. He felt her slowly dim and then, wisp by wisp, vanish from his consciousness as, after his first few bitterly homesick weeks in England, his wife and two children had dimmed and vanished.

'Exegi monumentum, aere perennius. . . .' Well, that was putting it rather too strongly. But this would be the standard —and authoritative—work for a long time to come. There was no doubt about that. Oh, no doubt at all.

Meanwhile Eithne battled against the wind, her chin tucked into the collar of her coat and her head turned downwards and sideways. There had been a bus but she had decided not to run for it, preferring to make her way home on foot and so delay the moment when she would burst in on Rose, perpetually knitting before the gas-fire, to be greeted by a squeal of 'Well—you're back early!'

A young man, a long scarf twisted around his neck, was standing outside the Curzon cinema, his muscular body supported on an umbrella that seemed on the point of snapping beneath his weight. It was not the young man seen in the train that evening but this one, too, had gazed at her on some occasion in the recent past, she could not remember when or where. Now, too, he gazed at her as she passed: first at her legs, then at her face, then at her breasts. Should she stop, making the photographs on display outside the cinema her excuse? For a moment she did so; and as she paused, the man himself straightened and began to wander over. But then, with a shake, she hurried on. Surprised, she realised that so far from this possible encounter filling her with excitement, it had caused in her a jolting kind of nausea.

Eithne had often described herself since the gradual crumbling away of her marriage as 'a bachelor girl'. When Rosie, who was seven years older and had long since acquiesced in a state of impregnable virginity, would give one of her shocked little squeals at the revelation of this or that of Eithne's adventures, Eithne would retort with a certain self-satisfaction 'Well, I like to play the field.' But now, overnight as it were, there in the middle of the field she had played for so long had risen up this mountain—the Japanese whom at first it was rather a joke to 'lead on' and whom now, she realised, she could not do without. Oh, damn that book of his, damn, damn, damn!

'So that's what it means! I'm less important to you than that stupid book of yours. That's it, isn't it?'

Nakamura, who had on this occasion eaten supper at Eithne's flat—Rose was out at one of her church meetings—quailed before the onset, cheeks sucked in and head lowered, while his fingers did up the buttons of the raincoat he had just put on. 'Eithne—you must try to be more understanding,' he said. He had the Japanese horror of scenes—they were crude, vulgar, ugly; but at the same time he could not help feeling obscurely moved by her impassioned voice and manner, as she confronted him with flushed cheeks and eyes that seemed to have grown suddenly small and sharp under the heavy, bluish lids.

'Every night it's the same,' Eithne rushed on. 'Do you think that I have nothing better to do than travel in that bloody train with you and then get you your supper?'

'If you prefer—' Nakamura began humbly.

'What can I find to *do*,' Eithne cut him off, 'when at half-past eight you announce that you want me out of the way so that you can concentrate on that wretched book of yours? It's too late to do anything. No one wants a date for an hour like that. I could have gone to the cinema with Clive—he asked me this morning—or I could have gone to Rose's meeting!' (Eithne had never in fact gone to a single one of Rose's meetings through all the years they had lived together.) 'But at this hour—! It's hopeless.'

'I am sorry,' Nakamura said. 'Very sorry.' Part of him wanted to get away from the congested face thrust towards his own and the loudly accusing voice; but the other part was irresistibly attracted.

'If it were another woman, I'd have something worthwhile to be jealous of. But a book! And your time is running out. Only six more weeks.'

'Six and a half,' corrected Nakamura, who always liked to be accurate.

'Well, six and a half. Do you realise that it's more than ten days since we—since we—' Eithne broke off, knowing that Nakamura shrank in shame and embarrassment from any discussion of their love-making or indeed from any reference to it. 'You can't be in *that* much of a hurry.'

'My mind must be clear,' Nakamura answered simply. Then with extreme difficulty, his hands twisting at the buttons of his raincoat, he got out: 'If we—we make love—then afterwards —afterwards I have no disposition for study. It is bad, I know, I should have better control of my mood. But alas, that is how it is, I cannot help myself. And as I have explained to you—'

She was staring at him, wondering how she could ever have managed to fall in love with such a—such a cold-blooded, self-absorbed *creature*. But that she was in love with him she was now in no doubt at all.

Then, her voice suddenly going slack and her body going slack with it, she said, 'All right. Go.'

'Go?'

'You want to go. Go. *Go*,' she repeated, with a momentary revival of the old vehemence.

'I will see you tomorrow?'

She almost replied, 'Hell you will!' But instead she found herself saying meekly, 'Yes, I suppose so.'

'Same time?'

'Same time.'

'Same place?'

'Same place.'

'Eithne—I am sorry. Truly sorry.'

'Naka—I am sorry. Truly sorry,' she mimicked back at him.

As soon as he had closed the door, she flung herself on the sofa and burst into loud, gulping sobs. It was perhaps lucky that Nakamura had escaped having to witness this noisy paroxysm of frustration and grief. When he had left Tokyo, he had had to chide his wife for allowing the university colleagues who had come to see him off to witness her with tears trickling down her otherwise rigidly composed face.

Professor Armour, who contributed to the *Statesman* and *Encounter*, frequently appeared on television and was perpetually shuttling between Sussex and the United States, had never until then taken any notice of Nakamura. It had therefore been a surprise for the Japanese when he had been bidden to a dinner-party to honour Dr Norfolk, on a visit from Berkeley; and even more of a surprise to find that of all the distinguished people present in the Park Crescent house—politicians, scholars and writers—it was with him, Nakamura, that Dr Norfolk seemed most eager to talk. The huge red-faced American and the little Japanese were separated at either end of the table; but throughout a protracted and curiously ill-cooked meal—the *poulet à l'estragon* shredding between the teeth, the mousse carrying a faint flavour of glue—Dr Norfolk would perpetually bawl down its length things like 'Now Professor Nakamura will no doubt confirm. . . .' or 'I hesitate to embark on this topic in the presence of Professor Nakamura. . . .' When the ladies left the men to their port, it was beside Nakamura that Norfolk placed himself, striding down the room in order to do so, while demanding some whisky.

Until that triumphant occasion Nakamura had suffered during his months in England a curious whittling-away of his self-confidence, of which he had been almost unaware. His colleagues at Sussex either patronised him or ignored him. He was merely one of a number of foreign scholars who burrowed away in busy obscurity at some totally unimportant subject of research. From time to time some dons kinder than Professor Armour would ask the Japanese in a jolly, encouraging voice, 'Well, how are things going, Professor Nakamura?' but when Nakamura embarked on an answer full of his habitual qualifications and periphrases the discussion would quickly be brought to an end. But here was a world-renowned scholar who was prepared to accord to him the kind of respect to which he had grown accustomed in Japan. Dr Norfolk had even read many of his papers, published in Japanese.

Professor Armour was unusually amiable as he said good night to Nakamura on the doorstep.

'You must visit us again soon. One sees so little of you.' He put his cigar to his babyish mouth and smoke wreathed out on the still evening air. 'It's all very well to spend all your time at your desk but you must have a thought for your colleagues too.' He put an arm round Nakamura's shoulder, as he guided him down the steps. 'Sure you don't want a taxi? Or I could ask the Liddles to drive you home.'

'No, no. I like to walk. Walking is good for me.'

'Spendid character, Harry Norfolk. He took to you. Thinks the world of you, one could see that at a glance. First-rate scholar. Absolutely first-rate.'

Beaming and waving, a portly but youthful figure in a heavily draped dinner-jacket and elaborately pleated shirt, Armour remained on the bottom step outside his house until Nakamura had turned the corner.

Yes, it had been a gratifying evening; one might say a triumph. But as, elated, he trotted off to the bus-stop—he had never been as late as this, might the last bus have already gone? —Nakamura found that all the details of what had passed in the sumptuous crowded house were fading from his mind, to be replaced by a joyful anticipation of returning to his book. The wheezing, watery-eyed American had asked him about it—

206

'We've waited far too long,' he had said in mock reproof, shaking a finger brown with nicotine, and when Nakamura had murmured, humbled, 'Yes, I regret. I am sorry,' the American had then retorted between snorts of seismic laughter : 'The real trouble in our game is not the scholars like yourself who take too long to get the stuff out but those who get it out too quickly.' He had then glanced at Armour, twirling his cigarette, one end sodden, between middle and fourth finger, in unmistakeable malice.

Seated in the bus at last, opposite a woman either so sleepy or so drunk that she swayed perpetually from side to side in imminent danger of falling, Nakamura pressed his hands together between his knees in an effort to stop them shaking with the excitement that kept welling up inside him, like an onset of fever. He had felt like this in the early days when he used to sit at the end of the platform at Falmer Station, waiting for Eithne to appear; and in his student years on the rare occasions when he and some of his friends would visit a brothel and would have to wait, as decorously polite as patients in a dentist's waiting room, for their turn to be called. Eithne was right, although during their recent scenes he had repeatedly denied it : the book really mattered to him far more than anything or anyone else, and the pleasure that he got from it exceeded any other pleasure known to him. Watching the saliva trickle out of one corner of the seamed mouth of the old woman swaying across the aisle from him, he saw it now with clarity.

When he opened the door of the darkened flat, pulling off his overcoat and dropping it over a chair before he switched on the light, it was as though he were entering the home of a beloved, whom he knew to be waiting in silence for him behind the closed bedroom door. He found himself moving on tiptoe, each of his senses sharpened to a thrilling alertness.

. . . The shock was at first like a stupefying blow. He stared

207

down at the desk, feeling a strange icy trickling moving along his spine. Then he began to rush about the small, crowded room, turning over papers, flinging clothes and books to the floor and even stooping to peer under the bed, where the dust lay in swollen grey sausages, into the shoe-cupboard and behind the paper-fan he had made to cover the empty grate. Suddenly, he whirled round, as though someone playing a practical joke on him were just behind his shoulder; then he tore the bedspread off the bed, and dragged the bedclothes to the floor.

His manuscript had vanished.

Who could have done such a thing to him? Who would want it?

Outside in the street, into which he rushed without his overcoat, he found two tall, ladylike policemen talking in a doorway. Breathlessly he explained what had happened, while they looked in turn down at him and into each other's pale, angular faces, wondering whether he was drunk or mad. 'My life-work,' he moaned; as he continued to moan when he had got them to enter the flat.

'Is anything else missing?' one of the policemen asked.

'I don't know, I haven't looked.'

'Well, may I suggest you look now?'

Both policemen seemed deliberately to refrain from calling Nakamura 'sir'.

Nakamura hunted among his belongings, pulling out drawers and then pushing them back, opening the little bamboo box in which he kept his cuff-links and studs and finally making sure that his camera and its accessories all still lay undisturbed at the bottom of the wardrobe.

'Well, it's a bit odd,' the less languid of the two policemen commented at the end of this search. 'Isn't it? Those papers of yours gone and everything else untouched.'

'What exactly *were* these papers?' his colleague enquired.

'Ten years of research. My book on Christianity in the Far

East.' As he spoke the words, Nakamura had to resist an almost overmastering desire to burst into tears. He put both hands to his mouth, finger-tips pressed to trembling lips.

'Now who would want something like that?' the same policeman asked, in a voice that carried with it a faint under-tone of mockery.

'If they were *scientific* papers—' his colleague took up know-ingly.

'No, no, they were not scientific papers. No, not at all. They were, as I say, concerned with my research into the spread of Christianity in the Far East.'

The policemen stayed long enough to ascertain that no door or window had been forced and to make some notes. Then they left, telling Nakamura to call at the station in the morning.

'You are very kind,' he told them, still tremulously agitated, as he let them out. 'If the thief can be found, I know that you will find him. I have always heard that the English police force is the finest in the world.'

Nakamura stood on the doorstep, watching them as, two tall, thin shadows in blue, they made their way off up the square. How their boots squeaked, in exact synchronisation as it seemed!

Back in his room, he again made another fruitless search of all the places he had searched already. For a moment he thought that a shoe-brush had also been taken and his heart rose at the possibility of a definite, if eccentric clue; but the brush was eventually revealed beneath the kitchen chair.

In a fearful access of desolation he threw himself on his bed, moaning against the sleeve that he pressed to his mouth : 'My book, my book!' Then, after what must have been several minutes of this keening, he jumped up again and began to scrabble his way back into his raincoat. He would go and see Eithne and tell her what had happened.

At that moment if the thought had occurred to him that she

might have had anything to do with the disaster, his conscious mind had repressed it.

Rose came sleepily to the door, leaving it on the chain as she asked, 'Who is it? What do you want? Who's there?' in a high-pitched, fearful voice.

'Nakamura.'

'*Nakamura?*'

They had met often enough, but Rose said the name as though she had never heard it before.

'Eithne's friend. Her Japanese friend.'

'It's very late.'

'I must see her.'

'Eithne's asleep.'

'Yes, but I must see her.'

Leaving the door still on the chain, Rose padded off. Nakamura had not seen Eithne for more than a week. Afternoon after afternoon he had waited for her on the platform in vain; until, taking courage, he had stood outside her office only to slink away, not sure whether she had seen him or not, when she emerged, vivaciously laughing, in the company of the young clerk she called Clive (or was it Keith?).

'What *is* all this?'

Eithne strode down the corridor, barefoot, in a pair of blue-and-pink striped pyjamas, the top two buttons of the jacket undone so that it seemed as though at any moment her ample breasts would burst out.

'Eithne—forgive me—but I must have your advice.'

'At this hour?'

Her implacable tone both repelled and intimidated him. It was then that the unconscious suspicion began to float upwards, like some greenly swollen corpse, into his conscious mind.

'Something terrible has happened.' He glanced at Rose, who stood at the farther end of the corridor, arms akimbo under her flat chest and eyes curiously bulging and defenceless with-

210

out their usual glasses, in the doorway of her room. 'My book —the manuscript of my book. Someone has stolen it. It's gone.'

'Stolen it! Who would want to steal such a thing? What use would it be to anyone?'

'That's what the police said. But it's—it's *gone*.'

Eithne gave an impatient shrug of the shoulders. 'You must have put it away somewhere.'

'No, no, I haven't, I haven't!' he cried out, exasperated by her terrible, contemptuous calm. 'Do you think that I could put it somewhere and not know where I put it?' Again Eithne shrugged, doing up a button of her pyjama-jacket and then raising the same hand to cover a yawn.

'Perhaps you took it to the university and left it there?' Rose suggested, advancing towards them.

'No, I never take it there—never! It is out of the question. Never would I take the whole manuscript there. Besides,' he added pathetically, 'it is too heavy.'

'Did someone break in?' Rose asked, feeling that she must provide the sympathy that Eithne was so mysteriously withholding. 'Is anything else missing?'

'That is the strange thing. My Canonflex camera is untouched. My pearl cuff-links—they are in fact Mikimoto pearls —are in the little box where I always place them. Who would leave such things and yet take my book? Who, who?'

'Who indeed?' Eithne said.

'You haven't let anyone have that key, have you? I mean,' he hastily corrected himself, 'no one has taken that key?'

'What key?'

'The key I gave you.'

'Of course not.'

'That is good.' But quite why it was good he could not have explained.

'It's ghastly for you,' Rose said. 'I see that. Would you like a cup of tea? Perhaps it'll cheer you up.'

'No, no. No, thank you. No tea.'

Again Eithne yawned, this time with no attempt at concealment. 'Well, I must be getting back to bed,' she said. Raising her arms above her head, first one and then the other, she stretched luxuriously, the pyjama-jacket rising with her rib-cage to reveal the flesh of her diaphragm.

'Sure you won't have some tea?' Rose coaxed. 'It'll only take me a jiffy.'

'No,' Nakamura said in a broken voice. 'No. But you are very kind. Very kind indeed. Forgive me. Such an hour. Disturbing two sleeping ladies. But I was so upset. Forgive me, please.'

It was Rose, her rayon dressing-gown rustling with every movement, and not Eithne who saw him out.

In the parched and frantic weeks that followed Nakamura found himself producing a number of versions of the story of how he had lost his book. All of them were prompted by the general disbelief, first voiced by the two policemen, that any casual thief would mysteriously enter the flat without forcing the door or any window and would then make off with something seemingly useless and valueless except to its author.

At the university Nakamura had first tried out on a woman student, always pestering him and the unwitting object of his dislike in spite of her mania for all things Japanese, the version of having absent-mindedly left the manuscript in a café, from which it had disappeared when, half-an-hour later, he had hurried back to retrieve it. But the tone, half pitying and half-contemptuous, with which she had drawled, 'Oh goodness, what an absolutely *mad* thing to do!' had convinced him that the story, if told in this manner, would only make him look ineffectual and silly. The next time, therefore, that he poured out the details of the tragedy—to Armour, who since the dinner never saw Nakamura without jovially asking him how he was getting along—he recounted how, travelling on the train from Falmer, he had, as he put it, been obliged to respond to a call of nature, leaving his brief-case containing the manuscript on the luggage rack above him; arriving at Brighton Station he had reached for the brief-case to find it was not there. 'I am afraid that the thief must have had a disappointment,' he concluded with a twitching smile. 'But for me it is a tragedy.'

Armour put a massive arm around the Japanese's shoulder, making him involuntarily cringe away from him. 'My God!' he boomed. 'Oh, what bad luck! Oh, I am sorry!'

The upshot of all this sympathy was that Armour eventually offered Nakamura a lift back into Brighton in his E-type Jaguar and once there, to his immediate regret, suggested that perhaps the Japanese would like a drink.

Nakamura, ill-at-ease with a bonhommie that even he could at once see to be factitious but at the same time not wishing to cause offence, lugubriously accepted.

Out in the garden—it was now spring and the day had been warm—Armour cradled a large glass of whisky on his chest as he lay, stretched out almost at full-length, on a vast wicker chair. 'Yes, that *is* bad luck,' he took up again. 'The nearest I've ever got to that was when I dictated a broadcast talk and the little idiot of a stenographer somehow mislaid her note book. Something comparatively trivial,' he added. 'Though annoying nonetheless.'

He went on to speak of T. E. Lawrence who had mislaid the original draft of *Seven Pillars of Wisdom* in not dissimilar circumstances—'and frankly, in the case of that piece of fiction, one can't help wishing that that had been allowed to be the end of the matter'—and of Carlyle, who had bravely set about rewriting the whole of his *History of the French Revolution* 'after J. S. Mill's maid—sensible girl—had consigned it to the flames.' There were other equally heartless anecdotes. But what made Nakamura most uncomfortable, like a hinted accusation, was the catalogue that followed of the scholars who, for one reason or another, had found it convenient to 'lose' manuscripts which either had never existed or existed in so chaotic or imperfect a state that publication of them would never have been possible. 'It's hard for a philosopher to say after twenty years of labour that his conclusions are balls. Far easier to have a tale of a master-work mysteriously lost or stolen. And the same goes for a novel. We all know of those individuals who have been said, for the best part of a lifetime, to have been working on an epoch-making novel. The fact that they are doing so appears to excuse so much that is otherwise un-satisfactory, drab and spineless in their lives. But as the day of reckoning approaches and the tattered sheets of paper in the bottom drawer of the desk lose even the surprise of contem-poraneity, then what is the solution? Theft—loss—fire! What else? . . . Now this business of the Sibelius Symphony is an interesting one. The old boy, as you probably know, liked to excuse the complete artistic sterility of his final years by drop-ping hints to this or that visiting notable that he was at work on a final symphony. But when he finally shuffled off that sub-stantial mortal coil—the cupboard was bare!'

Did Armour imagine, Nakamura asked himself, sick with desolation, as he struggled on his homeward way, that he, too, had invented the loss of his manuscript? Was that what he was implying? Was that what his colleagues, seeming so ready with their sympathy, were thinking had really happened? It was monstrous! In his mind, Nakamura heard them chortle to each other with gleeful malice: 'Eleven years, was it, that he was supposed to have worked on that magnum opus? . . . And of course he got that award on the strength of it. . . . I suppose he realised that it was worthless. . . . *If* in fact a single para-graph had ever been written.'

It was when he wrote to his octogenarian *sensei*, Professor Oda, and to his colleagues in Japan, that Nakamura first for-

214

mulated the theory that the manuscript had been appropriated by some rival scholar, either jealous of his reputation or eager to make secret use of his research. He had by now reached such a state of paranoia that there were long stretches of time when he managed to persuade himself that this unlikely hypothesis was in fact the truth. There was an elderly Chinese from Hong Kong, a Baptist minister with the name of Mr Ling, who was following at the university a course of research in a field not entirely dissimilar from his own. Since Mr Ling had, in the past, responded to all overtures of friendship with a baffling and humiliating coldness, it was not now difficult for Nakamura to adopt the suspicion that it was he who was the thief.

Occasionally Nakamura would also ruminate darkly on the possible rôle of Dr Norfolk in the mystery. Norfolk had visited Brighton on the night of the theft; he had known that the Japanese would be away from home, having dinner in Park Crescent; and he, perhaps alone of western scholars, would be in a position to appreciate the originality and importance of Nakamura's discoveries. Had there not been something false about the joviality with which, his face shiny and flushed with drink, he had bawled down the table his questions and compliments? Norfolk was known to be a rich man, quite apart from his academic salary; and for a man so rich it would be easy enough to find someone—an impoverished student even— to execute the theft.

Unable to sleep and barely able to eat, Nakamura would lie out on his rumpled bed—it was days since he had made it, though he was usually so tidy—to give himself up to these fantasies which at least had the consolation of allotting to him the role of tragically deluded protagonist in a tragedy of human vileness and betrayal. But then he would have to get up, to wander unhappily to the lavatory, and reality would supervene. Professor Oda might indeed believe that there had been some dastardly conspiracy—his letter, received that morning, bore witness that he did—but Nakamura himself could not believe it for any length of time. There was some other explanation; and the only possible explanation—though he shrank repeatedly from accepting it, pushing it far down into the abyss of his subconscious—lay in Eithne.

Since his late night visit to her flat, Eithne had made no attempt to get in touch with him. On two or three occasions when he had seen her in the grounds of the university, it was obvious that she had deliberately avoided a confrontation. He telephoned her but Rose invariably said she was out; he wrote and the letters remained unanswered.

At last, having resolved to make a surprise visit at a time, soon after she had got back from work, when it was likely she would be in, he came face to face with her on her doorstep in answer to his ring.

'Yes?' It was the tone of voice used to a canvasser or a collector for a charity. Evidently she had been washing her hair; and the towel wrapped round her head like a turban gave her an appearance both androgynous and menacing.

'I want to talk to you, Eithne. May I?'

'Have we anything to say?'

Still she blocked the doorway with her ample, vital presence.

'What has happened? Why do you treat me like this? Have we quarrelled?'

She gave a disagreeable smile and raised an eyebrow. 'I got bored,' she said. 'That's all. You bore me.'

Nakamura looked nervously over his shoulder, terrified that one of the neighbours might be eavesdropping on this exchange. 'May I not enter?' he pleaded.

'Rose isn't in.'

'But I do not wish to see Rose. It is you I wish to see.'

Eithne considered for a moment. Then she gave an abrupt sideways jerk of the head, so that water splashed from under the towel on to one eyebrow. Nakamura entered; the door clicked shut.

'Well?' she demanded.

'Why are we not friends any longer?' Nakamura asked, his voice still plaintive and abased. 'What have I done?'

'I saw that you had no more use for me—that you had other, more important things to occupy your attention. So'— she shrugged her shoulders—'I decided to efface myself. It was as simple as that.'

'But of course I had use for you. Of course!'

'Yes. As your cook. But no other use.'

'As my friend,' Nakamura said.

'Friend!' There was a terrible scorn in the words as they emerged from between her clenched teeth.

'Eithne—do not be angry with me . . . I came—I came to —to ask you—something. . . .' He faltered, his eyes gazing at her feet, and then cleared his throat with a dry, rattling sound, not once but twice.

'Well? Get on with it.'

'Eithne—my book—my manuscript. . . .'

Before he could go on, she shouted, eyes blazing under her towering head-dress: 'Your book! I'm sick of your book! Your book doesn't interest me! Do you understand? What do I care about that precious book of yours?'

'Eithne. . . .' The sweat was cold on his forehead and between his shoulder-blades; he could hardly get out the words. 'If—if you have my book—please—please—I beg of you—'

'*If* I have your book! Why should I have your book? Are you out of your mind? What possible interest might I have in that book of yours? Do you think I stole it? Do you?'

Head bowed, he let the words spark back and forth above him, in total submission to their sword-like swish and flash.

'I—I just . . .' he eventually managed to get out incoherently.

'No stone must be left unturned, every avenue must be explored. . . . As they say,' he added, in seeming apology.

'What an absurd idea! Why should your footling little work concern me in the least?' The towel was working loose with all this vehemence and she now plucked it off with a single gesture, allowing her thick, still damp hair to tumble around her shoulders. Ah, how beautiful it was—he had forgotten how beautiful! Suddenly he no longer thought about the book and wanted only to put out a hand and run his fingers through that hair, again and yet again. 'I'm sorry it's lost,' she went on, 'of course I'm sorry. Since I know how much it means to you,' she added on a nasty note. 'But if you're crazy enough to imagine that *I* had any part in its—'

'No, no!' Piteously he now denied it, his eyes still on that cloud of auburn hair. 'I just thought . . . wanted to make sure. . . . Maybe in joke. . . .'

'Well, in that case, I must get on with setting my hair.' Peremptorily she pulled the door open; meekly he went through it.

'Goodbye, Eithne,' he turned to say. 'Thank you. Please forgive me.'

But she had already closed the door and was pulling across the bolt.

Nakamura's colleagues eventually could not fail to notice how ill he was looking. Three parallel lines appeared mysteriously on either side of his mouth, which in turn seemed to have grown much wider and thinner as the flesh fell away from his face. His skin took on an orange hue, as though at the end of an attack of jaundice. Usually so athletically erect for a man of his age, he had now started to walk with a curious shambling gait, eyes lowered, chin on chest and shoulders bowed. 'It looks to me as though the poor man's heading for a nervous breakdown,' Armour told a colleague, who nodded in sage agreement and gave the opinion that the sooner Nakamura got back to his own country the better.

An advertisement placed both in the local evening paper and in the Personal column of *The Times* brought as its only result a visit from a journalist so young that his voice seemed not to have broken. He questioned Nakamura about his loss, expressed sympathy and said that his story would appear in the local evening paper in a day or two. But no story appeared.

Distractedly, Nakamura went through the ritual of preparing for his journey back to Japan.

Then, a few days before his departure, two letters arrived by the same morning post to bring him a little cheer. One was from Dr Norfolk, who began by expressing his regret at the news of 'the theft' and then went on to say that he had persuaded the American foundation that had originally financed the Japanese's year in England to pay him a similar sum for another year, in order to rewrite what—as Dr Norfolk put it— 'would undoubtedly prove a major contribution to Far Eastern studies.' The second letter, from Professor Oda, brought the news that the university had decided that, if Nakamura should desire it, he must be given a further year of absence from his post at his usual salary.

But the pleasure that those two letters brought him was only temporary. As, that evening, he sat at his desk trying to compose two suitable replies, he suddenly realised that he was sick with a mortal sickness: homesick; sick of research; sick of the book; above all, sick of himself. For the first time in his whole married life he felt an intense longing to be back in his home; to be seated at the table while his wife submissively brought him his food; to be out in his own garden with the azaleas in bloom around him and the tree-frogs croaking out of the depths of the dripping and misty greenness beyond.

He must go back, first he must go back. Then he would decide.

Having reached this conclusion, he ate a large meal for the first time for many days and slept a deep sleep.

In Japan a visiting professor would have been seen off by all his colleagues and friends. There was no one to see off Nakamura. The night before, Armour had given a perfunctory dinner for him—no liqueurs were offered, as on the occasion of the dinner for Norfolk and there were only six guests. Rose, of whom he had been seeing a little, had had dinner with him at a fish-restaurant the night before that; they had both been embarrassed by their habitual inability to communicate with each other and it was with mutual relief, if also with a certain sadness, that they at last separated, before ten o'clock, Rose pressing into his hand a package that turned out to contain an Edward VIII Coronation Mug. 'It's rather special,' Rose felt obliged to explain, 'because, you see, he was never actually crowned.'

'You are very kind,' Nakamura said. 'Always kind to me.'

'What train are you taking?' Rose asked, embarrassment making her change the subject.

Nakamura told her.

'I wish I could come to see you off. But I can't get away from the school at that hour. I'm so sorry.'

'Never mind. I will send you a postcard from our first port of call.'

'Will you?' Suddenly she sounded eager and hopeful. 'I'd like that.'

The porter grumbled about the number of small bundles and bags with which Nakamura was travelling. 'You'd do better to buy yourself a couple of large suitcases,' he advised with brutal candour. 'This is the surest way to have something stolen.'

For a flash Nakamura imagined, with a revival of his paranoia, that this was a sly reference to the loss of the book.

The bundles and bags had been arranged on the luggage rack and on the next door seat, Nakamura had divested himself of his raincoat, neatly folding it up and placing it on a suitcase, and the porter had slouched off, examining the coin in his grimy palm with a look of sour distaste on his face, when all at once there was a peremptory knock on the window beside Nakamura's cheek. He turned.

'Eithne!' he cried; but outside the cry came to her as no more than a noiseless moving of his lips and a radiant smile such as she had never seen him give before. Half-running, he made for the door at the end of the compartment.

As he neared her, her face upturned and the mouth drawn back to reveal the large, even teeth, his delight gave way to panic. How ill she looked, how thin, how grey! Her eyelids, bluish in the past, were now almost violet; her hair, usually so glossy, had grown brittle and dry; her neck looked scrawny and lined.

'Eithne!' Now the name he had cried out so joyfully the first time emerged on a soft note of pity and concern. 'How did you know? Oh, what a surprise for me!'

'Rose told me.' Her lips barely moved as the words came drily through them. She avoided his gaze. 'I came to say goodbye. And to give you a goodbye present.'

'A present! For me?'

'Yes, a present. For you.' Already he had noticed that she had a flat cardboard box under one arm. 'I think you'll be even gladder to have it than to have Rose's.' The stretched skin round her mouth cracked into a smile that was almost a grimace. 'Here you are, Naka. Here!' She thrust the box at him; and as, numbly, he took it from her, she called out 'Goodbye, Naka!', turned on her heel and began to hurry off.

'Eithne!' he shouted. 'Eithne!' He started to pursue her; but a whistle was blowing, a woman with a pomeranian managed to lasso his legs with the lead, he could not leave his luggage.

'Eithne!' he shouted again, this time in the face of the guard who was hurrying the length of the train, slamming door after door.

Then, clutching the parcel, he clambered back into the carriage.

'Aren't you going into dinner, sir?' the elderly Chinese steward asked.

Nakamura shook his head.

'Is this rough sea worrying you?'

'No, no. I'm just not hungry. Thank you.'

'Very good, sir.'

Nakamura got off the bunk, feeling slightly giddy as he raised his head from the pillow, peered at the belongings with which the other occupant, a Cingalese business-man, had littered the floor and table, and then stooped to take the parcel out of one of his bags. Although he had not yet opened it, he had no doubt of what it contained.

Always neat, Eithne had made up a package that was a model of symmetry and tidiness. Nakamura unpicked the knot, carefully removed the green string and then made a roll of it, before slipping off the paper. Nursing the manuscript on his chest with both of his hands, he then slowly crossed back to the bunk, sank down on its edge and started to read.

At first, he felt nothing but pleasure: in the clarity of his style; in the lucidity with which he had organised so many intricately disparate elements into an artistic whole; above all, in the originality of so much of the material he had managed to unearth. But into the pleasure there slowly began to seep a bitter, hopeless melancholy.

Each paragraph carried with it a reminder, often of events long since forgotten. Here, for example, was the passage about

222

the persecution of the Christians in Nagasaki: he had worked on it during his honeymoon in that city and he remembered now how his wife would patiently sit waiting for him back in the inn, while each morning and often each afternoon he would delve in the record office and in the museum. Here, beside a section about St Francis Xavier, there seemed to run, silently parallel, an account of his vexed journey to Peking, with the difficulties of obtaining a visa, the permission of the Japanese government and of his university, and the currency for his expenses. Here was that whole chapter written when his son was so ill with typhoid fever: while he laboured at it, his wife, pale and trembling, would keep coming in to him to announce 'His fever's getting worse,' or 'He's still passing blood,' until, in fury, he had shouted at her 'Why can't you leave me in peace?' Here too, were the last finishing touches, the ink a fresher blue, put in during the last weeks before the theft on the evening when Eithne had reluctantly left him. 'What will-power you have!' she would taunt him savagely on those occasions.

Suddenly he stopped reading the manuscript, in a piercing access of horror. It meant nothing; *nothing at all*. Sometimes in the forests about his home town on the Kii Peninsula he would come, as a boy, on a mammoth anthill. But when he kicked at it repeatedly until it split open, the baked mud, mined with its labyrinth of channels, would contain no life at all. All the seething, relentless energy that had gone to its construction had vanished, who knew where. The intricate factory had become a mausoleum. His book was the same.

Here, in his hands, lay the story not merely of the Christians in the Far East, but of his own ambition and ruthlessness and singleness of purpose. Here also lay the story of the people who had suffered for him: the docile, undemanding wife, with her innumerable trivial ailments from which she was slowly dying with the same weary patience that she brought to everything

223

she did; of the two children to whom he had always been a remote and minatory presence, to be avoided or placated; above all of Eithne, whose ample body had dwindled, whose eyelids had darkened with the weight of her grief, whose glossy coils of hair had dried like grass in the midsummer sun.

He jumped up off the bed and ran to the porthole, struggling to pull it open, while his breath came in gasps like an effortful sobbing. Wind and an icy spume lashed down at him. The pretty chintz curtains billowed out above his head, with a sound as though of ripping.

He went back for the manuscript; then struggled to throw it outwards into the plunging darkness.

But the wind that pressed against him like some vast invisible presence, clammy shoulders heaving against his shoulders plucked the pages out of his grasp and spun them back across the floor and on to the bed and over the pitiful possessions of the fat Cingalese. Some even seemed to be mysteriously sucked under the doorway, even though the metal lintel was so high.

Going down on his knees, Nakamura attempted to scrabble the pages up into a bundle. Through the open porthole a stinging spray came spattering across them, making the tiny characters blur and drenching his hair and shirt.

'Oh, Eithne, Eithne, Eithne!'

Suddenly tears were joining the spray, falling in large drops on his hands and on the Cingalese's pyjamas and on the sheets of the book that had been his whole barren life and also, he realised now, a terrible and prolonged kind of dying.